The three men were trapped within their own vehicle. No one could reach them, no one could help them. The flames and smoke made it impossible for anyone attempting to wrench open the driver's door. The petrol tank burst and seemed to blow what remained of the van apart.

The three men trapped, were human torches, they burnt alive, watched by horrified onlookers.

In the terrible confusion, no one noticed the masked man run from the bread truck. He watched for only a second, turned and ran back to the truck, and drove out of the underpass.

Eventually the screams of the dying men were silent.

All three bodies had been taken to the morgue, but it was two days before they were officially identified as . . . known criminals.

All three men had been married; these women were now widows . . .

Widows

LYNDA LA PLANTE

SPHERE BOOKS LIMITED
London and Sydney

First published in Great Britain by
Sphere Books Ltd 1983
30–32 Gray's Inn Road, London WC1X 8JL
Reprinted 1983 (twice), 1984, 1985
Copyright © 1983 by Lynda La Plante in
original scripts and novelisation

TRADE
MARK

Set in Century Schoolbook

Printed and bound in Great Britain by
Cox & Wyman Ltd, Reading

Prologue

On a cold November morning a raid organised by Harry Rawlins went disastrously wrong.

The raiders at a given marker in the Strand Underpass were to hold up a security wagon. A bread truck would act as a block, and ramming vehicle, in front. As soon as the security wagon halted, three men following in a Ford Escort van would hold up the traffic behind at gun point. One man would, by using explosives, blow the side of the security wagon. Each man would fill the other's haversack with money bags, running the last ten yards to the exit of the underpass to waiting getaway cars. The last man to leave the scene of the hold-up would wait until all three men had cleared the underpass. He would then drive off, meeting them in a pre-arranged hide-out.

The guards in the security wagon were completely unaware that they were sandwiched between raiders.

The police car giving chase to two young boys in a stolen car was also unaware that a raid was in progress. It was coincidence that the police, with siren wailing, followed the stolen 'joy-ride' car into the Strand Underpass.

The guards in the security wagon heard the police siren. The driver of the Ford Escort van turned for a split second to look behind him towards the noise of the siren. In that split second the security wagon slammed on its brakes. One of the raiders tried to warn their driver, but it was too late, the Ford Escort van careered into the back of the security wagon.

The explosives jerked out of the raider's hand towards the driver's seat.

The front of the van exploded like a time bomb.

A car following the raiders tried to brake but hit the

1

back of the van, locking the raiders' exit doors.

The three men were trapped within their own vehicle. No one could reach them, no one could help them. The flames and smoke made it impossible for anyone attempting to wrench open the driver's door. Then the petrol tank burst and seemed to blow what remained of the van apart.

The three men, trapped, were human torches, burning alive, and watched by horrified onlookers.

In the terrible confusion, no one noticed the masked man run from the bread truck. He watched for only a second, turned and ran back to the truck, then drove out of the underpass.

Eventually the screams of the dying men were silent.

The underpass was closed for the rest of the day as fire engines, police cars, and ambulances came and went. Later that night a tow truck removed what was left of the raiders' van.

All three bodies had been taken to the morgue, but it was two days before they were officially identified as:

HARRY RAWLINS

His body had taken the full impact of the explosion. The upper part of his body was literally blown to pieces. The skull fragmented. Both legs charred down to the bone. However, still attached to a burnt and mutilated left forearm was a gold wristwatch. The inscription read 'To Harry My Love', the date was a blurred 1962.

JOE PIRELLI

Was identified by his dental records held at Scotland Yard.

TERRY MILLER

Identified by a thumb and forefinger print on his left hand. The only part of his body not burnt.

All three men were known criminals.

All three men had been married, these women were now widows.

2

Chapter One

Linda Pirelli stood frozen, her dark hair framed her ashen face. She could hear her teeth chattering, clattering in her head. She wished she had someone with her, she wished for a lot of things; wished that this was a bad dream and any second she'd wake up.

When she saw his face, when they pulled the sheet from him, her teeth stopped chattering and she could feel something warm trickling down her leg. She heard herself whisper, 'Toilet ... I need the toilet ...'

The police woman gripped her arm, and she was gently guided from the room. Linda was taken home in a patrol car. The small flat, untidy as ever, was just as she had left it, as Joe had left it. She stood by the bed and stared down at the large framed photograph, at his arrogant handsome smiling face.

A bottle of whisky was by the bed, and Linda slowly unscrewed the cap and drank from the bottle, gulping it down. In a drunken stupor, she eventually slept, her raincoat and wet knickers thrown on the floor.

Audrey, Shirley Miller's mother, stood in the immaculate kitchen. She wondered where on earth her daughter kept the tea bags. She could hear her, upstairs, still crying, sobbing her heart out. Audrey sighed and opened the fridge, maybe some hot milk would do the trick.

Shirley lay in bed, her pink dressing gown wrapped around her shoulders. Her eyes were red rimmed from weeping. Beside her, a box of tissues; they littered the bed, screwed up into little balls. But every time she wiped her eyes, she started again, crying, repeating his name over and over. 'Terry ... Terry ... Terry.'

Audrey bustled in, the hot milk and buttered toast on a

tray. Shirley couldn't touch it, so Audrey polished it off. Shirley closed her eyes, the tears trickling down her face. Audrey looked at the silver framed photograph clenched in Shirley's hand. Terry's curly blond hair, his handsome boyish face grinning up at her crying, heartbroken daughter. Audrey sighed, she should never have married him, he was never any good.

She tried to ease the photo out of Shirley's hand, but she held it tight, even though by now she was sleeping.

Audrey sat back and looked down at her beautiful daughter. She'd get over him, in time, she'd be herself again, best just to let her cry, cry him out of her system.

Dolly Rawlins stood in her kitchen, ironing each collar and cuff she had carefully starched, just how Harry always liked them. Beside her was the laundry basket, piled with ironed sheets and pillow slips. Wolf, her little poodle, sat at her feet, his head drooped, but then he would jerk it up and watch her. Every time she moved he padded after her.

Dolly had been working all day, washing, hoovering, dusting; it was now after twelve o'clock and she was still pushing herself. Sometimes she would stop, stare, as if frozen, and she would feel the pain building up, so she began working again, anything, anything to stop that pain inside her.

At two o'clock Dolly dragged herself upstairs; the house was immaculate. Wolf trotted behind her. Dolly leant on the bedroom door, the bedside lamp gave a soft warm glow to the ornate bedroom, the matching bedspread and curtains, nothing out of place. She dug her hand into her apron pocket, and lit the hundredth cigarette of the day. As she gulped in the smoke she felt her heart heave inside her, she turned and went downstairs.

Dolly opened the mahogany doors to the stereo cabinet and switched on the record. It was already on the turntable, she had played it all day, it seemed to soothe her, the soft music, the deep rich tones of Kathleen Ferrier singing *Life Without Death*.

Dolly sat smoking with Wolf curled up at her side. She sat there all night, empty, lost. She didn't cry, she couldn't - it was as if someone had drained everything from inside her.

Audrey had arranged Terry's funeral, a quiet family affair. Just a few drinks back at the house, nothing special, besides Shirley was still in such a state that it was all Audrey could do to get her dressed and ready.

Greg, Shirley's brother, helped out as best he could, but he was unable to cope with his sister's weeping and sobbing. She had embarrassed everyone at the graveside, and had tried to jump in after the coffin. No head stone, well Audrey hadn't liked to ask for money, not yet, but she would arrange something, soon as Shirl' was back on her feet.

Audrey had high hopes of Shirley going back onto the beauty circuits, with her looks Audrey felt she could make it through to the 'Miss England' heats. In fact, she had already put her daughter down for 'Miss Paddington' but she would bring that up later, when it was all over.

Linda stood in the crowded Pirelli council flat. Everyone had been invited, all his precious family, weeping and carrying on, dressed from head to toe in black ... They'd put on a good feast - pasta, sausage rolls, you name it. Mama Pirelli had been working for days, cooking and preparing the room, lit candles ... in fact Italian was all Linda could hear spoken ... being an orphan she hadn't anyone of her own to invite, except the lads from the Arcade where she worked, but they never really knew Joe, so ... She was getting very drunk, she could feel them watching her, shaking their heads at her bright red dress, well she'd show them ... Then she saw her, seated at the other end of the room. Blazing with fury Linda pushed her way across the room ... Yes it was her, that little blonde slag she'd seen Joe with ... who the hell invited her, well she'd give her something to remember him by ... Linda threw her wine over the girl, and would have got into a cat fight if Gino, Joe's younger brother, had not pulled her away ... the room went quiet, they stared at her as she stood swaying drunkenly. Her mouth puckered like a child as she held her arms out, wanting some kind of comfort. Gino held her, whispered to her: he also managed to hold her right tit, but Linda didn't care. She cried openly, heartbreakingly. Joe had been a right bastard but she had loved him, and she still couldn't really take in the fact he was never coming home again.

Dolly was wearing a neat black suit, black hat with a small veil and she had smoothed her black leather kid gloves over and over, feeling her fingers through the soft leather. Wolf was beside her, she could feel his little warm body pushed against her hip.

Eddie came in, breezy and with his cheeks flushed from the cold. Harry's cousin was similar in looks, but whereas Harry was strong and muscular, Eddie seemed like a weak caricature. Eddie rubbed his hands, gestured for her to come out, everything was ready.

Dolly collected her black leather handbag, stood and smoothed her skirt. As she moved to the door, Eddie beamed at her. 'They're all here, hell of a turn out; the Fishers are here, not to mention the law ... can't even see the end of the line up ... must be fifty cars out there.'

Dolly bit her lip, she hadn't wanted it this way, but Harry's mother had insisted, everyone had insisted, telling her Harry was an important man, who had to be buried in style. Dolly checked herself in the mirror. Just as she got to the door Eddie stopped, and took from his pocket a small brown packet. He leant forwards in hushed tones. 'This is for you, Harry gave it to me, if anything ever happened.'

Dolly stared at the package. Eddie shifted his weight and moved closer.

'Just the keys to his lock-up, what have you. The law been sniffin' around my place ... know it's not the time, but, well, you take them.'

Without a word, Dolly slipped the packet into her handbag and followed Eddie out.

The line up of cars had actually brought out most of the street to their doors and as Dolly walked down the path she could feel everyone watching her. Car after car was lined up, waiting patiently to follow the hearse which was weighted down with hundreds and hundreds of wreaths and bunches of flowers. Dolly had never seen so many: hearts, crosses, gates, Madonnas ... the splashes of colour in contrast with the line of black cars.

Dolly alone was ushered into a black Mercedes Benz with dark tinted windows. As she bent her head to step into the car, she saw Harry's mother, in the Rolls behind, mouth the word 'Bitch', but Dolly ignored her, just as she had done throughout her married life.

Dolly sat stiff as unemotionally she gave the nod for Eddie to drive. Through the driving mirror he saw the trickle of tears running down her ashen face. She made no effort to wipe them away, nor move to show she was crying and in a clipped, tight voice she said, 'You told them there was nothing back at the house ... nothing. The sooner this is over the better.'

Harry was buried in the style his mother wanted, hundreds gathered at the cemetery, even more flowers littered the graveside. Throughout Dolly remained solitary, unmoved, and she was the first to leave the graveside with the crowds watching her walking towards the Merc.

Amongst the mourners was Arnie Fisher, in his cashmere navy coat, and his immaculate suit and shirt: as soon as Dolly's car moved off he nodded to a huge bear of a man standing on the outside of the crowd ... the man edged closer.

Boxer Davis pushed his way towards his boss. His suit in comparison was shoddy and threadbare and even his shirt looked grimy, stained. His big stupid face was concerned, moved by the ceremony, and his flattened nose dripped from the cold; he wiped it with the back of his

7

hand. Arnie Fisher took Boxer by the sleeve, flicked a look at the Merc and nodded for Boxer to follow. Boxer shuffled, slightly embarrassed. 'Don't you think I should wait a few days, Guv? I mean she only just buried him...'

Arnie stared unblinkingly at Boxer, again he jerked his head, then turned, conversation over.

Standing a few feet away from Arnie was his younger brother, Tony. Tony seemed to tower above everyone, even making Boxer look small in comparison. The cold sun glinted on the diamond in his right ear, he fingered it, then came to the end of some joke he was obviously telling and roared with laughter. Unlike his brother, Tony was a 'looker'; handsome strong features, the only thing similar to Arnie was the eyes, both had steely blue, icy cold eyes. Arnie was short-sighted so he wore rimless glasses - but you could see something between the brothers, something about those unfeeling, unemotional eyes. Boxer looked from Tony back to Arnie, nodded, and moved off, pushing his way through the already dispersing mourners.

Standing a short distance from the main crowd, Detective Sergeant Fuller watched. He leaned against a tombstone and made a careful calculation of everyone there ... and my God it was like looking at the mug shots down the Yard, all the lags were there - old timers and the new. He was very interested in the Fishers, and watched who they talked to, and like the mourners he, too, threaded his way between the gravestones towards the exit. Fuller was about to get into the police car when he noticed the mud on his shoes; irritated, he wiped them on the pavement. They had cost him forty pounds. Detective Andrews grinned at him from inside the car. Fuller was not amused, particularly as he now noticed mud on the hem of his trousers.

Uptight, Fuller opened the car door and sat inside. He took a clean white handkerchief and spat on it, wiping the knife crease on his right trouser leg. Detective Andrews watched and wondered if Fuller's underpants were snow-white Y-fronts: somehow he couldn't imagine him in small bikini knickers. Fuller slammed the door shut and jerked his head for Andrews to drive. His gestures were quick, sharp and he was methodically neat. Flipping open his ever present notebook he stared down at the list of faces he had spotted at the funeral; as the car moved off he turned and stared at the throng of people ... Arnie had disappeared. Fuller frowned and tapped his book. 'Let's take a look at the Rawlins' house, see who calls ...'

Chapter Two

Dolly sat in the plush velvet chair watching Boxer carefully pouring her a brandy. She noticed he was drinking orange juice, and sighed, why on earth had she let him in, big stupid idiot? - why him of all the people? - but she was somehow comforted, he had seemed genuine, moved in his funny way, and she felt lonely, terribly, terribly lonely ... even just thinking about it made her slip her hand to touch Wolf, sitting close to her feet. The tiny dog looked up and licked her hand. They drank in silence. Boxer became ill at ease, not sure if he should move his bulky body into one of the chairs. Dolly nodded for him to do so. He sat on the edge holding his empty glass. Dolly was tired, her head ached, she wanted him to go, but still he sat, coughed, touched his collar, then he blurted out. 'I'm working for the Fisher brothers now, Dolly ... they ... they want Harry's ledgers.'

Dolly looked at him and he got up and paced the room.

'They'll pay you good money for them, they want them.'

Dolly rubbed her head. 'I don't know what you're talking about ...'

Then he was beside her, bending down, his big moon face close to her. 'Yes, you do, you know about them, everyone knows the way Harry worked, he wrote everything down ... names Dolly, he listed names ... he pointed the finger, where are they Doll?'

She stood up angry. 'Don't you call me that ... you hear me ... and you can tell those two pigs I don't know nothing about no ledgers.'

Boxer gripped her, desperate he tried again, this time soothing, his voice sing song. 'The brothers have taken over, they sent me this time, but if I go back empty-handed it'll be Tony next, do yourself a favour darlin', tell me where they are.'

Dolly stepped back, her face twisted with rage, she shouted, 'I just buried him for God's sake ... GET OUT – GO ON, GET OUT ...'

Boxer put his hands up as if to say okay ... and Dolly hurled her glass at him, it shattered against the door ... she clenched her fists, her nails cutting into her palms. 'OUT BOXER ... OUT, OUT ...'

She heard the front door close behind him, turned abruptly and switched on the record player ... again the same song, the same heavy beautiful voice *What is life to me without thee, what is life if thou art dead* ...' It was then she remembered the package, she picked up her handbag and tipped out the contents.

On her knees she scrabbled for it, hoping, wanting it to be a message from Harry, just some little note to ... it *was* a note, wrapped up with a set of keys ... Harry's neat writing.

'Bank vault, Rotherhall ... double signature ... H. R. SMITH. Sign as Mrs H. R. SMITH. PASSWORD "HUNGERFORD".'

'Dear Doll,
Remember the day you signed at the Bank with me, it's all yours now. The keys are to the lock-up in Kings Cross, you'll find some things there, get rid of them.
Harry.'

Dolly clutched the paper, read and re-read it ... she tried to make out when it must have been written, but there was no date, no mention of love ... just the simplest instructions, but it was enough for Dolly to know ... the bank vault contained the ledgers.

Harry would have been proud of Dolly, she burnt the letter, and the keys she simply slipped onto her own key ring ... and as she carried Wolf up the stairs she repeated the password over and over to herself ... 'Hungerford ... Hungerford' ... the name was simple to remember, Harry's initials and Smith. As she got ready for bed she wondered how much money the Fisher brothers would give ... as she pulled the curtains across the bedroom window she saw the police car, just parked by the gate, waiting, watching, and she murmured to herself, 'Bastards'.

Chapter Three

Audrey was making tea in Shirley's kitchen, she could hear them thudding over the house. She took a good look at the washing machine. If Shirley gave her a reasonable price she'd have it, not the deep freeze though, but the washing machine. The kitchen was in a mess, every cupboard and drawer had been opened and checked through, piles of crockery still balanced on every available surface ... Audrey picked her way round the mess, the kettle boiled.

As Shirley entered, the front door slammed shut. Shirley slumped into a chair. She looked dreadful, her hair needed tinting and the roots showed through, she wore no make-up ... her face was red and blotchy from all the howling she still kept up. Audrey spooned in the tea, she saw that Shirley had lost a lot of weight, she shook her head, worried ... bugger had left her in a right old mess, three months behind on the mortgage, God knows how much she owed on the furniture. Still, she'd take the washing machine, that'd help out.

Shirley sipped her tea, leant on her elbows, eventually she nodded at the door. 'They've gone, God knows what they were lookin' for, they've even had all me carpets up ... I'll never get them straight again, even took me light fittings down ...'

Audrey 'hmmmed' and 'ahhhhd', she'd had the law do her own place over, that was when her old man was alive, it was a terrible feeling, like you'd been stripped. She poured more tea for herself, then Shirley was at it again, crying and sobbing. Audrey took her into her arms and rocked her back and forth. Shirley buried her head into her mother's neck, like she had done when she was a little girl.

Audrey dried her eyes with a tissue. Shirley sniffed. 'Don't know what I'm going to do, Mum.'

Audrey opened her old shopping bag and pulled out the white bathing suit, sequins all down the side, she showed it off, lying it across the table. Shirley looked. 'What you brought that here for?'

'I've entered you in for Miss Paddington.'

Shirley looked at her mother in disgust. 'Miss Paddington - you gotta be joking, you can take that back.' Shirley swiped at the white costume, the tea cup toppled over, the tea seeped over the costume, Shirley burst into tears again.

'What am I gonna do, Mum?'

Audrey held her daughter by the chin, fiercely she said, 'Win love, win!'

The law found hidden in a piece of piping a small packet of explosives, charges and detonators. Terry had hidden them beneath the sink in the bathroom, they found no money to tie him in with any other raids.

At Joe Pirelli's basement flat, the law found two hundred pounds hidden beneath the carpet, Linda Pirelli was astonished, she insisted they count it in front of her, in fact she had been as much of a hindrance as was humanly possible. The notes were matched with numbers recorded from a raid in 1978, but there was nothing in either widow's home to link with Harry Rawlins, nothing.

The law had been at Dolly Rawlins' for two days, nothing was left unturned, even plant pots were emptied and their soil sifted ... the garden had been dug over, bedrooms stripped, nothing had escaped them, and still they found nothing. There was not even a stray dry-cleaning ticket unaccounted for.

All the drawers from his desk had been dragged out, every letter and envelope, every picture. Dolly watched them as they mutilated her beautiful home, she had said nothing, just watched, her body tensed, but somehow she knew they would find nothing. Harry was too clever, too clever for the pigs. Detective Andrews was sitting on her upturned sofa, he was carefully taking apart a photo frame. Dolly snapped and she made a grab for it. 'You leave that, you bastards!'

Andrews looked to Fuller who was standing reading Dolly's private letters, Dolly turned to him. 'Tell him not to take that, it was the last photo we had taken – our anniversary.'

Fuller, without a look to Dolly, continued reading and told Andrews to take it down the Yard, they needed a more recent shot. He then knelt down and began feeling beneath the desk. Dolly had taken enough, she zig-zagged her way through the debris to the telephone, she turned to Fuller. 'This is harassment, I want to talk to your Commanding Officer, you hear me? What's his name? I'll have you for this, and I want his watch ... you hear me, I want his watch back, the only thing left of him.'

Fuller continued to ignore Dolly, she stood in a fury ...
'Who is he? I want his name.'

Fuller got to his feet, looked at her, and almost with a smirk he quietly said, 'Detective Inspector George Resnick, ma'am.'

The name hit home, Dolly replaced the receiver as if it had burnt her hand, she walked to the door and stopped. 'My husband's dead, isn't that enough for you?'

Chapter Four

The short squat figure of Detective Inspector George Resnick thudded down the station corridor, as always a cigarette stuck in his mouth, his overcoat open, his battered hat on the back of his head. Resnick carried a thick heavy folder under his arm, and as he passed offices along the corridor he bellowed orders for Fuller and Andrews. As he reached his own office, Resnick shouted for his secretary to bring him the lab reports from the previous night. He took his office key, opened his door and kicked it closed. The already cracked glass shuddered.

Alice hurtled out of her office clutching files and papers. Andrews collided with Fuller also on his way to Resnick. It was already nine thirty, Fuller had been waiting since nine for his order, tetchy, he straightened his already straight tie and tapped ... Resnick bellowed for him to enter.

The office was in its usual state of confusion. On every available surface balanced coffee cups, papers, loaded ashtrays – even the floor had piles of files stacked in lines. The filing cabinet was open revealing more stacked disorderly files. Resnick stood in the centre of the chaos smoking his tenth fag of the day, coughing his lungs up.

Alice began sorting out the mess on the desk. She worked fast, tipping ash into the bin and collecting screwed up bits of paper from all over the room. Meanwhile Resnick kept one eye on the file he was reading and barked out orders for Fuller to get the rest of the lads up.

Fuller watched as Alice cleared a space for the phone; it rang as he reached for it. Records were up in arms because Resnick had removed certain files without permission and without filling in the proper forms. Resnick threw a crumpled piece of paper to Fuller to fill in and send back to the 'nig nogs' in records.

Detectives Hawkes and Richmond arrived and still the bustle continued. Alice was almost clear and Fuller handed her the completed records sheet and drew up a chair. Andrews appeared with coffees and passed them round.

Alice, Fuller noticed, took Resnick's rubbish out with her; as if he had eyes in the back of his head, Resnick seemed aware of Fuller watching, and he turned with a flourish, 'Alice is taking my rubbish to the ladies doo dah, to burn. Don't allow cleaners in here, all right?'

Fuller flushed slightly at being caught out. Resnick didn't even notice, he pulled up his chair and plonked himself down in front of his 'lads'. He spread out the file, opened an envelope from forensic and tipped out large black and white photographs of the bodies from the raid, horribly mutilated, their faces burnt, naked, the men were grotesque ... the charred remains of Rawlins could not be recognised as being a human body.

'She didn't need to have him cremated did she?'

Resnick flipped the photographs to the men and, leaning back in his chair, watched Fuller's face. He had tried to like him, but there was something about Fuller that got right up his nose, even now he was sitting there as if he had a red hot poker up his arse. Still, he was a good officer, wish he could say the same for the idiot at the end of his desk, Andrews. Andrews had not been able to get himself a chair, but was perched on the end of the desk, already mopping up his spilt coffee. Hawkes and Richmond he knew of old, good hard-working plodders, still he would make do, he would have to.

Resnick eased his chair forwards and opened the previous night's reports, he flicked a look over them, lit yet another cigarette and, blowing out the smoke towards Fuller, tapped the report. 'Says here you think we're spending too much time on this Rawlins business, that correct? That what you think?'

Fuller bristled visibly, looked to Andrews for backup,

but Resnick was on him like a bird. 'Oi you, it's you I'm talking to, not him.'

Resnick gave a dismissing look to Andrews who was now staring aghast at the blow-up of Harry Rawlins. Resnick took it out of his hands and chucked it onto the desk, he stook up ... stuck his hands in his pocket.

Fuller watched Resnick pacing up and down: he spoke very fast, rushing out his words, and spitting at the same time, then he would gulp the smoke into his lungs and blow billows of it, streaming it through his nose. Fuller disliked Resnick, in his opinion he was a wreck, a 'has been'. Before being assigned to him he was working for Chief Detective Inspector Richards, he felt that he had stepped down a peg, and he didn't like it, couldn't understand it.

Fuller knew he was a bright boy, knew he was being watched, groomed for promotion. He just couldn't understand why suddenly he had been switched departments to work with Resnick. Everything about the man annoyed him. His scuffed filthy shoes, his stained shirts, the constant smell of B.O., a waxy smell, in fact there was very little about Resnick he could tolerate; Fuller also didn't smoke.

When Fuller was told he would be working under Detective Inspector Resnick, his heart had sunk, this would or could set him back months. He had made it his job to sniff out anything he could on the new superior officer, it hadn't been difficult, everyone knew the fat man's history, he was held up as an example for young recruits.

Resnick, like Fuller, had been groomed for steady promotion. He had two recommendations for bravery before he even made Detective Sergeant. It had all come tumbling round his ears like a pack of cement cards fifteen years ago. Resnick had been suspended from duty on the suspicion of taking bribes. He had been the 'tool' in a *News of the World* expose. There was even a photograph of Resnick, hand out, open, to take hold of a packet. His face was plastered over the newspapers for weeks, the scoop of the year, the crooked cop, receiving the pay-off. It took years of his life proving his innocence. The whole thing had been a set up from start to finish, a set up supposedly organised by one Harry Rawlins. It appeared Resnick was hounding him, both on duty and privately. Rawlins taught him a lesson, the lesson left a 'stigma'. It clung to Resnick like a shroud, and the climbing promotional stakes stopped, he never got further than Detective Inspector. Every year he put in for promotion, every year he had been passed over. Resnick proved himself innocent, but the powers that be never forgot, every time his name came up, the files and records dragged up the dirt, until that was the most memorable thing about a once possible candidate for the highest ranking position in the force.

Fuller came out of his daydream as he smelt the nicotine breath blasting over him.

'Oi, I'm talkin' to you.' Resnick proceeded to slap onto his jumbled desk file after file of unsolved robberies. 'A 3 Raid', the 'Euston Bypass', 'Blackwall Tunnel'. Resnick's stubby finger prodded each file. 'Take a look at the formation of those vehicles, each one's identical, and the men got away – we've nothing on any of them.' Resnick then had a coughing fit, the jowls on his face shaking, a puce colour rising upwards from his neck. 'An' you can bet your sweet life, all of them, every one was instigated by Harry Rawlins.'

Resnick waddled over to the drawing board, he jerked his head for his men to follow suit.

Like a bunch of schoolboys they clustered around Resnick's blackboard, a detailed drawing showed the raid that never took place. With a red felt tipped pen Resnick ringed the bread truck used by the men, the security wagon, and then the charred raiders' van, the death van.

Resnick felt Fuller's watchful eye on him, he had a desire to belt him one, but controlled it, he stepped aside and left the officers looking at his drawings.

Resnick helped himself to Andrews' coffee, it dribbled down his shirt front, but he didn't notice, he was watching

Fuller. Out came his neat black book, Resnick watched as he made careful copious notes. 'See you still haven't come up with that missing bread truck, how the hell can you lose that, a thing that size, bang in the centre of the West End?'

Resnick watched Fuller's mouth twitch with anger, he knew the lad had been out every day and night covering every inch of possible hiding places, but he just wanted to niggle him.

'He's our only link, the driver of that bread truck, he's the link to Rawlins' ledgers, he'll know where they are. Rawlins worked with a good hard-fisted team, I want that chap, and I want every man that ever came into contact with that bastard, Rawlins, questioned. Anyone who comes within pissin' distance of his wife, I want brought in and questioned, the round the clock on Rawlins' widow stays.'

Again, Resnick caught the twitch at the right side of Fuller's mouth. He had requested the use of the men on surveillance to help search for the truck.

'What about the other widows ... Sir?'

Resnick detected the slight beat before Fuller said 'sir', but he let it ride. 'Watch them for a few more days, doubt if they'll come up with anything.'

Resnick walked to the door, as he left the room he farted very loudly. He chuckled, he could just see that stiff prick's face twitching.

They heard Resnick's bellow of a laugh as he walked down the corridor.

Fuller opened the window in disgust.

Chapter Five

Dolly found it simple to lose the police tail. She went to Myra's hair salon in St Johns Wood Road, parked the car and saw Detective Sergeant Andrews stuck in the middle of two Jewish princesses arguing as to who had seen a free meter first.

Dolly slipped Myra a tenner, left Wolf in her charge and nipped out the backdoor; she was in a taxi half-way to the City as Andrews parked the police car.

Dolly had a nervous tickle in the back of her throat. The young prissy bank clerk stared blankly at her, then led her towards the private vaults. Dolly's heels clicked on the marble floor, again she coughed; the clerk turned and indicated the lift. She felt he gave a very heavy emphasis on, 'This way Mrs Smith.'

An hour later Dolly knew she had to go, she couldn't stay any longer, had to make it back to the salon. She found it hard to move, the contents of the strong box littered on the table in front of her. She had not had the time to count all the bundles of bank notes, nor touched the two small .38's; it was the ledgers that fascinated her.

The ledgers were dated, bound in heavy brown leather like ones she'd seen on the TV, usually in a Dickens play ... each one neatly labelled, going back for almost the whole of her married life of twenty years. Some of the names Dolly flicked through she knew were dead, but the latest ledger filled her with stunned amazement ... lists and lists of names, monies paid out, monies stashed here, there and everywhere ... also newspaper clippings, like a film star's scrap book ... cuttings neatly clipped and stuck in.

She had no idea Harry had been involved in so much heavy crime ... she shivered slightly. There in black and white, in his neat immaculate handwriting, was the outlay for the last raid ... in detail Dolly saw the security contacts, how many guns required ... like a play script ... she shut the book ... opened it again. My God he had even worked out crimes to be committed as far ahead as 1986 ... again she shut the book.

Dolly had made notes in her small black Gucci diary. She was reading it sitting under the dryer when one of the police officers assigned to watching her came into the shop. She smiled sweetly and he went out embarrassed.

Chapter Six

Arnie Fisher was in a fury, the type that when he had been a little boy his mother had had to shut him in a cupboard. The hard blue eyes flickered, the spit foamed at the side of his thin lips, he paced up and down and round the most enormous desk, the drawers were thrown around the room. Arnie had just had his office refurbished. The walls and carpet were a snooker table green and he had heavy brown leather sofas, a brown mahogany bookcase and a matching cabriole-legged coffee table. Sporting prints were stacked ready to be placed on the green walls, a chandelier was balanced on the mantle shelf, the gas log fire half in and half out of its hole. Arnie in his effort to be ultra tasteful had managed to create a hideous over-heavy effect – even the bathroom *en suite* had gold taps and a dark green bath and wash basin. He had elbowed the bidet as he didn't have enough room.

Arnie today was wearing pale grey; immaculate grey shoes, and a silk blue grey tie, which was now pulled half way round his neck in fury. Arnie was venting his full fury out on the desk top, he ran a biro right across it, then slapped it with his hand. His spittle shot out of his mouth and he dabbed it with a crumpled silk handkerchief.

The *en suite* toilet flushed, and Tony Fisher came out still doing up his flies. 'Eh, who you get to do this? It's a bleedin' antique and you go and get some ham-fisted git, it's varnished, it's bloody varnished.' Tony shrugged, seeming totally unmoved by the onslaught, even when he informed Arnie that it had cost a ton to do up and when the drawer flew through the air missing his head by an inch, he still didn't seem to give a toss. He just shrugged, he never worried when Arnie got like this, it always blew over. Only time you need be worried where Arnie was concerned was when he was nice to you, when he smiled that strange thin toothless tight smile. Right now his teeth were chomping up and down like a donkey's, right old wobbler he was chucking.

Boxer Davis arrived. Arnie got himself back in control fast, he went quiet, his hand gently rubbing up and down the varnished antique desk.

Boxer stuttered out the information that he had been to Dolly's. He had found nothing, had told her that Arnie was willing to pay hard cash for the ledgers. He said he needed a bit more time, she was still upset and would be easier to talk to when she calmed down. Throughout Boxer's explanation Tony kept edging forwards to interrupt. Arnie raised his hand, just a flick, but it was enough for Tony to keep quiet. Eventually Boxer wound down and stood, head bent, shuffling his feet, but he had no more information.

'Is that it? Is that it?' Tony crossed to Boxer.

Arnie now jerked his head for Tony to leave the room, a quick tight movement. Tony was about to argue, but there was that tight nasty smile and he knew better, he left.

Boxer shifted his weight from leg to leg, he leant on the upturned leather sofa. He was scared of Arnie, he hated himself for it, but this nasty little queen gave him the runs, you never knew where you were with him. Tony was different, he'd screw anything if it had all its limbs. Tony was punch-crazy, but he was under Arnie's thumb. You knew where you were with him. Boxer could feel Arnie's glinty stare boring into him. He made Boxer repeat his

21

information ten times, over and over, each time he would nod and twist his manicured hand for him to repeat, and repeat until Boxer began to stutter.

'You gettin' your knickers in a tizz wazz aincha', Boxer? Job too much for you is it, eh? Can't you handle it? Want Tony to take over do you? Eh? Eh?'

Arnie removed his glasses and began polishing them slowly. 'You got two weeks my old son, two weeks. If you don't come up with the ledgers by then I'll send Tony in, send him to see to the widow, an' you know how Tony likes the ladies, don't you?'

Then Arnie turned and the meeting was over. Boxer knew that the sole reason for Arnie giving him the job was because he had worked for Harry Rawlins three or four times. That was when he was 'up', a long time ago, but Harry had always given him the odd hand out. Boxer classed Harry Rawlins as a friend. He wondered what Harry had over the Fishers, what he had written down about the brothers. He suspected it wasn't anything complimentary, whatever it was it would be enough to put them away. They were just names to Harry – like him, like most of the villains in town, all of them listed. The law would have a field day.

Boxer crossed to the door, he was miles away, thinking, his dumb brain churning, it would be in his interest to get those ledgers, he was named, he could go under just like the rest of them.

He decided to see Dolly that night, whether she liked it or not.

The phone rang, Arnie picked it up, he went all coy, his body wriggled. 'Hello Carlos, I'm fine darlin', I'm fine.'

Boxer closed the door quietly, he moved down the staircase into the club. It was dark, seedy in the daytime, the smell of stale cigarette and cigar smoke hung to the red velvet curtains. The smell of beer was strong, pungent, sickening.

Tony Fisher lolled at the bottom of the stairs. 'Arthur Negus calmed down 'as he?'

Boxer skirted Tony, but he moved in front of him and

put his fists up. 'Come on, come on, show your metal.'

Boxer put his fists up halfheartedly, Tony slammed him one, hard below the waist. He buckled, holding his belly.

'You're losing your touch darlin'.' Tony was laughing his guts out as he ran back up the stairs; Boxer felt like puking his up.

Chapter Seven

Dolly saw the car from the bedroom window. She knew it was the law even though it was minus the trappings. The young officer sitting in the passenger seat kept on looking over to the house. About ten o'clock, Dolly saw one of the plain clothes men get out of the car and walk off, leaving only the young blond one still in the passenger seat. This is it she thought, I'd better move.

Dolly was seen five seconds later taking Wolf for a walk, innocent looking, just a coat slung over her shoulder, no handbag. Casually she watched as the tiny dog cocked its leg on every tree or wall – anything solid and standing the dog tried to pee over.

Andrews felt his eyes drooping, Dolly was still in vision near the corner, facing him. She called Wolf twice, the dog had pottered round the corner. Dolly stood, hands on hips, facing the blind side road, she clapped her hands. 'Come here ... Wolf ... here.'

Andrews smiled to himself; not exactly Barbara Woodhouse.

She had been gone round that corner quite a while, he waited, looked at his watch ... Christ!

Andrews ran to the corner, but there was no sign of Dolly, or her pooch, both gone. Andrews ran back to the car but it was useless, he had lost her. He could see Richmond at the top of the road carrying two cheeseburgers and milk shakes. God, Andrews thought, we'll be for it! Get out of this one!

Dolly had taken a cab ride to Liverpool Street, she walked the rest of the way, through the big arches behind Liverpool Street Station. Lock-ups, used by British Rail for storage, hired out by them for garage mechanics – huge caverns dripping water, cold, smelling like underground cellars – and everywhere like ghosts of the past, the wrecked silent cars, their windscreens shattered, their wheels gone, doors open. One by one she checked the locked and bolted doors, she was looking for number fifteen. Dolly was getting filthy as she passed wreck after wrecked car, brushing against her clothes. In the corner a group of winos lay in a drunken stupor, oblivious to her presence. She carried on.

Dolly stopped by a green sliding door, and peered upwards trying to see the number. She almost dropped Wolf, when deep growls then a high pitched harsh bark announced that a guard dog seemed to be hurling itself against the locked door. She could hear the chains rattle ... Dolly scuttled on, Wolf at a safe distance began to bark back. Dolly covered his face with her hand.

Number fifteen was scratched into the paint work of a small entrance door built into the huge doors of the lock-up. Dolly tried one key, then the other. The small door swung open.

Inside the lock-up it was like a gaping cavern, with the thunder of the trains above. Dolly closed the door behind her, put Wolf down and switched on a small pocket torch. By the light of the thin beam she edged forwards. The puddle was deep, thick slimy mud, oil streaked, and it covered her suede shoes. She swore and moved on. Wolf up ahead dodged the ghost cars, sniffing and wagging his tail.

Dolly made her way to the back of the garage. Again there were huge heavy doors, again a small inter-locking door. The annexe was much cleaner than the rest of the lock-up, a couple of wrecks pushed against the wall. Dead

24

centre was a van covered with a tarpaulin.

Dolly began checking over the area. She took out her small leather diary and switched on the overhead lights. They blinked on ... if her calculations were right, she knelt down by the van, pulled at the tarpaulin, broke a nail, and at the same time felt her knee slit through her stockings. Wolf scuttled to her side, and began digging frantically beneath the van. She pulled him off and bent down even further. She could see the neat hole covered by duck boards. She found two shot guns – Dolly replaced them, made a note in her book.

Built at the back a makeshift office had a zinc sink and a small Calor gas stove. Dolly pushed open the door. The office was filthy – dust covered everything – but it was eerie, as if the men had just left it that morning. The half filled coffee mugs, the torn biscuit packet and the open jar of Nescafe. This is where the men had worked, where Harry ... Dolly picked up the dirty mugs, took them over to the grimy sink. Cut out girlie pictures were posted up and notes scribbled on bits of paper. Dolly recognised Harry's writing. She turned the taps on ... The water took a time coming through, then spurted brown rusty water, gushing, soaking her: still she tried to ignore the feelings welling up inside. Then like the water, the tears Dolly had held back for so long burst from her, her body felt light, she gripped onto the sink trying to hold herself up.

If someone had been there and watched, watched a strength disappearing, cracking open, they would also have seen the way this woman held onto herself, gripping with all her might onto the cold sink. She wouldn't give way. The sobs were wrenched out of her, the tears poured of their own accord, she clenched her teeth, then it was over, she was back in control. Little Wolf was frightened and he whimpered at her feet. Dolly dragged herself up. 'All right darlin', all right, Mummy's all right now.'

Chapter Eight

Linda was watching a late re-run of *Harry O*. She was eating a Big Mac, with a half empty bottle of cheap plonk. When the phone rang, the message was brief, in fact Linda hardly said a word in reply. She replaced the receiver, thought, there's a turn up for the book; maybe she was going to bung her a few quid, she certainly could do with it.

She realised she had seen the episode before, went to turn over but all that was on was late news, snooker and a blank screen. Shit, she'd just have to stay with *Harry O*. 'Wonder why she wants to see me?' she mused.

Shirley was mixing her morning bran and yoghourt, it was already past twelve, but she just hadn't been able to get out of bed. The telephone rang from the hall and she nearly didn't answer it, thinking it would be her mother. Since Terry's accident, she'd not been able to keep her off the doorstep, any excuse ... it rang and rang.

Shirley was slightly taken aback. 'The Sanctuary?'

Yes, she knew of it ... she held onto the receiver after Dolly had hung up, but she felt a bit perkier, nice of her to call.

Linda had done as she was told, arrived on the dot of ten at The Sanctuary, and had then felt a right idiot hovering around waiting. When she'd seen the prices of the food bar she thought about nipping out to the cafe opposite. She'd not taken her clothes off, just sat waiting in the changing room.

She hardly recognised Shirley, she looked thin, worn out, but it was her all right, working out on the bikes. She wandered over, and was stopped by one of the attendants.

She had to call over, you were not allowed inside with clothes on. 'Oi - feelin' peckish?' Shirley turned and smiled and Linda nipped out and got a couple of bacon butties. She came back and changed into the towel, but didn't take her knickers off, or her bra; she was wearing her best, red satin, didn't want them nicked!

At eleven thirty there was still not a sign of Dolly. Linda had eaten both of the butties, and was now sucking a Mars Bar. She took a sneaky look at Shirley lying soaking in the jacuzzi, Linda dangled her foot in a bit further.

Twelve o'clock and still she hadn't appeared. Linda was getting tetchy. She was now sipping a coffee, moaning about the price of it. Shirley lay under the sun beds, Linda was getting on her nerves, she hadn't stopped talking. She embarrassed her. Twice she had fed the parrots even though the attendant had asked her not to and she spoke in a loud voice pointing out the other girls' figures. Laughing too loudly at her own witty remarks.

Linda was actually embarrassed by the whole place. She felt very ill at ease. They all seemed like ladies to her, snooty voiced skinny women. Suddenly Linda saw Dolly, she snorted. 'Gawd almighty, Lana Turner's here - take a look.'

Dolly, wearing matching bathtowel and turban, walked casually over to the girls. She nodded like the Queen Mother to a couple of attendants, then moved up the steps to the sun beds.

'I'm sorry I didn't send no flowers. Not in the rule book.'

Linda chewed her lip, she'd been all right until she brought it up, talking in that *Watch with Mother* voice. What did she have to mention their men for?

'Let's go into the sauna - we won't be disturbed there.'

Linda had never been in a sauna before. She was sweating, and could feel the colour running out of her bra. Shirley, well used to them, lay flat out along the top bench. Linda blew on herself, then waved the towel up and down. Dolly was going on and on about the ledgers, how the Fisher brothers wanted to buy them, how in actual fact they really belonged to all the widows. Harry made sure they would all be all right if anything should happen.

'Well, who's got 'em Doll?'

Dolly froze, she turned on the sweating Linda, telling her never to call her that, then she slammed out of the sauna.

Linda looked up to Shirley. She was feeling dizzy, dizzy and fed up. What on earth had got into Dolly? Why did she slam out like that? Shirley bent down and patted Linda's shoulder. 'Just shut it will you, can't you see she's all upset? it must have been terrible for her, worse than it was for us. She'd been married twenty years, she must be feeling terrible.'

Linda stood up and snapped, 'An' I'm not, is that it? Just 'cos I don't show it, don't mean I don't feel.'

Shirley tried to calm Linda, but she wasn't having any of it, she wanted to go out and give Dolly a piece of her mind. It was all bravado. Suddenly Linda crumpled up, she hugged her knees, burying her face, and said in a muffled voice, 'I went to dry me face this morning, got soap in me eyes. I picked up his dressing gown, I held it, I could smell him. I could still smell his body, it wasn't the towel, it was his dressing gown.'

Linda couldn't finish, and she sobbed. Shirley's mouth twitched, felt the tears springing up, and the next minute she was sobbing too.

When Dolly re-entered there they were, the pair of them, in floods of tears. Dolly tried to keep herself in check, but then she started. They all had a good cry, easing the tension, but not for long. Dolly blew her nose, and dropped the bomb shell.

She, Dolly, had the ledgers, but wanted to sound out the girls, because they had two alternatives, either sell to the Fishers, or ... both Linda and Shirley were in no way ready for what came next ... 'Or we'll pull the job Harry had lined up.'

Linda started to laugh, hysterically. Shirley just sat with her mouth open, not sure she had heard correctly.

But Dolly was deadly serious, in fact she began to get angry and snapped at Linda. 'You don't think we could do it? Okay by me, we'll sell to the Fishers ... but we won't get more than two per cent. On the other hand, this job's worth near a million.'

Shirley was still unable to take it all in. Linda, sharp as ever, knew that if a job was worth a take of that amount it would be a heavy one. That means guns, but she shook her head. 'Do us a favour ... what d'ya think we are?'

Dolly had had enough, she picked up her vanity bag, and went to the door. Linda tried to stop her, but she shook her hand away.

'Just think about it. I'm not stupid, I wouldn't have suggested it if I didn't think we could do it ... have a few days to think. I'll contact you, don't try and get in touch with me, I'm being watched.'

Linda tried to get Dolly to give a few more details, but Dolly was already half out of the door - she didn't look back. The door closed behind her. Linda looked up to Shirley, she felt dizzy - 'Gawd, I'm gonna faint.'

Chapter Nine

Shirley had not really given Dolly's suggestion much thought. She had enough worries. She was getting pestered by the mortgage man, and the H.P. clowns had called twice. She'd have to sell the washing machine, Audrey was after it. She even toyed with the idea of getting a job, but she couldn't really do anything. She'd never done a day's work in her life, Terry wouldn't let her, and she'd only been sixteen when she married him. Maybe she could do a typing course ... The days drifted on, still no word from Dolly, nothing.

Linda had given it all a great deal of thought, and had

come to the conclusion that Dolly had blown her bottle. She hadn't heard so sod it, life must go on.

Linda's daily slog down the Arcade was becoming hard to bear, day in and day out, then the nights, sitting in that bloody glass booth, dishing out the change. The law were in again, pestering her, pushing her around, always asking the same questions. 'Harry Rawlins this ... Harry Rawlins that ... did she know anything about the ledgers?' It was driving her nuts.

Charlie was getting worse. Charlie, the limping grease pot she had to work with, hovering after her. He was trying to be nice, just got on her nerves, everything was getting on her nerves. Then she blew. It was just after she'd been practising on the shooting range, something she did every day ... she was able to get a bulls eye every time now, so even that had lost its interest. Charlie had just overstepped himself, he had squeezed his smelly little body into her booth, pressed his spotty face close and asked her to go out for the night with him, he'd got two tickets for a late night movie. He winked and leered at her. She knew what he was after, what they were all after, she'd seen them drifting in, the riff-raff, the layabouts. Suddenly she wasn't Pirelli's property any more, she was a freebie. Suddenly, she was just a scrubber who worked the Arcade, she no longer had the back up of being Joe Pirelli's missus ... and so she turned all her venom on Charlie. She would have hit him, her fist was all ready to swipe him, but the phone rang, and it was Dolly.

Shirley had been waiting in the ladies' toilet in Regents Park for over half an hour. The attendant was in and out of her closet watching, cleaning the foul toilet seats with an equally filthy rag. Where the hell was Dolly? She had said three, it was long past that.

Dolly eventually breezed down the steps, took out her make-up bag and began to freshen up her lipstick. Shirley hovered at her elbow. Dolly calmly informed her that the police tail was outside holding Wolf ... then she grinned, cocky. Shirley twisted her hands, nervous, and kept on

30

whispering that she didn't think she could handle anything dangerous. Dolly snapped her vanity bag shut, took out a fat envelope and handed it to Shirley. 'There's enough here to cover your mortgage for a few months and more besides, you'll get that every month ... the meeting is next Thursday.'

Shirley held onto the envelope, muttered that she couldn't make it Thursday, she was busy ... Dolly looked.

'I'm going for Miss Paddington ...'

Dolly patted her shoulder, already on the way out. 'Won't last all night will it? You be there, eleven thirty – if you don't come we'll know you're not with us, okay?'

Shirley still hovered, she looked at the envelope, and could feel the wad of money.

'You just pay me that back if you're not able to make it ... Okay?'

Dolly, with a frosty smile, walked out. This time Shirley really needed the loo, she almost wet herself with nerves.

Detective Andrews, feeling a right arse, stood with Wolf on a lead. Dolly thanked him and took it from him. Andrews shook his head, she was something else, this woman. Still he wouldn't put that in his records, wouldn't put that he was left holding the baby, so to speak. Another moment longer he would have seen Shirley leave the ladies loo, but he was already trailing after Dolly as she fed the ducks.

Chapter Ten

Audrey was tight lipped and getting more and more agitated. First Shirley had said she could have the washing machine, then she had said she couldn't. She'd arranged a van and everything, and now here she was wearing a costume that must have set her back a bloody fortune, and she wasn't saying anything, she must have got the money from somewhere – then it hit her. Oh God, not her Shirley, she couldn't be. 'You turning a few tricks, Shirley? That where you got this money from?'

Shirley almost swiped her. Audrey had never seen her so angry, so she kept it shut – maybe she was nervous because of competition. Audrey looked around, there were quite a few professionals she could tell. The ones with all the leg tan, it wouldn't be easy, but her Shirl' was out on her own. Audrey preened herself, she was a good looker all right, she'd looked a million dollars in the evening gown parade ...

Freddy entered the dressing rooms, the girls started yelling and shouting, and Freddy began reeling off the numbers of the finalists. Shirley and Audrey waited. Then he shouted Twenty Three, Audrey jumped into the air, Shirley smiled. The girls not picked moaned and blew raspberries at Freddy. He was sweating, trying to get them organised for the walk down. Belting out on the tannoy was a dreadful rendering of *Feelings ... ohhhh my life is feelings.*

Audrey gave Shirley the last once over, hugged her, told her to lick her lips then rushed out front. Greg was keeping her seat, she could have bitten her tongue, just as she turned she said, 'Terry and me will be ...'

She saw Shirley start, her eyes widen and Audrey quickly covered herself. 'I mean me and Greg. Your brother's got some friends, we'll be shoutin' for you.'

Audrey took one last look as she left. Shirley was standing last in line, her beautiful body, her exquisite face, she was twisting her number card round and round in her fingers.

Linda arrived at the lock-up about fifteen minutes early, and she was freezing. She walked up and down. A dog began barking and when she peered through the cracks she could see a huge Alsatian tied up with a chain lead.

Dolly had been driving up and down the flyover for over an hour, they were still on her tail, blast them. She just couldn't shift them. She'd driven half way to Oxford and back, still they were there, every turn, every light, there they were; it wasn't going to be easy.

Dolly remembered a film she had seen, and smiled to herself as she remembered. She put on speed, round the Shepherds Bush roundabout, along Notting Hill Gate, straight down Bayswater Road, and reached Marble Arch. They were still there, still behind her. Then she zipped into the traffic line and took the right turning towards Hyde Park; keeping on the inside lane. Four cars behind she could still see the police car. She overtook a heavy goods truck, nipped in front and then whipped into the Dorchester's U path; she was out of the car, Wolf in her arms, within seconds. She crossed to the doorman, handed him the keys with a £10 note.

'Park it, darlin'. Be back in an hour.'

Dolly entered the Dorchester before the doorman had time to think. He turned after her, then moved towards the Merc. As he bent into the driving seat, the police arrived, their light flashing. Andrews jumped out of the still moving police car, hurtled over to the Merc and he grabbed the doorman. 'Where did she go? Which way?'

Dolly was already in a taxi going in the opposite direction as Andrews wandered around the Dorchester. God he'd done it again, this time he'd get a bollocking ...

By the time Dolly arrived at the lock-up Linda was frozen, and in no mood to mess around.

Shirley was late and Linda wanted to start without her. Dolly just lit up and sat on some packing cases. She quietly opened her black leather diary and made notes, Linda couldn't get a word out of her. She paced up and down ...

'Put the kettle on if you want something to do.'

Linda pulled a face and went into the annexe. It was tidy and the mugs cleaned. Dolly had already been at work.

Shirley stood in the spotlight. She felt an idiot, couldn't think of anything to say, the damned girl in front of her had said everything she and Audrey had worked out. I mean, she had said she wanted to be a nanny, wanted to look after the children ... she'd even said she liked disco dancing and roller skating ... What could Shirley say now? She heard the announcer going blue in the face, trying to get her to talk. Eventually Shirley heard herself saying something about reading, novels, then as if through a haze she heard this fool in his frilled evening shirt asking her, 'What novels?' ... Her brain wouldn't function. She just stood there ... Then he began about boyfriends. Did she have someone special out there, someone to go home to? and all she could think of was Terry. She could see his face, it kept looming in front of her: first it was Terry smiling, then it was Terry, the Terry she'd had to identify. The Terry all burnt, all distorted ... Shirley couldn't speak, she could feel the panic rising up in her, she licked her lips, could taste the gloss, but nothing ... She wanted to die, she wanted the floor to swallow her up.

After the competition Audrey was silent, her lips pursed like a dried prune. She knew Shirley could have won, she had it all going for her, standing there like a dummy. That bloody Terry, she'd never thought anything of him, never was good enough for her Shirl', and here she was eating her heart out over him. Audrey blurted it out. 'You should start doing something with your life my girl, you don't get many chances and when they come, grab 'em ... you should grab 'em.'

Shirley dropped Audrey off. She could feel one of her false eyelashes coming loose, she didn't have the strength to fix it, sod it ... She gave the nod for the cab to drive off. She did not even say goodbye to her mum, just turned her head away. Shirley could have won, she nearly won, Audrey had pictured herself going on holiday for two to Spain, and all those prizes. Here she was, nothing, not even the soddin' washing machine, as she plodded up to the nineteenth floor, the lift out of order again, she sighed. Shirley was definitely getting money from somewhere. She sighed ... Ahhh, sod it.

Linda was on her second coffee when they heard the bang bang of the main garage doors. Shirley was late, but she had come. Dolly was relieved, she was just about to call it off. Linda had gone to guide Shirley through the debris of cars, Dolly could hear them both step into the puddle and swear. Linda's voice going on at Shirley for being late, as they entered the annexe; Dolly could see that Shirley was upset. Linda, however, was rabbiting on about Shirley's gear, joking about the slap Shirley still had plastered all over her face.

'Gawd, what you come as? Look at her ... all dressed up like a dog's dinner, look at the gear.'

Shirley dropped her suitcase and burst into tears. Linda threw up her arms in despair. Her mouth gaped open when Shirley wept and sobbed out how she had only come sixth, how she had made a fool of herself in front of everyone, how she had been awful to her mum.

Dolly settled Shirley down, patting her head like a child's. She ordered Linda to get some coffee. Linda stomped off in a fury muttering about how she'd been there half the night, and all she'd done so far was act as a bloody canteen.

One hour later the scene was very different, still the same three oddly mixed women, but now the atmosphere was tense, electric ... Dolly had gone over every detail, her quiet voice droned on and on, but nothing was left unturned. Dolly had made neat drawings for them to see, it was one hell of a difficult job, a security raid.

Linda leaned forwards, she had bitten every nail off on her right hand, and was starting on the left. Shirley was still, just a strange feeling in the pit of her tummy ... both girls focused on Dolly ... the quiet voice persisted.

'Main problem is the weight, you see, we got to carry it on our back from here ... right up to here, that's where we'll have the getaway car parked ... it's a run of about

35

twenty yards. Doesn't look much but we'll be carrying a hell of a lot of money on our backs.'

Dolly looked up and into the two alert serious faces. In the gloom, they both looked young, innocent ... Linda chewed her nails. It was Shirley who spoke first, her hand shook as she pointed to the drawings. 'What happens if we get aggro from these cars at the back?'

Linda snapped that that was her problem, she was the back up, she was the one handling the shooter. She looked to Dolly who gave her a brief nod. Linda sat back, cocky, self assured. 'I say we can do it!'

Dolly lit her tenth fag of the night, she blew out the smoke, stared hard at Shirley, then flipped open her brief case. She took out two sets of keys. First she turned to Linda dangling the key. Linda, with a smile, grabbed it and stuffed it into her pocket. Keys to the lock-up, keys to their headquarters. Dolly held out the key for Shirley – was she in or out? Shirley hovered for only a second, then she, too, took hold of the key. Dolly smiled, sighed and opened her bag, took out two thick heavy brown envelopes. 'Here, you get yourself wheels. That's the first thing. Make sure they're taxed and MOT'd, pay cash. After we're through, we dump 'em.'

Linda couldn't help having a look inside. She swallowed, must be about two grand in there. Her eyes glinted, she was itching all over.

Dolly shut her brief case and stood up. Wolf pestered around her feet and she scooped him up, then looked to Linda. 'You lock up. Never call me, I'll always get in touch ... you both know what to do. We take this in stages. So stage one: let's get ourselves sorted out with motors, then you, Shirley, you start out as the buyer, all the gear will be down to you.'

Then she was gone, her footsteps echoing down the stone flags ... Linda bit off her last nail, spat it out and looked at Shirley. Shirley was visibly shaking, the dog began barking from next door and she jumped. Linda ruffled Shirley's hair and grinned, Shirley took hold of Linda's hand for comfort, she got none, Linda withdrew it and jerked her head for her to leave. Shirley whispered, 'Are you nervous?'

In the dark Linda's face looked like a cat, her dark eyes, her black thick curly hair, a slightly crazy wild cat; her eyes sparkled, then she grinned and it eased her whole face up, a funny wide lop-sided grin. 'I'm shitting meself darlin', but I feel alive, like I'm tingling all over.'

Shirley looked down at her long slender hands with the perfectly manicured nails, they were shaking and her gold wedding ring glittered. She noticed that Linda no longer wore hers.

The police were still waiting at the Dorchester, Dolly couldn't help a hooded smile as she again tipped the doorman and got into the Merc. She drove home like a cat with cream, up the drive into the garage.

Dolly locked the garage doors from outside, allowing Wolf to have a pee in the garden. Usually she would have entered the house through the connecting door in the garage to the kitchen. She still couldn't keep the smile down as she noticed the police car positioned outside across the street. She was getting adept at losing them, she took out her front door key and let herself in.

The chill ran right through her body, like an icy blast from her crotch to her head, her eyes stinging ... in the darkened hallway she saw the debris, everything smashed, carpets torn, vases knocked over.

The lounge door was open, her heart felt like it would burst through her shirt. She saw a figure bending over the stereo, then she heard the click, click of the record going down, then, 'What is life to me without thee, what is life if thou art dead.'

Dolly slowly pushed open the lounge door – the room was destroyed, the stuffing hung out of her beautiful sofa, pictures smashed ... Dolly felt a flood of anger and she kicked at the door – it swung open.

Boxer Davis sat in the corner of the room, he held the picture frame in his hands, his suit and hair covered in the fluff from the stuffing. Somehow he looked so ridiculous that it eased Dolly, she wasn't afraid anymore. She walked over and shut the record off, in silence she stood with her back to him. Wolf whimpered, running round the room, getting tangled up in the torn cushions. Dolly heard Boxer move behind her.

'It wasn't me Doll, honest.'

Dolly, blazing, whipped round on him, she screamed, 'Don't you call me that ...'

Boxer was in a state, almost in tears. He begged Dolly to listen to him, that he hadn't done this, it was Tony Fisher, he had come here, come to talk to Dolly. Finding no one at home he'd done this, destroyed the place ... Tony wanted Harry's ledgers, they think Dolly knows where they are ... Boxer was pleading with her, pleading with her to tell the Fishers. They weren't offering money any more, they were giving her a warning; unless they got the ledgers, next thing it would be her they would destroy.

Boxer hovered around her almost crying with the shame of what had happened to her home, again and again he told her he had nothing to do with it.

Dolly sat on her torn velvet chair and told Boxer she didn't know anything about the ledgers. Her insides screwed up when Boxer said that the Fishers would start on the other widows. They know one of the women must know something ... Dolly wanted to hit him, hit him straight between his idiot blinking eyes, sitting on his haunches in front of her, patting her knee like a great ape. She had to have time to think it out, she couldn't take on the Fishers, she didn't know what she was going to do, she needed time, needed somehow to keep the Fishers away from them.

Dolly had no one to turn to. She heard her voice talking to Boxer asking how he had got in, did he know the police were watching her place? They had searched for the ledgers, they wanted them, if they had been here surely they would have found them, and all the time her head was saying, *time, time, I need time*. Like a race track, her brain was tick, tick, ticking ... But she was smiling at Boxer, he was showing his methods of breaking in, the old plastic card, boasting how he could still turn a house over. She had to have time, she had to go over those ledgers again to see if there was anyone she could ask for help, anyone she could trust enough.

She heard herself asking Boxer if he could help her get the house back together, heard herself arranging a meeting for the next day, how they would look for the ledgers together.

At long last, she was able to get him out, get him out so she could think. She bolted and double locked every door in the house and she sat with a cup of coffee well into the night, thinking what she could do. There she sat as all her beautiful china and cutlery lay smashed and strewn everywhere, sat whilst the frozen food melted, sat where the stuffing lay strewn from the cushions, sitting in the wreck of her beautiful home.

Dolly knew she had to begin thinking like Harry had done. Harry, what would he have done? Harry ... Like a dead weight Dolly stared around her home, the Capi de Monte collection Harry had bought her, smashed. She held the head of one of her pieces. Harry, what would Harry do? She knew she had to get to those ledgers again. She flicked the curtain apart and saw the law still outside – fat lot of good they would be. She flipped the curtain back again. Then she saw his face, the cracked glass, the frame broken, but there he was, his handsome face smiling up at her, like it was a message, like he was trying to tell her something ... Harry ... Harry. Dolly knelt on the floor and picked up the broken frame. She stared at his face, softly and with her whole heart and soul she whispered. 'I loved you ... I loved you ... I love you.'

Dolly had the best night's sleep she had had since the 'accident'. She slept soundly like a baby. It was as if Harry had come back to her, he was going to guide her all along the way. She was doing this for Harry and he would watch over her. Harry wouldn't let anything go wrong, just as long as she had him, she didn't care what happened. Nothing mattered ... Harry had come back, he was living, he was alive inside her.

Chapter Eleven

Linda was down the auction before the place had even opened. With her manual she inspected car after car. Not sure what she was looking for she moved along the lines of vehicles for sale and decided the best model would be a Ford Capri. She liked the red one and began chatting up a dealer, getting as much information as possible on the car she fancied. He was very helpful, fancied her, thought her easy pickings, and she didn't seem to mind when he put his arm around her. Definitely going to give her one he thought ... sexy little thing. He said he'd take a look at the engine for her ... she rubbed her body against him and smiled.

Linda was too busy getting the low down on the Ford Capri to notice Arnie Fisher arrive in a silver Jag.

The auction had started, the 'specials', the high priced motors, went first.

Arnie, carrying a deep red brief case, bustled his way through the maze of cars. Arnie saw Carlos, stopped, stared straight at Carlos and straightened his silk tie – 'Any way you look at it the boy's a looker.' Carlos was leaning over the bonnet of the Roller Arnie had spotted a couple of days back. Carlos looked up, and smiled.

'Yes, any way you look at it he's a looker.'

Carlos waved Arnie over.

Arnie noted that Carlos was wearing a reasonable suit. The boy was learning fast, didn't go for the rough trade look; no, he liked his boys neat, tidy, with class. Carlos was something else, bit of the animal in him as well. Arnie noted that perhaps Carlos had too many gold necklaces on, but he would put him right later that night.

Carlos was enthusing about the Roller, one of the best he'd seen, just needed the odd touch up, tune the engine and she was perfect. Arnie leant into the engine, more so that he could press his body against Carlos, he hadn't the foggiest about engines, all looked the same to him. His glinty eyes noted that Carlos had also made an effort to clean his nails; yes, the boy was going to go places, he was getting very fond of him, would put a lot more business his way.

Arnie handed over the brief case and patted Carlos on the cheek with instructions to buy the Roller.

Carlos bid, bought, and paid for Arnie's new toy, all over and done with in a flash: together they left the auction.

Linda Pirelli, with the aid of the now boiling over dealer, got a good price on the Capri. As the boyo moved in to get his goodies, his arm slipped beneath Linda's coat. Without looking at him, counting out her money, Linda quietly told him to, 'Piss off, or she'd start screaming there and then ...'

She turned and gave him a cold icy stare. He got the message and backed off ... she heard him muttering 'soddin' bitch', but he kept well away.

Shirley was having a lot of aggro from Greg. I mean the car was the right price, and everything, just that she wasn't sure if it was nicked. Audrey, on her fifth cup of tea, insisted that Greg must have nicked it 'cos according to the *Exchange and Mart*, she, Shirley, was getting too good a price on it.

Greg and Audrey were still going at it hammer and tongs when Shirley thought what the hell, went upstairs and counted out the money. She handed it over, all seven hundred and fifty quid. Audrey missed her mouth with the tea cup, and it dribbled down her chin.

Greg handed over the keys and log book and left. Audrey still hovered; again and again she asked where the money had come from, how come Shirley was chucking it about. Eventually Shirley had to lie. She said she had found a suitcase, one of Terry's ... Then Audrey was satisfied – even more so when Shirley bunged her fifty quid – well, she had to, Audrey had gone on and on about how she had to pay the chap with the van she had ordered when Shirley had told her she could have the washing machine. Audrey was still clutching the fifty, as if it would disappear, when they went outside.

The Mini Estate wouldn't start the first time, nor the second time. It eventually went on the third try, but it leap-frogged down the road. Shirley swore and said she'd have to get Greg to fix it. The brakes seemed a bit stiff and the windscreen wiper fell off. Apart from that it wasn't bad; do nicely for stashing all the gear in the back. Shirley was feeling more like herself, and thought she might go and have her roots done, go a bit blonder, and might even have a massage.

Linda put her foot down, seventy – eighty – she took a look in the mirror and put her foot down again, eighty five, ninety ... smoke drifted from the bonnet, it then began to billow and she pulled the car over onto the lay-by, got out and kicked it.

Dolly had just got back in time for Boxer. He was hoovering the lounge – the damage wasn't as bad as she had first thought – but she would have to have the sofa and chairs re-covered. The carpet stains had come out.

Dolly was wearing an apron and a scarf tied round her head. Every so often Boxer would lumber in and ask if she had found anything. She would shake her head and carry on, he wasn't being all that helpful, but he would be, he would be. Dolly smiled to herself, and called out if Boxer fancied some bacon and eggs. She almost surprised herself, humming; she was humming as the eggs sizzled.

Linda was on her knees, why is it the tower block lifts are always out of order? What is so bloody stupid, it's usually the kids that live in them that wreck them, I mean they're only doing themselves in really. She paused for breath, she had a loaded bag of groceries. She put the bag down, took out her compact and fixed her face, put some lipstick on. It looked odd, made her face seem even paler.

Linda stood at the end of Papa Pirelli's bed. The man was dying; he had been dying since she had known Joe, the sunken eyes, the rattle of his breathing. Today he looked even greyer. They said he took Joe's death very hard, but Linda noticed no difference, just this time he turned his head away from her so he couldn't see her face.

Gino was as effervescent as ever, beaming at her in his stained shirt, his waiter's jacket flung over the back of a chair. Funny how unlike Joe he was, much smaller, still the dark handsome looks, but somehow Joe's face had been stronger, leaner. Linda noticed that Mama Pirelli had already, without a thank you, taken the groceries into the kitchen. She could see her bulky figure at the sink, she was chained to that sink. It was a pity they never thought of putting a slap of paint around the flat, or opening a window for that matter; it was stuffy, too hot, and the smell of stale food hung over the whole place, it clung to Gino from the restaurant.

Gino got up and hugged her, always a little too eager to touch her. She backed off slightly. From the kitchen Mama shouted in Italian. She knew Linda couldn't understand a word, knew it annoyed her. She could speak perfect English if she wanted to. Whatever she said made Gino angry, so it must have been something rude. Linda opened her bag and took out an envelope. Gino tried to stop her, knowing it was more money. She always gave them a hand out when she came round, she got no thanks for it, but still she did it ... but this time she wanted something in return. She knew one of their lot had a garage somewhere, she needed a mechanic.

One of her duties was to learn all about car maintenance. She took it seriously, and wanted to learn. Not at night school like Dolly had said, be quicker with a friend, someone who would cut corners, and the Capri was still playing up.

Gino scribbled the name down of someone who might help. Mama came out of the kitchen wiping her hands, ignored Linda and gabbled in Italian to Gino. He

answered her back in Italian. Linda could pick up the
word 'slut'. She chucked the envelope onto the table,
picked up her handbag and the note from Gino and
crossed to the door. 'You tell Anna Magnani I'll not come
again, that's the last handout you get from me!'

Linda was gone before Gino could stop her, she could
still hear the two of them arguing as she ran down the
stairs . . .

Chapter Twelve

Boxer was sitting stuffing the eggs and bacon down as if
he hadn't eaten in weeks. He pushed the plate back,
slurped his coffee down, then sat back. He grinned,
patting the jacket of the suit Dolly had given him, then
got up and straightened the trousers. Although Boxer was
about the same build as Harry, the suit looked too tight.
Boxer's belly hung over the waist, but to him he looked a
million dollars. He kept on touching the material.

'Pure wool, this, very nice, very nice.'

Dolly had also laid out a couple of shirts, trousers, none
of Harry's best, just his working clothes. She couldn't part
with anything else, they were all still hanging in his
wardrobe, all pressed and cleaned, shirts neatly stacked
and folded. Dolly wanted everything left just as it was,
she had even polished Harry's shoes and washed his
socks. She stared at Boxer, bit her lip, now was the time to
do it. She coughed and poured another cup of coffee. 'Sit
down Boxer, I got something to tell you. It's about the
ledgers, you see . . . I know where they are.'

Dolly had been awake all night planning what she
would say, rehearsed every word. She began by asking if
Boxer's wife, Ruby, was still around, knowing she wasn't,
knowing she had left him years before and taken his son
with her; she wanted to get Boxer at ease with her. She

also asked if he was well and truly off the bottle. Boxer got a bit irritated, after all he had come to talk to her, not the other way around. He was working for the Fishers and if he didn't come up with something soon he would be out of a job. Even Boxer was named in those ledgers, he could get into trouble, never mind anyone else.

When she told him, his mouth gaped open, he felt a chill run up his spine and he spilt his coffee.

Dolly told Boxer that Harry had used four men on the raid, one man had escaped, that man had the ledgers. She knew where he was, but she couldn't tell him, it was too dangerous, because that man was Harry Rawlins. Dolly had buried another member of the gang. She had told Harry about Boxer, and he was prepared to take him on his payroll. He wanted Boxer to work for him, just like old times. He was to keep on with the Fishers, keep them at arms' length so to speak, until he was ready to come back and take over again.

Boxer listened intently, his mouth open, then he slapped his thighs and roared with laughter. 'Old Harry, what a man.'

He kept shaking his head. 'What a turn up for the books.'

Dolly gripped his hand, it was imperative he kept his mouth shut. Was he on their side?

Dolly watched Boxer stroll down the path, assured. He even nodded to the police car still parked alongside the house. She didn't know how long she would have, but one thing was for sure, Boxer could keep his mouth shut. She had a lot to do. She had to go to the bank, get some money to pay him, and, most important, she had to get hold of the girls and warn them.

Dolly sat at her little desk and began making notes of everything she had to do. Uppermost was the rumour she had begun to spread with Boxer, but more important was the fact that she now knew it would be impossible to do the raid with only three women. They needed another member. Maybe it would mean delaying the raid itself, it was going to be difficult, but somewhere in the ledgers she would find a name, someone they could use.

Dolly's house was left untidy probably for the first time in her life, the lounge was still a mess, even the hallway, but Dolly had too much on her mind to worry about that. She also had to do her stint at the Convent. She didn't want anyone suspicious about her movements and she must look as if she was carrying on as usual. It made things difficult trying to fit everything in, but somehow it was giving her extra energy – she was feeling fit, strong, in fact she was beginning to feel alive again. She turned and smiled at the photo of Harry, even more she felt him with her now, her body ached to hold him, she shut her eyes.

The night before the raid, he'd come into the bedroom and she knew he was up to something; he was always the same before a job, tetchy, nervous. He had prowled round the house, in and out of rooms, sitting, getting up again, making coffee, constantly checking his watch. Harry had not made love to her for months, then that last night he had slipped into bed beside her, he had been rough with her, but she didn't mind, the touch of him, the smell of him, she had held him in her arms like a baby. After she heard him get up and go into the spare room, she had lain there awake for hours holding herself, smiling. Even after twenty years he could make her whole body shudder inside. His tight muscular body with not an inch of fat on him, she was as proud of his body as he was. She'd take furtive looks at him when he shaved, watching his muscles tense and relax ... his hands, Harry had long strong hands, the nails cut short. Dolly had to stop her daydreaming, she had wasted enough time. Something inside her was grateful for the last night, the last time he had been near her he had made love to her, that was all that mattered. He had loved her.

Linda Pirelli stood at the open garage door as a young kid in filthy overalls came up to her. She asked for Carlos, the boy turned and yelled.

46

Carlos was on the phone to Arnie Fisher, and was arranging the pick up of a brown Jag he had just finished. He turned, didn't recognise the bird, and nodded for Johnny to see what she wanted.

Linda was persistent and she waited for Carlos to finish his call. She couldn't hear what he was saying but she could see him. Linda noted his body, watched as he scratched his head, ruffling his thick black curly hair. Carlos had an old boiler suit on open almost to his waist, as he turned still talking, Linda got a full look at his face. She took in every detail; he was a dish, with big dark eyes, unshaven, scruffy, but there was something very sexy about him. Before he had even spoken to her, Linda had said to herself, 'I'll have him.'

Carlos wasn't interested, he only did contract cars. He was dismissive and got onto a trolley and lowered himself beneath the car. Linda moved closer and bent down, knowing her skirt was open, she knew he could see between her legs.

'I'll pay you to teach me about motors, I want to learn.' Carlos eased himself out, he looked at her, thought she was a bit tarty for him, pushy, but there was something about her. Before he really knew what he was doing he heard himself telling her to get in, he was going to do a test run on the car he was working on. She was in the passenger seat before he could open the door, she grinned and he couldn't help smiling back, cheeky little cow.

Linda sat with the safety belt on as Carlos flung the car round the motorway, he really knew how to drive. She knew he was trying to put the wind up her, but it took more than a hundred and twenty miles an hour to do that.

Carlos kept brushing her thigh when he changed gear, she made no effort to move her leg. He wasn't all that tall she thought, mind you, she always looked at men and compared them with Joe. Joe was, or had been, six foot three; this chap, she reckoned, was about five nine, but he was all right. She also liked whatever cologne he used – as he bent his head she could just smell it faintly ... yes, she would definitely try it on with this one.

Carlos found himself teaching Linda everything about her Ford Capri. She'd got a good buy and it needed only a slight bit of work. He cleaned the plugs. All the time she was at his elbow, whatever he did, she wanted to repeat it and she was getting covered in oil. She made him laugh she was so intent on learning everything in one half hour, she was even under the ramp with him. He couldn't quite make her out, he knew she was coming on strong, but at the same time she seemed genuinely interested in the engine. He shrugged, let it ride, why not?

Four hours later they were still there, the Capri was running as smoothly as a baby. Johnny had left. Carlos noticed that the Jag had been collected, so he hadn't too much to do, although Arnie's Roller still stood waiting to be done over. Carlos wiped his hands on a rag, Linda's legs stuck out from beneath the car, good legs, her skirt was tucked into her knickers, they looked like red satin, she wore no stockings. As she eased herself out he looked down, her legs either side of him. 'How much do I owe you?'

Linda drove, Carlos beside her. They went up over the flyover. He checked every dial, then gave her the nod to put her foot down ... the car roared forwards, hundred, hundred and twenty ... Linda flicked him a look, he was more intent on watching the bonnet, the dials, than noticing the speed ... yes, she would really try it on with him, she fancied him rotten.

Linda wished she had made some effort to clear the flat. The mess was everywhere and she just managed to slip into the bedroom and toss the duvet over the bed, clear up a few pairs of knickers and washing left strewn around the room. She could hear Carlos in the bathroom, she pulled the curtains and went into the small lounge. She poured two large drinks ...

Carlos was stripped down to the waist, and was using Joe's razor. She placed the glass down on the sink, brushing past him; he took no notice, miffed she went out.

Linda downed her drink in one go, then took another

shot. She wasn't sure how to go about it. I mean she'd given him every 'come on' possible and he had ignored her ... he was standing, leaning against the door, he was even better looking than she had thought. He raised the glass and drank and she could hear the bath running. God he was certainly making himself at home ... without a word he turned and went back into the bathroom.

Linda followed. He was standing looking at some bath salts and held them up. 'What do you like? This or this?'

Carlos indicated another bottle of Badedas, Linda shrugged. He tipped in the blue salts, then crossed over to her. 'You wanna stay with me or not?'

For an answer Carlos began to unbutton her shirt, at last she thought. She couldn't wait to get out of it, pulling at the buttons, trying to hold him to her, at the same time trying to wriggle out of her skirt. God she had the hots for him so much she couldn't stop herself. He picked her up and dropped her straight into the bath.

Linda was so furious, she hurled the bath salts at him.

He got out of his trousers and stepped into the bath with her ... Linda could see a thin white line where he must have had swimming trunks – he was beautiful.

Dolly was getting into a panic, she had tried to contact Linda and Shirley all morning; neither answered. She had also had 'Kojak' on her heels everywhere she went. She was getting used to it – just annoyed her – even followed her to the Convent. The Mother Superior had been kindly – talked about her 'loss', how dreadful to lose the loved ones – but asked if she would still come in as before. So she had done the kids' dinners. It was going to be useful. The Mother Superior's office was never locked and it meant that Dolly could make all her calls from there. It also meant that they would take messages, must give that number to the girls ... girls 'where the hell were they?'

Dolly eventually tracked down Shirley in a beauty parlour. She was wired up, face-packed and God knows what else. Dolly was brief. She had to have a meeting tonight, it was urgent: be at the lock-up by eight fifteen.

Dolly lost Kojak via the backdoor and breathed a sigh of relief. She would have to go round Linda's herself. She picked up a cab and, with Wolf under her arm, set out for Kilburn. Detectives Hawkes and Richmond radioed in that they had lost Mrs Rawlins.

Resnick was on his way to the Sunshine Bread Company. They had traced the bread truck used in the raid. At long last Resnick had something to start moving on. So far, this was all they had.

Detective Fuller drove like a maiden aunt, until Resnick yelled at him. With light flashing and siren blasting they arrived in the bread company yard.

The truck used in the Rawlins raid was cordoned off. Wall Titherington from Forensic was already working over the inside with a group of men. He looked up as Resnick arrived. 'Here he comes, thinks he's in some Sam Peckinpah movie.' Resnick had given orders that some kind of office interview room should be set up for him. He was to question every driver, mechanic and company worker using the yard, anyone with access to a bread truck.

The makeshift office was set up in the Ladies' cloakroom annex. This was the only place large enough to accommodate desks, phones, Fuller, and the men Resnick required.

Andrews was positioned outside the cloakroom taking dabs from every worker in the building. Andrews was very quiet, the black ink already half-way up his shirt sleeve. Resnick had given him a warning; if he didn't pull his socks up he would be out wearing hobnails. The hamburger incident had somehow got back to Resnick and he was furious. It was also interesting to note that Dolly Rawlins had not only skipped away from Andrews, but his second team, Hawkes and Richmond. He made a note to go over just how many hours Mrs Rawlins went missing.

Dolly had yet again lost Hawkes and Richmond. The taxi

waited for her as she went down the steps to Linda's basement flat. She rang the bell and kept her finger on it. Kept ringing until she saw the curtain flick aside.

Linda was in a flat spin. She tried to wrap the sheet round herself. She whispered desperately to Carlos to keep quiet. As Linda ran to open the front door she was in a panic.

Dolly hardly waited for Linda to open the door before she stepped in. 'Why the hell don't you answer your phone? Get dressed, I want a meeting, now, come on it's urgent.'

Carlos sat up and pulled the duvet over himself; as he did so he knocked over the glass on the dressing table.

Dolly froze, she stared towards the closed bedroom door. 'You got someone in there?'

Linda, guilty as hell, admitted that she had, said he was a mechanic.

Dolly gripped her hard ... 'He see me? ... Did he see me, slut?'

Dolly made Linda feel grubby, ashamed; she slumped against the wall, Dolly looked to the bedroom, she gave Linda five minutes, she'd be waiting outside.

Linda had cried, Carlos couldn't make her out; one minute she had been all over him, the next she wanted him out, didn't want him to touch her. When he asked about the caller, Linda began shrieking it was no one, nothing, she had to go out.

Carlos angrily got into his trousers. Linda, already dressed, hovered at the door. She had to go, could he let himself out? She was almost frightened; he nodded, he felt like a tart. He was getting very uptight, he turned on her, hand out he asked for forty pounds, for his work on the car.

He couldn't make her out, she opened her bag and began counting out notes; she was shaking. He went over to her, held her gently, put his hand over the money, he didn't want it. Linda looked into his face, she kissed him, holding onto him, then she was gone.

Carlos finished dressing. At the side of the dressing

table he noticed a photo frame, face down, he picked it up. Joe Pirelli's face stared coldly back at him. There was something dangerous about the man's face, his eyes, dark and heavy, his broad shoulders. Carlos replaced the photo and was on his way out when he stopped, looked down at the phone, got out his book and made a note of the number.

Dolly never spoke in the taxi, not a word, sitting hunched up in the corner.

Linda went through various emotions, ending up with the feeling, 'What the hell is it to do with Dolly? If she, Linda, wanted a screw she would bloody well have one, it was no business of Dolly's.' But all the time she felt guilty, as if she had been caught out by her mother, doing something she shouldn't have done. Besides, he was nice, she liked him, she crossed her legs, she was still wet inside from him. She looked sidelong at Dolly, her fact twisted in a bitter little smile. When was the last time Dolly got her rocks off? Judging by the look of her about twenty years ago. She wondered what Harry had ever seen in her. He was a good looking bloke, mean bastard though. Well, she wasn't going to take any verbals from Dolly about this... no she'd give as good as she got ... she just wished she didn't feel so bloody guilty.

Shirley had no idea what was going on between Dolly and Linda, but there was something. Linda had sat, head bent, foot twitching. She had not said a word, and every time she opened her mouth to speak, Dolly glared, so Linda shut up; the tension was heavy going.

Shirley was showing Dolly the gear she'd bought, rather proud of herself ... she'd already got two black jump suits, plimsolls and one ski mask. The hoods were proving difficult to get hold of, they had them in every colour but black; fancy eye holes, the lot. But Dolly had insisted on plain black, nothing to trace it. Dolly looked over Shirley's gear; she sighed, lifted the ski hood, chucked it down again, abruptly telling Shirley it was too

large, eye holes too big and they didn't need a mouthpiece.
'The less they see of our faces the better.'

Shirley turned this way and that showing off the
jump suit. 'Good fit, all black just like you said, Dolly.'

Dolly pulled at her hair, sighed again and with hands
on her hips said, 'What do you think we're supposed to be?
A fashion parade! Look at the legs. I can see your ankles
for one. It's fitted, I can see your bust, look at the bloody
zips everywhere, what did I tell you? Boiler suits, make
'em at least four sizes too large. We gotta dress
underneath it, get it off in two seconds. Might even pad
ourselves out, useless, absolutely useless.'

Shirley stood, feeling an idiot. Everything Dolly said
was right, but she might have put it a different way. She'd
spent two days *schlepping* everywhere for this gear, all
the way to Harlow ... Windsor, even up the M.1. Shirley
muttered to herself and went over to her little corner, took
off the jump suit; twenty five quid down the drain.

Throughout this Linda had sat, chewing her nails,
swinging her foot: now she sighed, crossed her legs and
started chewing another nail.

All three eventually were settled. Dolly lit another
cigarette, Linda booted Wolf off her leg. He was always at
it that bleeding dog, he'd hump a table leg. Dolly gave
Linda a nasty look, she made Wolf sit next to her and
opened her bag: the meeting was on.

Dolly informed the girls about their needing a number
four. This was the first time they were aware that one man
escaped from the 'accident'. Linda was stunned. She
sprang up, red in the face, shouting, 'You mean some
bastard left our men burnin' to death an' just pissed off ...
he left them, did nothin'?'

Dolly sighed again, told Linda to sit down; she was
really beginning to get on Dolly's nerves. Linda was still
standing, ready for a fight. She leaned over the orange
boxes and smirked into Dolly's face. 'I got a right to know,
some bastard's out there, I'll get him, I'll kill 'im, you
might not care about your man but I ...'

Linda didn't get out the rest of her sentence, Dolly was

up and at her, so fast she almost surprised herself. Linda felt the blow on the side of her head, she stumbled, holding her ear, her head was throbbing ...

'Don't you ever insinuate I don't care, I saw how much you did this afternoon, so SIITTTT-DOOOOWNNNNN.'

Shirley shook. God, Dolly had a temper, she'd never seen her go off the handle like that, in fact she could hardly believe it had happened. Dolly was smoking, checking over her notes as if nothing had happened. Linda was crying.

'Why is it you're always right an' I'm always wrong?'

Dolly, without looking up, told Linda that as she was forty-five, and paying the bills, she was right, take it or leave it. Dolly then looked up, all motherly; she patted Linda, told her she was sorry. Shirley, without being told, put the kettle on ... Linda moved her orange box further away from Dolly, out of reach.

Shirley waited for the kettle. She asked if the fourth member would be another girl. Dolly said she was checking up in the ledgers, she'd find a suitable one. Linda, game as ever, was at it again. Why shouldn't she find one? She knew lots of girls. Again, Dolly put her down, she seemed to really have it in for Linda. Shirley knew something must have gone on between them, she couldn't think what ... she carried the tea over.

Dolly took hers black with no sugar, she sipped at the hot tea, they'd all got new mugs now, each a different colour. Dolly's was pink, Linda's a pale green – already the handle had chipped after she had dropped it – Shirley's was primrose yellow. They drank in silence. Dolly fiddled with her note book, lit another cigarette. Shirley moved her orange box aside, she hated smoke, made her eyes all red.

Then Dolly came out with what she had told Boxer. The lie that the fourth man was Harry Rawlins, that it was Harry who had escaped, Harry who had the ledgers, Harry who would be getting very uptight about any harassment of the widows.

Dolly finished, placed her tea mug down. Neither girl said anything. Shirley was still trying to understand what on earth Dolly was talking about, I mean why on earth spread a rumour like that? Dolly smiled and looked at her watch ... 'Bet you any money Boxer Davis is at the Fishers' place right now, spillin' the beans, an' when they found out what he's got to say ... they'll leave us alone.'

Linda asked quietly how Dolly could be so sure about Boxer. Dolly slipped on her Harris Tweed and smiled. She knew old Boxer, never could keep his mouth shut, he'd talk, he always did.

Dolly scooped up Wolf, and was on her way to the door. Over her shoulder she said she would contact soon as she'd come up with another girl. She stopped. She'd written a phone number down, where she could be contacted, she instructed the girls to learn it, then burn the paper.

Linda looked at the notelet, handed it to Shirley. They heard the door slam behind Dolly ...

'You'd better eat that, I ain't got a match.'

Shirley nearly did, but then caught sight of Linda's face.

'Joke, it's a joke.'

The girls, against orders, left together. Linda had left her car at home, so Shirley gave her a lift to the arcade. All the way there Linda moaned and went on and on about Dolly. Why should she be boss, why her and not one of them? Shirley didn't join in; personally, she thought that Dolly was the boss. She parked, Linda got out, moaned at having to go to work. Linda actually could be a pain in the arse, thought Shirley, watching her walking along the road. She started the car, backed and was doing a U-turn when she saw Linda enter an off licence. 'Mmm,' she thought, 'she'll be the worse for wear tonight, she was in one of those moods.'

Shirley drove home, wondering what was on TV.

Linda was well and truly pissed by ten o'clock. but she always said however drunk she was, she never gave the wrong change. Charlie kept looking over nervously; if the boss was to come in now, see her legless in the box office, singing at the top of her voice, he'd probably get the sack and all. Charlie kept looking over, she was knocking them back. Well, he thought, if you can't beat 'em, join 'em. Charlie took his beaker over and peered through the small money hatch ... Linda was singing to the music, eyes closed. He helped himself, he took a sneaky look at her, she was a bit crazy, something must be buggin' her.

As Charlie moved off, he saw Bella O'Reilly enter the arcade. Bella was dressed to kill; a yellow satin skin-tight top, tight black jeans, her jacket slung over one shoulder. For a moment Bella stood surveying the scene, all six foot of her. She was wearing high heels making her even taller. Behind Bella hovered her pimp, Oil Head. He was joking with a couple of Chinese, his black Fedora twisting round in his hands. You could see the glint of his rings, obviously doing a deal. Charlie had told him about plying his trade round the arcade, but he had just laughed. Oil Head used to laugh a lot, you never really knew if he was laughing at you or had some private joke of his own: either that or he had done his nose in again.

Bella paused for a moment and took in the dump. Like a performance, she started swaggering round the machines, loud mouthing a couple of youths who gave her the come on. Whatever she had said, they recoiled and turned their back on her. She saw Linda and swayed over, all the time giving the chat to whoever cared to listen.

Linda gave a whoop when she saw her, held her hand out of the small hole in her booth. Bella slapped it, held onto it, then did a quick bump and grind.

Bella and Linda had known each other from way back, not that Linda had done any real hooking, more of an amateur, and before she had met Joe, but somehow Bella had always seemed in a class of her own, big enough to take care of herself. Bella bent her head towards the gap, her hair was cut close, cropped to her head. She wore a head band, yellow and gold, cheap, sold in the markets. But somehow on her, it had class, like an African princess. The two old mates chatted. Bella filled Linda in about what she'd been up to in the past few months. She'd gone over to try Mayfair, got into trouble and Oil Head had bailed her out. She owed him one so she was working for him, just until she got herself back into the swing of things. She was also doing her act, two spots a night down the clubs. The two stood, heads bent, looking at each other. Linda looked at Bella's arm, see if she was on anything. Bella straightened up ... 'Not me sugar, that was my man, never touch the hard stuff.'

Linda knew that she had. Bella stopped fooling around, leant in and held Linda's head between her strong hands.

'I know what it's like, he did the big O.D. three months back. I'm on my own, too. Heard about Joe, he was one of the best. You need me sugar, I'm back at my old pad, any time.'

Oil Head whistled for Bella, he had a client. Bella went off, turned, and shouted that she was at the International if Linda wanted to see her later. Charlie went up to Linda, he was still looking towards Bella, watching her patting the little Chink's head, she linked arms with him and they sauntered off. Charlie scratched his balls ... 'I could give her one ...'

Linda, uptight, told Charlie that if he tried it, Bella would give him one he couldn't get up from. Charlie, on the defensive straight away, said that he wouldn't soil his hands, anyone could have her, if they had the right change. Him? He wouldn't soil his hands. She looked too much like a fella for his liking anyway ... Linda laughed, poured another drink. She liked Bella, liked her a lot.

Chapter Thirteen

Arnie Fisher poured champagne. He carried the glasses over to the sofa. Carlos was sprawled out reading a magazine. He sat close to him and put his hand on his thigh. Carlos took the glass and swung his leg down; Arnie leant back.

Arnie was looking very dapper, in a new cream silk suit. He got up and admired himself in the mirror, turned, and, smiling, asked if Carlos would like to have one made up for him. It'd suit him! Suit his dark looks. Carlos nodded and sipped the champagne. Gloria buzzed to come through and without waiting for an answer she entered, dressed up to the nines, her huge tits busting out of the forty-six C cup. She leant on the door. 'Boxer's outside, wants a word ... let him in, shall I?'

Arnie adored Gloria. If he had been straight he would have had a scene with her. They got on well, he could yell and shout at her and she didn't give a toss. Good girl was Gloria, been with him for years, used to be a hostess downstairs, got a bit old for the racket, and went upstairs to the office. Her typing was still haywire, and she couldn't spell, but somehow she got things in order, and she looked good out there at her desk.

Gloria crossed to the champagne and helped herself to a glass, stood back and admired her figure in the mirror. She had another look at Carlos, nice looking fella, didn't know how he could stand Arnie pawing him, but then they were all the same these poofs. He was doing very nicely out of Arnie, she'd seen the suits, the eau-de-Cologne, the added business going his way. She wondered how long he would last, usually they never made it beyond two months.

Arnie was a fickle little bastard, but this one, this Carlos, it'd been near that already and they still seemed to be going strong. Gloria turned with her champagne ...

'I'm off home now, okay? Shall I show him in?'

Carlos had already stood up, as if he knew Arnie wouldn't want him in the office, but Arnie patted his arm, it was only Boxer Davis. 'Wheel him in,' he said.

Gloria wiggled out and Boxer entered, he took Arnie off guard slightly. He had had his hair cut, parted, and it was flattened down on one side, made his ears stick out, but more than that, the whistle. Boxer was actually wearing a near decent suit. Boxer looked at Carlos, Arnie waved him in; he didn't offer him a drink. Arnie sat back on the sofa and crossed his legs, he fiddled with his shoe. Boxer hovered and he stared at Carlos. Arnie eventually uncrossed his legs. 'So what you got?'

Boxer blurted it out. He'd been at the Rawlins' place, had some information, which was worth a lot of money. Boxer kept looking to Carlos, not wanting him to listen in.

'It's private.'

Eventually Arnie gave Carlos the nod to get some more champagne. As he left, Boxer sat down. It irritated Arnie, big oaf, what the hell had he come as ...?

Boxer told Arnie, told him about Harry Rawlins, told him everything Dolly had told him not to. He didn't want to, but 'this prick' made him feel so dirty, so useless, he wanted to show him: he, Boxer was back in the big time. He and Harry Rawlins could wipe this little turd out, he would show him.

Arnie's reaction was not what Boxer had expected. He took his glasses off, repeated what Boxer had told him, almost word for word ... 'Harry Rawlins is still alive eh?'

Arnie suddenly started to shriek with laughter, high-pitched, screeching laughter, his head back along the sofa. Then he looked up, squinted at Boxer, his face turned nasty, his eyes icy ...

'You stupid git, get out ... go on out ... still alive? ... do me a favour, I was at his soddin' funeral, along with the law. Who does she think she's kiddin' eh? ... eh?'

Arnie was up on his feet, Boxer backed from him, Arnie moved closer, jabbing Boxer with his finger, prodding him, his bony finger sticking his ribs. 'Get out of my sight, understand, you're through, you had your chance, you've blown it sonny, understand, you've bleedin' blown it ... an' get that rag off your back, go on, git down to the yard an' start clearin' beer crates, back where you belong ... Tony was right ... should have let him take care of it a long time ago ...'

Boxer wanted to hit him, wanted to hit him so much he could feel his hands clench, then the door opened and the boyfriend came back. All Boxer could do was snarl that Arnie could take his beer crates and stuff 'em up his arse, it was big enough.'

Boxer got to the door, Arnie was furious, his eyes popping out of his head. The boyfriend stood like a spare part holding the champagne, but Boxer still wanted the last say . . . he looked round the door. 'Oh yeah, you can tell Tony that Harry didn't like him messin' his home up, I warned him but he wouldn't listen. Harry's very angry.' Boxer nodded, and then shut the door.

Carlos, seeing Arnie was ready to explode, put his arm around his shoulders. Arnie pushed him away, and strode after Boxer, but as he reached the door, he pulled himself together, he turned to Carlos, his face contorted with rage, but his voice was icy. 'I'll have him, I'll have that stupid git.'

Carlos thought he was glad he was on the right side of Arnie. Seeing him now, the little man meant business. Carlos knew Arnie could be pretty lethal; he was frothing at the mouth, his hands clenched, his eyes behind his rimless glasses were like two yellow piss-holes in the snow – funny 'cos he thought they were blue.

Dolly was puzzled to get a message at the convent: urgent–meet at headquarters tonight.

Shirley was already in bed when she got the message: be at the lock-up, urgent, tonight. She also thought that Linda sounded pissed, she wasn't sure, but she slurred her words.

Linda *was* pissed, but sobering up. She held a cracked cup of black coffee. From outside the dressing room P. J. Proby belted out, 'Hold me, honey, won't you hold me', the recording was cracked and so loud she could hardly hear herself speak.

Bella was fixing her leather boots on, she had a whip fastened at her side, she was next on, and Linda was becoming a bit of a pain. The boss didn't like strays back stage, and drunk ones did not help. Bella needed this job, good money. She watched Linda gulp the coffee and saw

it trickle down her cheek. Linda lurched over, 'Well ...
what you think, you wanna' join us?'

Shirley couldn't believe her eyes, there was Linda,
looking dreadful, her makeup all over her face, sitting on
one of the orange boxes, telling this coloured chick
everything about the raid. She was too stunned to speak.

Linda had waved her to one side, done the introductions
as if, this whatever her name was, 'Wonder Woman' ...
Shirley had even seen Linda showing this woman the
chain saw. Christ, if Dolly was to find out, they would be
for it. She tried to get Linda to one side, but it was useless.
Linda was sitting there talking at the top of her voice
about what they were all going to do ... telling her about
the raid.

Shirley got up and made some coffee, not for herself, for
Linda. If what she said was true, and she had contacted
Dolly as well, then God help her. Dolly coming in and
seeing Linda in this state would hit the roof.

Shirley watched the two as she made coffee, Linda was
now showing Bella the shot gun. Bella, interested, looked
over her shoulder. Linda fell over, picked herself up and
rubbed her elbow. The sooner she gets some more black
coffee down her the better, thought Shirley. Shirley
handed her mug to Linda and as she reached for it, she fell
over again, sitting on the floor. She giggled and Shirley
helped her up. The other girl, Bella, whatever her name
was, had the nerve to walk into the annex and make
herself a cup of coffee. At least it gave Shirley time to grab
hold of Linda and whisper what on earth she thought she
was doing? Then they heard the outer door clang shut, the
Alsatian start up his barking next door ... Linda
soberish, paled visibly. Bella stayed in the annex
spooning sugar into a mug, Dolly's pink mug.

Shirley had never seen Dolly look so awful. Her hair
needed washing, she was tired, her face drawn, haggard
almost. Dolly wore no makeup, maybe that was why.
Suddenly she looked her age, older even than Audrey,
Shirley's mother. There again, thought Shirley, she is

old enough to be my mother. God, there was going to be one hell of an explosion. She was right.

Linda felt sick, terribly sick, she swayed slightly. Her mouth was dry, she could taste the whisky churning in her stomach. Dolly stood, hands on hips, fighting to control her anger. Somehow she had thought something had gone wrong, maybe even the Fisher brothers; the phone message had said 'urgent'. She had dropped everything, and nearly brought the police tailing her to the lock-up. It had taken her over an hour to lose them.

Dolly moved closer to Linda, bent her head, stepped back and spat out. 'You're pissed.'

Of course, Linda argued that she wasn't, she'd just had a few. Dolly advanced towards her, Shirley backed away, even though she was nowhere near. Dolly frightened her, the veins stood out on her neck, she was looking past Linda to Bella.

Bella was standing at the doorway of the annex. She was so tall her figure seemed to cut off the light. She smiled a greeting and walked towards Dolly, hand outstretched.

Shirley had seen Dolly when she had had a go at Linda earlier that evening, but she was different now, tougher, something almost mannish about her. When she eventually spoke, it was like a growl. She flicked a look to Bella and back to Linda.

'Who the hell is this?'

Linda's words tumbled out over each other trying to explain that she'd brought Bella to be the number four girl, she wanted in. Linda said she'd told her everything.

'You've told her?... YOU'VE TOLD HER?'

Linda started to cry, but Dolly stood her ground. She turned to Shirley, back to Linda, then ignoring Bella completely she began to walk out. 'It's off, that's it, over, finished. You've done it this time, I quit, and I want paying back every cent I've put into this so far, and you get that tart out of here NOW. You and that slag OUT... OUT.'

Linda stepped in front of Dolly, pleading with her just

to talk to Bella. She was perfect for the job, she could do it. Linda was blubbering, trying to keep hold of Dolly's arm. Dolly jerked herself free.

Bella had remained silent throughout. Now she put her coffee down, picked up her bag and passed Dolly so close she could have touched her, but she just walked to the door.

'Eh ... you ... just a minute.'

It was Bella's turn to whip round on Dolly. Her deep voice was controlled, but her dark eyes were blazing. 'I got a name, not tart, slag. You want to speak to me my name is Bella, Bella O'Reilly, Mrs Rawlins, and you can stuff your job ... but you're a fool, I'm right for it – where you think you're going to find someone who'll just step in, what's more, someone who'd want to?'

Maybe it was the calmness of Bella, the toughness. Whatever it was, Dolly made the first approach. Dolly took Bella's arm and led her to one side of the lock-up. She spoke quietly, head bent, not raising her eyes to meet Bella's. She asked questions and to each one Bella replied just 'yes' or 'no'. Shirley could hear the word 'guns', but whatever went on between the two women couldn't be heard by Linda or Shirley; they stood watching like two school kids.

It seemed an age before the two women broke. Dolly went over to the orange boxes and sat. She began to undo her coat. Bella stared towards her; Linda looked to Dolly and then back to Bella. Lighting a cigarette, Dolly said, 'How many more you told, Linda?'

Linda was like an eager puppy dog. She shook her head, repeating over and over, 'Just Bella.'

Then it was Dolly's turn to have a private chat with Linda, like a headmistress. She was obviously laying it on thick. Linda stood, head bowed. She cried, wiped her eyes, her voice was muffled. Shirley heard her promise not to do it again, ever. She'd never drink again. Then she was leaning back on her heels, squatting down by Dolly.

Shirley shuffled her feet, she felt like Miss Goody Two Shoes, then Dolly called her over and Linda stepped back.

'Well, what do you think?'

Shirley knew then that Bella was in with a good chance. She also looked strong enough to hold the chain saw. She nodded, 'okay by me!'

Dolly held her hand out. Bella stepped forwards, Bella was to be the number four girl.

Chapter Fourteen

The three girls had been working alongside each other for over four weeks, buying, collecting, training. They rarely saw Dolly as she was still having a lot of trouble with the law. They trailed her everywhere, but the girls were free. Shirley went on daily shopping expeditions to buy the kits, shopping all over London, making sure that nothing was traceable. Always paying cash, each garment was cut, no buttons, belts, ties, nothing that could come loose or catch on anything.

Bella kept herself fit at a gym, she learnt to handle the chain saw, the engine, taking it apart and putting it back together again.

Linda kept up her good work on the motor, she learnt about engine stripping, speeding, and the more she learnt, the more often she met with Carlos, in secret afternoon sessions. Linda was becoming very fond of him, she liked him.

The law, meanwhile, had also gone one step ahead, and one back.

They had the bread truck used by the Rawlins' gang. Two days of extensive enquiries, every man and woman in the company had their prints taken, a long, tedious procedure.

Resnick had narrowed the field down to the two mechanics who worked the company haulage and repair yard, but these had eventually been eliminated. Neither had seen the truck driven into the yard, neither could recognise any of the men from the Rawlins' raid ... They had never seen Harry Rawlins, Terry Miller or Joe Pirelli enter their yard. They had not seen the driver who replaced the truck. However, one man had been made redundant three months before; Len Gulliver, fifteen years with the firm, worked a fiddle with his two lads, had a spare set of keys to the yard. Resnick gave orders to move out and pick up Len Gulliver. For the first time in weeks he actually thought they were getting somewhere, in fact he was almost pleasant, put a 'tenner' on Len Gulliver being their lead.

Resnick was right about Gulliver. His wife was able to identify Joe Pirelli as actually coming to the house to talk to her husband. She was even able to recognise Harry Rawlins as the man who remained outside in a dark grey Mercedes Benz.

Resnick could feel his insides churn, he couldn't wait to get his hands on Gulliver himself. Mrs Gulliver was surprised that no one at the bread company had told Resnick, but then they had treated her Len no better than a dog. Fifteen years he worked for them: and just like that, finished, out, don't want you any more, two hundred quid for fifteen years service. Resnick nodded in agreement. Poor man, dreadful, but he really would like to see him.

Resnick met Gulliver. He was in the back room, his coffin all ready for the funeral the next morning. Mrs Gulliver was still complaining about the bread company as Resnick and Fuller left, they could hear her going on behind their backs.

'Got him in the throat, cancer, but if you ask me, it was that bread truck company that put the nail in.'

Resnick knew this meant they were back where they started. Fuller also knew, but right at this moment, he couldn't stop himself. He got a fit of the giggles, kept on repeating what Mrs Gulliver had said. 'Gotta be a classic that ... classic.'

Resnick managed to wipe the grin off Fuller's face when

he held out his hand for the ten pound bet. His good humour was very short lived. As he got into the car, Andrews informed him that Alice, his secretary, had been on the blower, twice. He had apparently had an appointment with the Chief. Resnick swore, Fuller started the car, he enquired if it was something important, knowing full well that Resnick had arranged an appointment to review his chances for promotion. The whole squad knew; Resnick's promotional stakes were, as ever, pretty low, even lower now that he had missed his appointment ... and the Super there too! Through the mirror Fuller gave a hooded look at Andrews sitting in the back. Resnick caught it, but took it on the chin. He instructed Fuller to take a look at the Rawlins woman's house, see if anything had cropped up.

Green Teeth put in a call to speak with Detective Inspector Resnick; no one could find him, he said he'd call again. The chaps drove slowly past the house. In darkness, curtains drawn, the patrol car was standing at the curb. Hawkes nearly bolted through the roof when Resnick banged his window, they had nothing to report, nothing, no movement, nothing.

Resnick went back to the station. Again 'Green Teeth' called. This time he spoke to Resnick, told him he had something for him, something about the Rawlins ledgers.

Arnie Fisher was in a blazing row with his brother Tony. Tony had been up North doing a bit of business with a delivery. All he had to do was make sure the delivery was on time, the truck unloaded and the goods (booze) stored ... simple, neat arrangement with contacts up in Manchester. No rough stuff, simple cash transaction, just required one of the big boys to do the entertaining lark for a couple of nights, keep the chaps up there happy.

Arnie had a good thing going with two clubs up in Manchester. Shipment of over twenty grand's worth of booze coming to him for less than twelve, can't be bad. Somehow Tony had blown it, somehow the idiot had put his foot in it somewhere.

Tony had gone up North, in the Jag done over by Carlos. All he had to do was act Mr Big, entertain, right? And he had acted Mr Big Shot. Unfortunately he had also given one of the contact's wives a thorough going over. Pretty little blonde with big tits. He had been fingered, got into a fight, and just when he should be shaking hands and departing up the motorway back home, he is having a fist fight in The Golden Slipper. Fist fight gets out of hand, the law are called, Tony does a runner in the Jag. Speeding, he smashes up a stationary vehicle and heads for the M.1.

Now Tony explains all this aggro in his own terms, just a 'bit of a problem' no mention of the blonde piece, no mention of the fight, just that perhaps the motor might have been spotted by the law and would need a little attention.

Arnie is blazing, because Tony has not even got a detailed run down of all the booze in storage. He's had a message on the blower that the lads up there are none too happy ...

Tony lounges in the swivel chair, he's been trying to get Arnie to tell him what's been going with the Rawlins business. Arnie still fiddles and fusses with his booze lists. Tony blows, 'The law get hold of them ledgers, sweetheart, you an' me go down for fifteen, an' you're needled about ten bottles of bleedin' cherry brandy.'

The brothers bicker and row, as always; Arnie trying to keep Tony on an even keel. Eventually, he tells him that he can take over from Boxer. No one has seen Boxer for two or three days. Not since he told Arnie that Harry Rawlins was still alive.

Tony's mouth gaped, then he laughed. He could see that Arnie was edgy. He told him not to worry, he'd get hold of Boxer, get down to the bottom of it.

Arnie digs his hands into his pockets, he doesn't want any trouble, any Harry Rawlins kind of trouble. He takes his glasses off. 'Maybe Boxer's got the ledgers ... he was very cocky ... got a new whistle on.' Arnie put his glasses back on ... Half of him wants to let Tony have his head, go

and finish everything off, get the ledgers, see the idiot
Boxer, but there is something niggling him. Doesn't even
know what it is, but as soon as he sees Tony looking at
himself, combing his hair, he knows. He crosses and
stands behind him. 'Don't do nothin' crazy now ... we got
a good business going, don't go crazy, don't touch 'em ...
the widows, just ask a few questions.'

Tony grins, and pats Arnie's cheek. As he moves to the
door, it opens and Carlos enters. He's come to collect the
Jag. Tony is on him like a bird. 'You knock darlin' ...
understand me? Knock before you just walk in ...'

Arnie smooths Tony out, he waves Carlos in, again he
takes Tony's arm and warns him to be careful. Tony leans
on the door, looks at his brother. 'Listen petal, Rawlins is
dead, we got nothin' to worry from him, only thing we got
on our backs are the ledgers, an' if I'd had my way we'd
have had 'em by now ... I'll pay that cousin of Harry's a
visit, number one. Then I'll pay the widows a little visit;
then deliver that idiot Boxer ... don't worry, I'll sort it all
out ...'

Tony gives a kissing pout to Carlos and slams out.
Carlos looks at Arnie questioningly. 'Trouble?'

'Nothing, just got a few loose ends to clean up. See,
when Harry Rawlins snuffed it he left a few widows
behind him, his lads, Miller and Pirelli ...'

Carlos stared and thought: Pirelli. He said nothing,
smiled a toast to Arnie and drank the champagne.

On the sofa was a large tissue wrapped box, Arnie
nodded for Carlos to open it. It was the white silk suit, the
one he had promised ... Carlos held it up, smiling. 'Pirelli
... I heard that name someplace?'

Arnie fussed and fiddled, putting the jacket on Carlos.

'Yeah, he was one of the big timers, Rawlins' mob, his
wife runs the arcade down the road, real slag; but Joe, he
was heavy duty.'

Arnie stepped back admiring the fit on Carlos ...

Carlos remembered the photograph, the one at the side
of Linda's bed but he said nothing.

*

Eddie Rawlins was sitting in his disgusting office. A shack stuck in the middle of a wrecked car yard. In some areas the cars were piled three or four deep on top of each other. The colours still bright. Eddie liked colours, often used to sit in his office staring at the colours, he had decided that the day he made enough money for a Roller it would be sky blue ... Silver Cloud, sky blue ... 'Yeah, nice that.'

Eddie had been given a tip for Haydock, three fifteen ... he had flipped through the papers and came up with a couple of possible runners and was on the blower to a mate with a little shop near Epsom. Not too much, just a fiver here and there. Eddie was careful, the careful sort that would only put a fiver each way on a pony, then be taken in by a con for a hundred quid buying the wife a 'hot fur number' that usually turned out to be as pony as his horse.

Eddie heard a car draw up, but the window wasn't at the right angle for him to see anyone crossing the yard. The window was so filthy you couldn't see out of it anyway. Eddie carried on yakkin', he looked up when his door opened ... he still kept on yakkin', but his stomach turned over, his visitor was Tony Fisher.

Eddie tried hard to act nonchalant, replaced the receiver casually, took his feet off the desk and reached for a bottle of Scotch. He went over to the filing cabinet to get glasses, and took a quickie through the stained window. Tony was alone, his car parked out by the wrecks ... Ford Granada, terrible shit green colour. All the time Eddie's head is buzzing, but the rabbit kept on dribbling out.

'Bad business, nobody doin' much, how's things with you? Nice club, nice place ...'

Eddie was, by now, pouring the drinks. He missed the glass completely when Tony, sitting, relaxed, opposite his desk, asked about the Rawlins' ledgers.

Tony Fisher was actually very good at his line of work, in fact he was everything he tried for. His fancy clothes, his muscles, his manicured hands, even to the diamond in his ear, carefully assembled. He crossed his legs, the

Gucci shoes were polished. Arnie had tried to give him class, but the diamond in the ear gave him away. Tony thought it made him sexy, and in his way he was, and it did, but his eyes let him down, they were shifty, sly, gave him away completely. Tony Fisher looked at your forehead when he spoke, he never met you eye to eye. He was flicking looks all round the filthy squalid hut knowing the effect he was having on Eddie. Eddie was terrified. The feeling made Tony feel good, it was always the same. He uncrossed his legs and leant forward taking out his handkerchief, he stood as if to take his glass, but he grabbed Eddie by the hair and stuffed the handkerchief into Eddie's open, scared mouth. It was all over in a matter of minutes, Tony had hauled Eddie against the wall, butted him in the face, removed the handkerchief and gently wiped the blood from Eddie ... he leant his head close, whispered, 'Tell me about Harry Rawlins' ledgers – what you know about them?'

Eddie, in tears, pleaded, said over and over he didn't know what Tony was talking about, he'd never seen the ledgers. Tony was opening the door, he turned, inspected his bloody handkerchief and tossed it into the bin. 'Boxer Davis seems to think your Harry's still alive. If you find out anything, let me know.'

Eddie waited until he heard the car drive off, then he picked up the phone, he touched his still bleeding nose. Eddie explained what had happened, his voice was high-pitched, hysterical, as he repeated what had just taken place. Then he listened intently, he sat down, he tried to interrupt, but was cut short, eventually Eddie agreed to find Boxer Davis.

He replaced the receiver and examined his face in a cracked mirror stuck on top of the filing cabinet. He stared at the phone. Eddie didn't like Bill Grant, he was another 'Tony', didn't like working with him at all.

From where Eddie was standing he saw the rows of wrecks, the sun was glinting, sparkling down on the colours ... still the best was the blue of an old Cortina ... Eddie sighed and took out his car keys, he locked up, and weaved his way across the yard, he got into an old Rover, metal grey.

Chapter Fifteen

The girls were all busy at work in the lock-up. Shirley over in her corner was busily sorting out two pairs of overalls she had bought, carefully cutting out the labels and burning them in a trash can.

Dolly was sitting with route maps, like an accountant, pouring over his figures. Bella and Linda were respraying a white Ford Escort van, both women were filthy, covered in paint, with the machines going – they didn't hear the front main gate of the garage bang. Little Wolf did, he started to yap, then the Alsatian from next door started to bark. Dolly froze, signalled for the girls to keep quiet, Linda moved to the duck boards to get out a shot gun. Bella held her back, Dolly was already on the move. The lights were turned out, again they heard the bang, bang from the main gates.

Dolly had Wolf in her arms, she edged open the small door built into the main gates, edged just a crack. The girls stood grouped in the inner annex doorway listening. They could hear Dolly murmuring, a deeper voice answering back, then the click of the door being closed.

Dolly walked slowly back to them, she was frowning, dragging on the ever present cigarette, she blew out the smoke. 'We got problems ... any of you ever heard of a Bill Grant?'

The girls looked at each other and shrugged, they followed Dolly back into their inner sanctum, she picked up her bag, stubbed the cigarette out. 'He said he was a friend of Harry's, lock-up further down, wondered if I wanted to lease this place ... said he was a mechanic.'

Again the girls looked at each other, what was so terrible about that?

'Harry would never let it be known this was one of his places. I'll have to check him out ... see if I can get to the ledgers.'

Dolly left, the girls continued to work. Shirley could hear Linda moaning to Bella about Dolly, seemed that 'they always had to do the dirty work, how come they never had a blimp at the ledgers?'

Shirley was nearly through, she pressed down the ashes in the bin, straightened up and checked her watch – if she left now she could see 'Dallas'.

Linda and Bella watched Shirley leave and continued spraying, both had to go on to work later that night so there was no point in going home. Linda really had a moan, Bella said nothing, but she listened. A lot of what Linda was saying was true, they did all seem to be doing the running around, but then Dolly was paying them. Something was niggling Bella, but she kept it to herself. She just began keeping her eyes open, began watching Dolly, as from that evening.

Dolly found no trace of Bill Grant in the ledgers. She went on to work at the convent. She was on 'dinners' the next day and decided to get all the potatoes done, give her more free time in the day. There was no real need for her to go to work but she couldn't keep still lately, liked to keep herself busy in the evenings. She also liked the law to have a fair crack at tracking her down and keeping to some kind of a routine, made it a lot easier when she wanted to lose them. They were outside now, well they'd have a long wait, she would take her time in the kitchens, nothing else to do.

Linda was pretty knackered when she arrived at the arcade. She was just going in when she saw Carlos walking past; she stopped and kissed him. She was pleased to see him, he looked very smart, said he'd tried to call her earlier that afternoon. They arranged to meet the following day, they were still chatting when Charlie came up. Linda was late, he hadn't had a break yet. As he was talking he was having a good look at Carlos. So this was why Mrs Pirelli had been so friendly lately, she must be getting her oats. She was fairly eating him now, splothering all over him. Charlie was jealous as hell, for years he'd been after Linda, never got a look in. 'Oi, i'n't it about time you got in and did some work?'

Linda gave Carlos a kiss again. Across the street, Boxer Davis passed. He had a bag of fish and chips. He stopped, recognised Carlos, saw Linda reach up to kiss him. She disappeared into the arcade, and Carlos moved off. Boxer stood watching, then he crossed the road just as Charlie was nipping out for his break. Boxer stopped him.

'Eh, that Joe Pirelli's missus?'

Charlie nodded, and moved off, he knew Boxer, knew him of old, always ready for a hand out, well he wasn't gettin' anything from ... Charlie stopped, turned, he took in the suit. Boxer must be doing all right for himself, looks half-way decent. Just in case Charlie might get in on anything Boxer might have going, he shouted after him. 'See you around Boxer ... anytime.'

Boxer turned and beamed, he waved. Something definitely going on, thought Charlie, maybe he's got some kind of racket. He continued on for his sandwiches, hands stuck in his pockets. He wished something was soddin' going on for him, his leg had been playing him up something rotten. He dug around in his pocket until he had a gentle grip on his balls. Comforted, he went on his way, head bent, slight limp, faint grin on his face.

Chapter Sixteen

Resnick sat in the back of the police car, seething. He had had yet another bugger of a day, no results, nothing ... he knew his 'guvnor' was beginning to review the whole case, he knew he had to come up with something, but he had nothing. Resnick lit up and inhaled deeply, he saw

Fuller wince as the smoke curled into the front seat – just let him try and open that window, just let him try.

Resnick was spoiling for a fight; twice that day he had asked to have a word with the Chief. The station was bedlam, the painters and decorators trolling all over the place. Resnick hated the idea of the new communal annex, it wasn't his style. Judging from what had gone on so far with this Rawlins business he was beginning to think he'd lost his touch. He shut his eyes and sighed. He went over everything they had got so far, it always ended up with a big zero ... someone, somewhere has those bloody ledgers, he knew it, but whoever had them wasn't making a move.

Resnick flipped open his brief case and studied the reports; the Rawlins woman had become adept at losing her tail. Mind you, with the lads he'd got on his team that wouldn't be too difficult. He turned over, staring at Dolly Rawlins' notes: Hairdresser ... The Sanctuary, salon, bank, hairdressers, convent, convent ... certainly had her hair done a lot, also went to the bank a lot. The car halted and papers fell on the floor. Resnick swore at Fuller, he stuffed the papers back in his brief case.

'Regents Park ... Sir.'

Fuller knew how to get under Resnick's skin – the constant use of 'Sir'. Resnick opened the car door, and flicked a look at Detective Andrews. He was staring into space, bloody miles away. God, what a bunch ... he slammed the car and shouted over his shoulder to give him ten minutes.

Resnick wandered through the park gates, maybe he'd strike lucky. 'Green Teeth' usually had a titbit about something, maybe he could give 'em a leg up – they certainly needed it.

Linda was counting out the change when a hand thrust a twenty pound note through the kiosk window. She was about to give the owner a mouthful when she saw who it was: Tony Fisher. Linda felt her stomach lurch, but she

74

smiled, and Tony pressed his face closer to the small glass. She could smell his eau-de-Cologne, heavy, sweet. He stared at her forehead, then his face disappeared. He moved round to the small door of the booth.

Linda clocked that Charlie was back, she also clocked that when he saw it was Tony Fisher, he turned away. Little turd she thought. Tony was very pleasant, if you could ever call him that. Wanted to know if he could take her out, have a chat. Linda made up to him, she'd love to see him, always wanted to go into his swish club. She saw him swagger slightly, she moved closer to the door and leaned, showing her figure. 'I'm not off until twelve ... how about coming back then?'

Tony undressed her with his eyes, inside she curled up, but she kept the smile on her face all the time. It nearly slipped when he began asking questions about Shirley. Where did she live? Did she still see her? ... Linda didn't know how she kept it up but the chat kept flowing. 'Shirley? ... Oh no, I've not seen her in ages, might be back with her mother, stuck up cow, still thinks she's Miss World.'

Tony backed off, he left Linda the twenty pound note, strolled to the exit, patted Charlie on the head, then turned. 'See you about twelve then darlin' ...'

Linda sagged onto the stool, Charlie rushed over, told her she must be out of her mind foolin' around with him. 'You know who that was don't you ... that was Tony Fisher.'

Linda tried to contact Shirley, she got no reply. She called Bella, told her to try and contact Shirley, warn her to stay out of sight. Tony Fisher was on the war path.

Bella tried to call Shirley, no reply. She eventually put a call through to Dolly, hoped to God she was still at the convent and could get the message to Shirley. Bella was told that Dolly was not available, but the message would be passed on.

Bella couldn't really tell some nun or other that a friend of Dolly's was in danger of being beaten up. I mean it wouldn't sound quite right, so she left an urgent message for Dolly to contact Bella, repeating that the message was urgent.

Shirley felt fresh and clean, she'd had a bath and washed her hair. She began cleaning her nails. She'd had to cut them very short, kept on breaking them down at the lock-up. Sitting in the steamy bathroom where it was warm, cosy, like a womb, it made her feel safe. The radio was playing something classical, she liked that, not sure what it was, but it was nice: trumpets.

Fuller and Andrews had circled the park so many times they were beginning to get dizzy. When they picked up Resnick they had to make another round trip. Resnick was in need of a Gents. Fuller waited as Resnick relieved himself behind a tree because no conveniences were open. Fuller was still, to his annoyance, unaware as to what had taken place with 'Green Teeth'. Detective Andrews, sitting in the back, grinned. He suggested that perhaps all their 'guv' had done was feed the ducks. Fuller hunched further into his seat. He looked out of the window with disgust. 'I'd like to feed him to something, certainly wouldn't be effing ducks.' Resnick was very subdued when he got back into the car. He eventually repeated the information from 'Green Teeth'. 'Appears Boxer Davis is suddenly very flush. He's spreadin' it around town he's working for ...'
Resnick couldn't say it. He lit a cigarette and stared out of the window. 'Says he's working for Harry Rawlins.'
Andrews rubbed his head. 'What? "Green Teeth"?'
Resnick snorted and spat out. 'Boxer Davis, you idiot. It's a load of old bollocks, but, well, he is throwing money around, maybe he knows something we don't.'
Resnick scratched his nose. 'That's not sayin' much though, is it?'
Fuller yawned. Andrews looked to Resnick, leaning his arm along the back of his seat. Resnick glared at Fuller. 'Well, get a bloody move on, pick him up!'

*

Boxer was counting out the money Dolly had given him. He was tickled pink. He stacked it all up in neat piles. Dolly had said get out of town for a couple of weeks, until Harry needed him.

Boxer picked up the faded brown photograph of himself and his son. The little boy was perched on his dad's shoulders waving at the camera. Boxer rubbed his flat nose. Maybe he could look up Bibi, see if she would see him. Little fella must be what? Eight? He shook his big ugly head, he couldn't even remember how old the boy was.

Boxer carefully placed the photo in an old battered suitcase. He felt so good, so damned good. He shook his head and chuckled, he could still see Arnie's face. Boxer muttered to himself. 'You can stuff those beer crates up your arse, it's big enough.' Boxer stuffed some cold chips into his mouth and laughed, they tasted awful, so he scrunched the paper up and chucked them into the already overflowing waste basket. The waste bin was like the rest of the bedsit, battered, dirty. Boxer surveyed the room, well, he'd be out of the place soon. He was glad. Harry would see that he had a decent place. Boxer eased his huge frame into the one easy chair. 'Harry', he closed his eyes.

Boxer could see him, clear as day. The first time he had met Harry Rawlins it was at the ringside, he'd looked down and seen the row of empty chairs for the 'specials' filling up. Harry, cigar clamped in his mouth, looked straight up to Boxer. 'There's a grand riding on you tonight, my old son.'

The door banged, Boxer opened his eyes. He knew who it was, he could hear her puffing and panting outside his door.

'Eh, Boxer, you in? Boxer?'

Boxer didn't answer, he looked with loathing to the door. It was Fran, Fran the ten ton landlady, the huge, over made-up, foul breathed, Francese Welland. When Boxer was sober he couldn't face the fact that when drunk he could sink into her bulk, even love her. Boxer had been sober for five months.

'Boxer, I know you're in there.'

His doorknob rattled as she tried to get in.

'You've got a visitor, open the door.'

Boxer opened up, his face creased into a huge grin. Standing behind Fran was Eddie Rawlins. He shut the door in Fran's eager interested face. Boxer tried to tidy the table. Eddie took out of his pocket a bottle of malt whisky, Boxer's favourite. Boxer shook his head and held his hand up, but then reached for two mugs – it was, after all Harry's cousin.

Fran could hear the phone ringing and ringing, she shifted her bulk and then heaved her way to it. Fran shouted up for Boxer ...

Boxer was well pissed, the chair toppling over as he went for the door. Fran stood panting on the landing. 'It's for you, dear – deaf are you?'

Boxer caught her in his arms and kissed her and, with his arm flung round her shoulders, he went down the flight of stairs to the telephone. Fran went all girlish and giggly, and whispered in his ear.

Boxer answered the phone and Fran eased her way downstairs to her room, she lolled in the doorway smiling up at him. 'I got a bottle of gin down here Boxer!'

He waved to her, smiling stupidly, then went back to speaking into the phone. Fran went into her room and closed the door.

Dolly tried hard to hear what Boxer was saying. His words were slurred. He mumbled something about Pirelli, and the Italian. He had seen the Italian ... then the phone went dead.

Dolly re-dialled and still the phone was dead. Dolly chewed her lip, she was tired. First the panic call from Bella, now she couldn't get hold of Boxer!

Dolly tried again, only to be told by some woman that he had just gone out! Dolly was in a quandry as to what to do.

*

Resnick and Fuller were at the third known address for Boxer Davis. Seemed Boxer did a moonlight every five to six months. Fuller craned forwards to watch Andrews coming down the steps of yet another seedy rooming house.

'Not here, but I got an address he's supposed to be at.'

Resnick snorted and pulled his hat over his eyes.

'It's Ladbroke Grove.'

They moved off, and Resnick's head lolled onto Fuller's shoulder. He began to snore, Andrews looked through the driving mirror and grinned. Fuller's face was a picture.

Boxer was well and truly legless, hardly able to stand up. Club after club, round after round of drinks. Eddie and he were now in the dingy basement of the Sportsmen's Club. The walls were covered with faded photos of ex boxers and wrestlers.

Boxer was the centre of attention. He was reliving his last bout blow by blow. They had all heard it before, but cheered and egged him on. Eddie kept the drinks flowing into the big hand.

Boxer was onto the final round, his head jerking, his arms flaying. He spilt his drink onto a small round bald man. Boxer kissed the top of the little man's head and slung his arm round the man's shoulder.

Eddie watched the staircase. The jeans and plimsolls came down, Eddie was given the nod. No one noticed, Boxer had everyone's attention.

Boxer insisted his new little bald friend now accompany them. The barman showed Eddie the fire exit doors, he knew the 'Champ' would not make it up the stairs. Propped up between Eddie and Baldy, the threesome burst through the exit doors into the back alley, Bins and crates of beer were stacked either side of the doors. An old wino was busily picking his way through one of the bins.

Boxer fell to his knees as the cold air hit him. Eddie looked to the alley exit. The headlamps blinked on once, then he heard the car reverse. Eddie now had to get Baldy away. 'Let's get to the dogs, eh? You fancy a spin down the City?'

Eddie and the little fat man left Boxer slumped in a heap by the bins. They were about two yards from the exit of the alley when they got into a cab. Eddie saw the car edge towards the alley.

Boxer staggered to his feet, holding onto the bin. 'Wait for me ... eh ... wait for me.'

The head lamps went on full blast, Boxer put his hand up to shade his eyes, he swayed, the lights went out. The tramp flattened himself against the wall, the car seemed to fill the alley, the engine roared. The tramp saw the bins fly up into the air, heard a pitiful moan and ran for his life.

Three times the car reversed and screeched up the alley. The bumper crashed against the brick wall. The bins and bottles banged and shattered. The neon lights blinked on and off. The loud rock music thudded.

No one would have known he was there. It was the trickle of blood, slowly seeping onto the brightly lit pavement that eventually led them to Boxer, the 'champ'.

Dolly pushed and shoved her way through the crowds of cheering men. They were calling and shouting abuse towards the small stage. A ramp led down from the stage through the crowds.

Striding down the catwalk, clad in black leather and wielding a long whip, was Bella. She was like a panther, cracking the whip above her head.

Dolly looked up and watched. Bella was beautiful, there was a wildness about her, an overpowering sexiness. She swayed to the music, arrogantly staring ahead. She began stripping off. Dolly was shocked; off came the black leather bra, Bella's body was oiled, she glistened, naked but for a tiny G-string and thigh length boots. Bella moved her crotch sexily. Dolly clutched her handbag, her eyes popping out of her head. Bella was tossing her head, her mouth open in a grimace, like an animal. She stared hard at Bella's face, the eyes had a completely impassive bored stare. Bella was detached above them all, untouchable. Dolly was proud of her, for that moment, proud watching the whip crack over the men's heads. Dolly felt Bella's strength, not one of these gawping men would ever touch that inner core. Maybe that was what Dolly had seen that night at the lock-up. Dolly had seen the real Bella, she understood the desperation to get out of this, this kind of life.

Dolly had to shove and push her way to the stage exit, she just caught Bella as she was going off. Already the next act was on, Bella forgotten. A drag queen was prancing up and down the catwalk. Bella got on her knees and bent down to speak to Dolly. 'Tony Fisher is on the war path, he's after Shirley. She's not answering her phone.'

Dolly was shoved from behind and turned round to thump the guy. She looked back to Bella. 'I can't take care of everything.'

Bella looked hard at Dolly. 'Seems the rumour hasn't paid off.'

Dolly said she would do what she could about contacting Shirley. She was about to leave when she asked Bella if Linda was seeing an Italian. Bella shook her head, stood up, she had two more gigs to do that night.

Dolly watched Bella walk off stage, she turned, she could see the law standing watching her. She was so knackered she felt like asking for a lift home.

Linda was tired, working all day at the lock-up, and at the arcade every night was beginning to take its toll. She'd already made two mistakes counting out the takings. She wanted to be out of the place before twelve just in case Tony Fisher came back.

Charlie was hovering round the entrance, staring out along Wardour Street, ambulances and police cars seemed to be having a field day out there. Linda was just finishing counting a stack of change when Charlie shouted. 'Back in a sec, gonna see what's up ...'

Linda could have throttled him, she had to start all over again. She had just finished when she was back, flushed, running, she'd hardly ever seen him run, not with his bad leg, but she was fairly doing a Seb Coe.

'Bomb ... is it a bomb?'

Charlie pressed his face against the glass, 'Boxer ... it's Boxer Davis, someone done the poor bastard in, he's like a minute steak, I've bleedin' never seen anythin' like it ... blood up the walls, blood everywhere.'

Linda went icy cold, she stared, she heard her own voice. 'Boxer ... Boxer?'

'Yeah, I only saw him earlier, thought he was lookin' good, I said to myself he must be onto something big see, and then ...'

Linda went to the exit and stood with the rest of the gawping spectators. The blue lights of the ambulance were spinning round and round, the police siren wailed. Linda felt sick, terribly sick, she turned to make her way back to the booth. Charlie was describing, in all its gory detail, the body of Boxer, she kept hearing him repeat it.

'Minute steak ... minute steak ...'

Linda wondered if Bella had been able to contact Shirley, she was in a dither as to what to do. Seemed Dolly's rumour had got right out of hand.

Resnick ran up the stairs, but even before he stepped into the room he knew something had gone wrong.

Fran, Boxer's landlady, lay on his bed, her face was beaten black and blue, blood was streaming from her nose, and a cut above her eye. She was lying like a beached whale, moaning.

Resnick couldn't get any sense out of her, she was weeping and wailing, rocking back and forth, she didn't know who had done this to her, she didn't see his face.

Resnick spoke to Fuller, told him that no one takes a beating as severe as she'd had given to her, and not see the bastard's face.

The ambulance arrived to take Fran to hospital. It was radioed through that Boxer Davis was in intensive care, he was still alive.

*

Linda went round to one of Bella's clubs, she waited for her and told her the news. Boxer had been in an accident, and from what she'd heard, the accident was intentional.

Chapter Seventeen

Shirley started the car, it was dead as a dodo. Right, she thought, I'll have him for this, I'll really have him, but on the third try it jumped into life and she spluttered down the road. Audrey was frozen, her feet were killing her, even the fur lined boots didn't help in this weather. She blew into her mitted hands. Awful business, not done a thing since eight-thirty. She didn't like to keep drinking coffee as she had to keep leaving the stall to take a pee; that meant asking 'Mushroom Features' on the next stall to take care of hers, and she knew what that meant. Ten pence for Audrey, ten pence for himself.

Audrey saw the car pull up, very nice, flash, wasn't sure what the make was, lovely brown colour. She knew Tony Fisher of old, his mother and her mother had worked down the garden together, before it was all cleared. Now she'd heard she was doing the cleaning for a big firm up at the Aldwych.

Audrey watched Tony go over to one of the stalls. Handsome bloke; the coat he had on his back must have set him back a few hundred. She shrugged, his mother was cleaning offices and there he was parading round like a fashion plate. She shook her head and bent to straighten her paper bags; she looked up, he was coming towards her. She smiled, he nodded, cheeky bugger she thought, who the hell does he think he is putting on airs with me? She touched her woolly hat, and nodded to 'Mushroom Features'. With a look to Tony, the squirt turned his back on Audrey, all along the line you could see the stall holders take one look at Tony, then busy themselves. Tony nodded to the apples, Audrey weighed him a pound and gave them over for free. She wished she had gone to the lav, this boy put the willies right up her.

'Where's your Shirley these days?'

Audrey was no fool, no one comes down asking questions without wanting something, and it usually is something you don't want to give, so she busied herself with the oranges. Audrey was thinking; had her baby got herself involved with the Fishers? She had suddenly been very flush. The next minute Tony had a grip on the edge of the stall, he was going to overturn the lot.

Shirley didn't see Tony's face, she walked up to the stall from behind. She wanted to find Greg – that brother had sold her a duff motor. Then it was too late, Tony was smiling, looking at her forehead and guiding her towards the shit brown car, very pleasant, just wanted a chat. The grip on her elbow was hurting, Shirley gabbled that she was back living with her mum, said it loud enough for Audrey to hear.

Soon as they'd moved off, Audrey was running like a hare, out of the gate towards the pub. One of the stall holders, laughed, thought it was her bladder again, but Audrey was frightened, scared for her baby.

The shambolic mess of Audrey's kitchen disgusted Tony as he picked his way through laundry bags and stacks of washing and rubbish. The ironing board was laden with clothes waiting to be ironed. The kitchen table had the remains of the breakfast, probably a week of breakfasts by the amount of dirty dishes. Only surpassed by those stacked in the sink, and covering the draining board.

Tony took off his cashmere coat, folded it and placed it on the ironing board, he pulled a chair out and sat. Shirley was shaking, she couldn't hide it, she wasn't clever like Linda, she was scared and she knew she was showing it.

Tony watched her. He had fancied her since he first saw her, must be over five years ago when she was just a kid. Why'd she'd married that mutton head Terry? He had brought her down the club, to a private party. Shirley must have been only sixteen, but she was well stacked even then, fresh, eatable. Tony crossed his legs and eased his crotch, he was turning himself on just thinking about it.

She was shaking, like a quiver, all over her. He could see her hand as she opened the fridge door, the milk was off. He watched her bend her lovely head and sniff the bottle. 'It'll have to be black.'

Then she was filling the kettle, every movement was sexy, and the more flustered she got, the more sexy he found it. He sucked his knuckle, it was red, raw, scratched, he licked it.

Shirley had to squeeze past him to get the coffee, he grabbed her and sat her down on his knee. She sat stiff backed, he could smell her, fresh, like fresh lemons. Close, too, he could see her clear fresh skin, she was like a delicate flower. Tony began to undo her shirt. She tried to stop him, held his hand but it was like a child's hand, no strength, he ignored it, just undid another button. Shirley got off his knee and went for the coffee.

Tony laughed, Shirley was trying to spoon out instant coffee, button up her shirt and pour the boiling water. Her hand was shaking so much she was helpless. Tony lit a cigarette and crossed over, he took the kettle out of her hands and poured the boiling water. Shirley tried to move away from him, but she was trapped, he just placed his free arm around her waist. 'What you know about the Rawlins' ledgers?'

If Shirley had been frightened before, she was now terrified, she forced her voice out. 'Nothing, I don't know anything about them.'

Tony drew on his cigarette; his arm still loose around her waist. Then it tightened, he pulled her shirt away from her breast. He held his cigarette close, almost touching. Shirley screamed and tried to break from him. He held her tight, she wriggled, the cigarette was knocked out of his hand, he suddenly blazed. He hit her hard across the mouth, so hard he released his own grip on her. She crumpled in a heap onto the floor, her lip was cracked and a thin trickle of blood oozed out. The colour was poppy red, red against the ashen pale skin. Tony gripped her by the hair, he began to unzip his trousers, forcing her head down.

Greg had never been one for good timing, now it was perfection. The back door was flung open, and there he was. Shirley had never loved him so much in all her life. Greg stood in his leather gear, his studs and his pink and yellow hair. Behind him, Arch, with his 'mohawk' and his leopard T-shirt, and Fruity Totty's shaved head and eye makeup ... the three were like some bizarre movie-go-round, standing in the doorway, looking like Toyah on a poor night ... but being there was enough to stop Tony, he zipped up his pants.

Greg stepped further into the kitchen. He was scared out of his head. He looked to Shirley, 'You all right?'

Greg's two mates stared hard at Tony Fisher. Both stepped back as Tony put out his hand. He laughed at them, and reached for his coat. Tony slipped the cashmere round his shoulders, then turned to the two boys. He walked to the door. 'I got a good memory for faces.'

He tapped Fruity on the cheek and left.

Fruity was the first to crack the tension. He looked down at his clothes. ''E can remember me face, in this gear?'

Greg held his sister, probably for the first time in years. She was shaking, trying to cover herself. Greg took her through into his bedroom and sat her down. Greg was embarrassed to see Shirley like this. He had no idea how to help her, he knew she was frightened. He just sat with her, holding her hand.

Arch tapped on the bedroom door and came in with a cup of coffee. Shirley couldn't drink it, he had used the milk.

Chapter Eighteen

Resnick had been waiting all night outside the ward. They wouldn't let him in, not even to see the poor bastard. He had smoked his way through a whole packet of cigarettes. Eight beakers of coffee, well, one chicken soup and sugar. Resnick was stiff and tired and hungry.

The doctor came out. He didn't have to say anything. Resnick knew by the look on the man's face that Boxer hadn't made it. The doctor watched as the small, squat man walked out. He turned to the seat where he had been sitting and shook his head. It was a wonder he was still on his feet with that much smoke inside his lungs. Above the seat where Resnick had been sitting was a large sign: 'No Smoking'. Surrounding the seat were fag ends, ash and squashed coffee beakers.

Resnick opened a fresh packet of cigarettes. He had half eaten a pork pie and given up. The pastry was 'cementish'. He lit up and flipped open the surveillance reports. The only thing that Hawkes and Richmond had to report that was slightly out of the ordinary was that Rawlins' widow had paid a visit to a strip joint.

Resnick burped, tasted the pork pie in his mouth and dragged heavily on the fag. He was all in, he would call it quits for the weekend. Resnick tapped the desk with a pencil, the only thing he had was the landlady, Boxer's landlady. She must have seen who beat her up, he wanted her down the Yard over the weekend, take a bloody roll up bed if necessary. He wanted her to go over every mug shot until she came up with the man who beat her. It meant no weekend leave for the lads, but if they didn't come up with something soon they were in the shit.

Resnick opened a bottle of Scotch. He poured a measure into a beaker on his desk. He almost swigged the green mould floating on top. He stared at it. Maybe 'Green Teeth' was right, maybe Boxer Davis did know something about the ledgers. Resnick picked up another beaker, inspected it and poured another measure. He drank, turned and stared at the photographs stuck up along the wall. What would any of those men be doing with a contact like old Boxer? Resnick sighed and shook his head.

Resnick picked up three darts from his desk drawer, he stared again at the three faces. Rawlins, Miller and Pirelli. Maybe Boxer was the only person the escaped raider could turn to. So, if that was so, and suddenly Boxer starts blowing his cover, then he had to be removed. They had found a considerable amount of money at Boxer's. The beakers were wiped clean. Whoever was there, whoever beat his landlady was a pro. Resnick took aim with one of the darts. It stuck in the wall above Terry Miller's head, then fell to the floor. Resnick poured another drink and swigged it back.

Fuller saw the light on in Resnick's office, he was very uptight. The weekend was ruined. He had arranged to take his wife to a 'Tenants Meeting Social'. All weekend leave cancelled, well he'd see about that.

Fuller had already put in for a transfer, but until he got it, he would just have to keep control of his temper. He would ask the fat man nicely, see if he'd waive the weekend clear for him.

Resnick barked 'Enter', and Fuller stepped into the untidy office. Resnick was sitting staring at the three photos on the wall. A dart was sticking out of the filing cabinet.

'Er, it's about the weekend leave, Sir. I actually had something planned and wondered if it would be possible for ...'

Resnick ignored him, he picked his tooth with the third and last dart. He then jerked his head towards the dead men. 'There was a fourth man on that raid. Now we know where these three are ... but the one that skipped it?'

Resnick turned his beady eyes on Fuller, his voice for a

change was quiet. 'I think he was the one that gave Boxer Davis' landlady that thrashing ... she's scared ... but I want her to identify that man ... so ... even if it takes all day, all night, all weekend, I want her down at the Yard going over the mug shots ... all right?'

Resnick took aim with the dart, it hit Harry Rawlins straight between the eyes.

Fuller stood for a moment, looked to Resnick, then back to the dart sticking out of Rawlins' face. He shifted his weight, maybe the fat man is right, on the other hand ... he shrugged and turned to leave. Resnick asked Fuller if he was going for a few jars down the local.

Fuller didn't answer, he shut the door with a polite, 'Goodnight, Sir.'

Resnick poured himself another drink, he sighed, wondered if the lads were all in the boozer. He remembered the time when he would hear 'Eh George ... coming for a snifter?'

In the old days, no one left the station without giving him a yell, not so now, nobody gave a bugger and it was going to get worse when they moved into the new annex, everyone looking at everyone else. Goldfish bowl, living in a goldfish bowl. Resnick slowly put his coat on, plonked his hat on the back of his head. He felt lonely, terribly lonely, but then had done for years, so what the hell.

Chapter Nineteen

It was a lovely morning, sun shining, Linda put her foot down. The car could really move, she loved it, she loved Carlos. She had left him fast asleep, curled up like a baby. She'd told him she had to visit a relative in Brighton. The radio was on, she began to sing at the top of her voice.

Shirley drove into the Little Chef, up into the garage and

petrol area, she got out and lifted the bonnet. Something was burning, she could smell it ... if she was late Dolly would go mad, still, she was half way there.

Shirley touched her cracked lip, it still hurt like hell when she smiled. She touched the radiator, it was red hot.

Bella had been taking care of 'Oil Head's' bike for a week now. He didn't expect to go down, but they'd given him six months. So now Bella had his bike, not that she would have it long as she knew he was behind on his payments. Still, they had to find it first. She opened the throttle - lovely clear road, lovely clear day - it would be her first ton solo, she had been riding bikes for years.

Bella, in black leather from head to toe, began to pass everything on the road; she loved it.

Bella arrived at the deserted beach first. She heaved the bike back on its stand on the dirt track, and walked to the edge of the cove. Below, Bella could see the small area of the beach, the tide was out, she smiled. Dolly thought of everything, she bet she had checked on that.

Bella made her way down the small wooden path onto the beach. A couple of boats lay on their side, and about twenty yards up, an old Morris Minor, the wheels gone, the seats torn and covered in mildew. So this was to be their rehearsal ground. Bella walked up and down, she began collecting sticks. Her job was to mark out the twenty yard run they would have to make with the money on their backs.

Linda was next, her car hurtled onto the gravel, skidded to a stop. Bella looked up and waved, Linda began unloading the boot. She had brought sacks, rugs, she stood at the end of the steps, arms full. Bella smiled, Linda was shouting, talking away as usual. Bella couldn't hear, but she guessed the gist.

'What she picked this place for, I don't know. She must be barmy, how we gonna rehearse the raid here?'

The wind was blowing Linda's dark, curly hair, putting some colour into her ashen face. An odd face, she could veer from downright plain looking into an angular beauty, her hawk nose, and high cheek bones, her dark alive eyes. Bella got back to her duty.

The two girls conferred, and began working together, Linda stacking sand into sacks, making sure they were round about the weight they would have to carry. Each sack she knotted and lugged over to one of the rugs that she had spread out in front of the Morris. The rug was to be the security wagon.

Shirley arrived, the rain began, lightly, spitting down. Shirley unloaded haversacks from her boot.

Linda noticed Shirley was wearing one of the jump suits Dolly had down as being no good. Linda made a mental note to ask if she had another, they looked quite nice, well, anything was a step up from the filthy jeans and plimsolls she had on. Linda was also wearing an enormous sweater, one of Joe's. It hung round her knees and the sleeves kept slipping down making her look like a scarecrow.

Shirley began stacking the haversacks into the Morris Minor. She wished she'd brought a heavier jacket, the sea air was cold, her nose started running.

By the time the Merc arrived the girls had set up the beach for a rehearsal. They were also getting cold and wet, and the rain had started belting down.

Dolly stood on top of the cove and looked down. She could see from there the outline of the twenty yard run. Bella had marked it out with a series of sticks. A finishing line depicting the end of the underpass was drawn into the sand. Stones, bricks and rubbish were marked out for the lead truck.

Dolly made a note to remind Linda that it was getting to be too close not to have the truck lined up. It was Linda's job to find a suitable truck. So far she had come up with nothing.

Shirley was huddled in the Morris, she was going over the straps on the haversacks.

Bella was up by the edge of the tide prodding some seaweed with a stick. Linda shouted that Dolly had arrived, she turned, grinning, holding up the stick. It was uncannily shaped like a sawn-off shotgun.

Dolly made her way slowly down to the beach. The picnic hamper was heavy and Wolf kept getting under her feet, plus, she was carrying an umbrella.

Linda watched Dolly make her way towards them. She shook her head. Again they had done all the hard work, and here she was arriving like the queen mother. Dolly gestured for Linda to join her, Linda made her way towards her.

Dolly was still on the move when Linda came up, her hair wringing wet, dripping, the sweater getting further and further down her knees. She looked almost water logged, unlike Dolly – immaculate as ever, her matching rain coat and wellies – she handed over the picnic hamper.

'You hear about old Boxer then? He got it up by the arcade.' Dolly nodded and kept on the move. She stopped and turned, looking at Linda for a moment. 'This friend of yours, the one I found you with, he Italian is he?'

Linda shook her head, she felt a twinge of guilt, but then she thought what bleedin' business is it of hers anyway?

'You still seeing him are you? This mechanic?'

Again, Linda shook her head, but Dolly stared ...

'Look Dolly, he was just a one night stand, there was nothing in it, I've not seen him since, just like you told me, I've kept meself to meself ... all right? there's no one.'

Dolly looked hard, trying to detect if she was lying, Linda held her gaze, then Dolly began to walk towards the girls.

'He was run over, Boxer, hit and run just up by the arcade.'

Dolly, without turning her back to her. 'Yeah, I heard ... accident!'

Linda trotted alongside Dolly.

'Eh, you think that rumour o' yours worked then? You think the Fishers'll leave us alone then?'

Dolly said nothing, just kept walking.

'Old Boxer musta run straight to 'em, you were right, couldn't keep his mouth shut.'

Dolly stopped, the wind was pulling at her scarf. 'He

was a fool, but I never meant, I never thought … poor Boxer, couldn't keep his mouth shut.'

Dolly began to inspect the layout, bit like an Army Major, prodding the sacks full of sand with her brolly. 'Too heavy, take some sand out, we're not carrying gold bullion.'

Shirley began tipping out sand and retying the bags.

'This the security wagon then?'

Dolly nodded to a large plaid blanket, the corners held down with bricks.

'We thought we'd use the old wrecked Morris as our van, practise cutting through with the chain saw later.'

Dolly looked at the wreck, the haversacks were stacked ready to put on. The heavy truck, still to be found, was marked out with sticks and rocks, seaweed, anything Bella could find. Dolly turned to Linda. 'You're going to have to get that truck soon you know, we must know what size it is, you can't leave it much longer.'

Linda nodded, thought to herself. If she so much as asks me about that just one more time I'll clock her one. Linda actually prided herself on her professionalism. She had been on the look out for the right truck for weeks, knew exactly what she was looking for, even had a possible line up, but she said nothing, for a change.

The three watched as Dolly, in her bright red wellies, walked the twenty yard run. This was to be the run they would have to make carrying the money on their backs in the haversacks. The run was drawn into the sand, sticks and more stones made it look like a small runway, the finishing line was Bella's crash helmet and Linda's bags.

They saw Dolly turn, shade her eyes, and then begin the walk back. All the time she paced it out with long strides. Linda joked that she looked like Mussolini, Bella nudged her, grinning. In a funny way she did, the red wellies sticking out as she marched towards them.

'Right let's get cracking, I'll give you all your positions. Linda you drive our van, the wreck, just mime it for today.'

Linda snorted, and looked over to the Morris. 'Well, I wasn't thinkin' of racin' it was I?'

Dolly ignored her, turned to Shirley. 'You try the chain saw, practise with the engine, see if you can cut through ...'

Before she could finish, Linda butted in. 'Bella's doin' the saw, Dolly, that's Bella's job.'

Dolly tapped the wet sand with her wellie, head bent, and shook her head. 'Bella drives the truck, the one up front, until I say different.'

'But that's bloody stupid. Bella's the only one of us so far that's been able to handle the saw, Shirley can hardly lift it. Where are you going? Aren't you in the front truck doin' the ramming?'

Dolly sighed, she was getting angry, you could see by the way she clenched and unclenched her hands.

'Whoever drives that front vehicle is in the most dangerous position, whoever drives it has to hold the guards by shot gun, whoever drives it is the last to leave, that is the most dangerous position, right? RIGHT? Bella was last in, until I say different THAT's the position she takes.'

Dolly began to take her coat off, she folded it neatly and began putting on a haversack. She wore her Dance Centre track suit. The rain had already soaked her hair, it was plastered to her head, and she looked faintly ridiculous.

'This is a bloody waste of time, I mean, it's obvious isn't it? Bella, it's obvious you should carry the saw, why don't you say something?'

Shirley picked up a haversack and began putting it on.

'If Bella doesn't drive the front truck it means Dolly does so why don't we just do what Dolly says and start rehearsing?'

Linda let out her breath, seething. 'She thinks it's a bloody amateur dramatics play, it's crazy!'

Bella tapped her on the shoulder and winked, she then walked back up the beach and began winding the stopwatch. She stood by Dolly's picnic hamper, wouldn't say anything, somehow she knew she wouldn't have to.

94

Linda, Dolly and Shirley sat in the wreck of the Morris; Linda in stony silence having a sulk.

'Okay, we got four minutes from start to finish; first let's just try timing getting out and starting the chain saw.'

Bella watched, it was like the Marx Brothers. She could hear the bickering and arguing going on further down the beach. Shirley had dropped the saw three times, once on her foot, so she was hopping about, screaming with pain.

Linda had thrown her haversack down, and was refusing to budge. Only Dolly kept on. She managed to get the chain saw out and start it. The sound of it cutting the side of the wreck reminded Bella of the dentist. She opened the hamper and helped herself to a sandwich.

Fifteen minutes later the three had settled into some kind of routine. Dolly was the one handling the saw. They began heaving the sand bags into each other's haversacks. Again, it was like watching a comedy sketch, they did nothing but argue and shout at each other. That took another fifteen minutes. Bella was beginning to get freezing cold, she stamped her feet, helped herself to a beaker of hot coffee.

Dolly stood with her haversack loaded up, staggering under the weight, with Linda arguing with Shirley about how many bags each should carry.

'Let's see if we can make the run, we should do it in under half a minute.'

Linda kicked at a sand bag. 'By the time we've got out and cut through with that bloody saw, they could have got the police, fire, ambulance, and Christ knows what else.'

'JUST time the run, Linda.'

Now Shirley was beginning to get angry, her mouth still hurt from the punch Tony Fisher had given her. Her foot was thudding from the chain saw, she was cold and hungry. Bella heard Dolly yelling for her to time them running down the beach. She held the stop-watch up.

No matter how many times they did the run, Dolly always lagged behind. She didn't have the energy, she was puffing and gasping for breath. She was as stubborn as a mule, but she wouldn't give up. Every time they made it to the finishing line, she paused, clasped her side, heaved for breath and asked what time they had done.

Bella was beginning to feel sorry for her, it was obvious she couldn't do it. Linda and Shirley were over the finishing line half a minute ahead of her each time. Still Dolly wouldn't give way, time and time again she turned and went up the beach.

'This is ridiculous, Dolly, it's bloody stupid. I know I can do it, Shirley knows she can do it. What's the point of all three of us running up and down like yoyos. YOU'RE the only one holding us up, you try it on your own.'

Dolly stood for a moment, she was heaving for breath, but eventually she nodded, turned and walked back up the beach.

'She's bloody spastic, look at her, what a waste of time.'

Linda helped herself to a sandwich, Shirley sat on the ground rubbing her foot. Only Bella watched Dolly, watched her very carefully, the woman was pushing herself, her determination was unbelievable, she just wouldn't give way.

'She's ready.'

All three turned, Bella held up the watch, one hand raised above her head, she gave Dolly the signal.

This time she was coming within the time limit, but it was awful to watch, the veins standing out on her neck, her arms flaying at her side. She was running so hard her lungs seemed to burst, and just a yard before the finishing line she caved in. Her legs buckled under her, but she forced herself on, trying to fling herself across the finishing line.

Dolly collapsed in a heap, her breath came in sobs, heaving, rasping sobs. Linda looked at her, then turned to Bella.

'What time you make it?'

Dolly struggled to take her haversack off. The pain in her side was burning her up, still she couldn't get her breath. Shirley knelt down beside her, she whispered 'It's no good Dolly, you can't make the run.'

Dolly staggered to her feet, picked up the haversack and handed it to Bella. Bella gave her the stop-watch. Linda was smirking as Bella stripped off her bike leathers. Beneath, Bella wore running shorts. She'd show her, just watch Bella go. Bella lifted the haversack and strolled down the beach.

'She used to run for her school.'

All the time, Linda kept up the dig at Dolly. Shirley could have hit her, sometimes Linda was evil, really evil. Dolly said nothing, she poured herself a beaker of tea.

Bella was worried they might have damaged the saw. She picked it up and tested the engine, starting and restarting it. Satisfied, she looked back up the beach and got into the wrecked Morris Minor.

Dolly watched in silence, her eyes flicking from the stop-watch back to Bella. They watched her move out of the wreck, actually cut a hole large enough for a shot gun to be pushed through. Linda began shouting for Bella, jumping up and down, waving her arms in the air.

Bella ran to the marked out security truck, she lifted up bag after bag of sand, pacing the time it would take for her to fill Shirley's, then Linda's haversacks. Linda screamed, 'GO. GO. GO.'

Bella ran towards them in long easy strides. With her tight hard muscular legs the weight on her back had no effect at all, it was an effortless easy run.

Dolly never mentioned the actual time, she didn't have to, it was obvious to them all. Shirley and Linda hugged Bella, congratulating her. Dolly walked up the beach alone, she called to Wolf, who was rolling in a dead seagull.

It was strange that it should turn out this way, strange because if the girls had watched their men rehearse they would have seen an almost identical pattern emerge.

Terry had been at the airstrip for two hours, setting up the vehicles. Jimmy Nunn was an old mate, having a bit of a hard time. Jimmy was an exracing driver, banned for dangerous driving involving another driver. Married, and on the dole, he needed a job. Terry thought he might be the man they were looking for, but he could make no decision without Harry's approval.

Terry had taken Harry to meet Jimmy over three months ago and nothing more had been said. Harry liked to talk to new boys, liked to get to know them before working with them. Harry had made several visits to Jimmy's, but had not given the red light yet. Today he would watch Jimmy at work. If he liked what he saw, Jimmy would be the driver for the security raid.

Jimmy was testing the engine of the bread truck. Terry had arranged delivery of it, it was a good strong incongruous vehicle with double doors at the back, and heavy enough to take the impact of ramming the security wagon. Jimmy tested the engine, rev count, he put his foot down, got out and lifted the bonnet ... didn't sound too good, but it would by the time he had finished with it.

Jimmy was a good looking fella, about thirty-three, big, six foot. Jimmy had no record, but he had been on a couple of jobs, so came with a good reference. Terry knew he would be okay, he liked the way he worked, and he was certainly giving that engine the once over.

Joe Pirelli was standing in a clearing some distance from the airstrip. Terry heard Joe cleaning out the shot guns, quick blasts. Joe was fanatical about his 'irons', they were greased and tested. Joe was a professional, and Terry had always liked working with him, he never put a foot wrong, seemed to have nerves of steel. Joe also had a temper, violent, you always knew exactly how far to go with Joe. When you saw his eyes flicker, a strange jerky flick, that was the warning, and then he was lethal.

Terry knew Joe had done some heavy numbers, he knew better than to question him – that was Joe's business. For the past three years they had worked closely together, but Terry had never become friendly, never socialised, even though he would have liked to. One of the Boss' rules; if you worked for Harry, that was the way it was, and the way it had to be for everyone. Joe was walking back up the airstrip, he carried his 'irons' in a long leather bag, almost like a squash case. He went over to a Lancia and placed the guns in the boot. Terry watched him. Joe was tall, six three, maybe even more. He had dark Italian looks, and was obsessed with physical fitness. He was lean, with rather a hawk nose, and then those strange eyes, odd colour, hazel maybe. Joe was a very tough man, Terry was glad he was to be on this job with him.

The two men checked their watches, then looked over the dummy security van. Everything was in order for the rehearsal, they were just waiting for the Boss. Harry Rawlins liked everything to be ready for his arrival, and Joe and Terry carefully went over every detail; the money sacks were weighted, the vehicles positioned exactly as they would be for the raid itself. After the rehearsal it would be their job to clean the cars, and take them to the lock-up.

The bread truck now sounded as if its engine was running smoothly, Jimmy got out of the driving seat and gave the thumbs up.

Jimmy, from where he was standing, watched the two men talking. They frightened him slightly, well, Joe more than Terry. He wanted to be in on this team, wanted it very much, he admired Harry Rawlins, and knew he'd been carefully vetted for the job. He knew he was still on trial. Jimmy checked his watch, it had stopped again, he tapped it and looked up.

The silver Merc was so quiet he hadn't heard it arriving, it seemed to float down the runway. As soon as Terry and Joe saw it approaching, they automatically stiffened: he was here.

Harry Rawlins looked more like a city banker than a man about to rehearse a security raid. The fawn cashmere coat, the dark suit, the brief case. Harry was wearing dark glasses, he left his car door open and joined Terry and Joe. The three men went over the vehicles. Harry, without a word, just nodded as Terry pointed out details. Harry nodded towards Jimmy, then looked over to the B.M.W. getaway car . . .

Terry crossed over to Jimmy. 'He wants to see you drive.'

This was Jimmy's chance, he ran to the B.M.W. and started her up. Harry was impressed, Jimmy could certainly throw a car around.

Jimmy was sweating, the car screamed up and down the airstrip, careered into a spinning turn and then past the three men. He saw Terry grinning and giving him the thumbs up sign.

Harry went back to his car and took his coat off. Jimmy watched as Harry neatly and methodically changed his clothes, folding each garment up and placing it on the seat of his car. Any other man would somehow have looked faintly ridiculous standing there, half undressed, but there was something so neat and organised about the way he changed. Eventually, Harry stood in a track suit, he was bending down, tying up his plimsolls when he ordered Terry to try the explosives.

Terry had them already prepared, it was over and done with in a matter of seconds. Terry went behind the security wagon and, boom. He walked back again, grinning. 'I could get me granny through.'

So then they were ready. Harry quietly went over the instructions. The raid was identical to the way the girls had set up theirs, only this time, explosives instead of a chain saw. Each man put his haversack on, and Jimmy was handed the stop-watch. He walked back up the marked airstrip, the men had to make the same twenty yard dash as the women . . . Harry said the whole raid had to take less than three minutes.

Jimmy watched as they got into the cars, and drove back down the runway, he backed the bread truck up, and then they were in convoy. Harry wanted to see the way Jimmy could stop and start the bread truck. The three men sat in the car watching as Jimmy slowed down to almost a stop, then he jerked, stopped again – and then travelled naturally, put on a burst of speed, and slammed on the brakes, with a smell of burning rubber as the truck halted. Harry nodded from his car, he was pleased, and tapped Terry's leg, 'The boy's good ... very good.'

Jimmy got out of the bread truck and looked back, he gave the thumbs up and standing, started the stop-watch. The three men moved like lightning. Joe out of the van first, he stood with a shot gun holding up what would be oncoming traffic. Terry was already slamming the explosive to the other side of the van, Harry was climbing over the roof of the security wagon.

Boom! Off went the explosives. Harry moved into the security wagon. Terry was first out with his haversack loaded, he replaced Joe and took up the shot gun, then Harry emerged from the truck, followed by Joe. All with their loaded haversacks full of weighted 'money' sacks ran towards Jimmy. Joe was first over, then Terry, Harry was way behind when he crossed the finishing line, he was panting, he gripped his side as if he had a stitch. Told him timing, he said, 'Let's go again.'

Jimmy could see that Harry was holding them up, he knew that Terry and Joe knew, but neither said a word. Jimmy saw a look pass between them, Harry missed it, he was bending over gasping for breath.

Jimmy watched the men rehearse meticulously for over half an hour, then Joe, Terry and Harry went into a huddle. Harry's face was tight with anger, his jaw worked, you could see the tiny muscle at the side twitching. He had to admit that it was him that was holding them up, he took the haversack off and held it out to Jimmy. 'Lemme see you run kid.'

Terry and Joe were embarrassed for Harry, who stood sweating, staring at the stop-watch. They didn't bother to do the run, they just wanted to see Jimmy. Without a word, Harry timed Jimmy six times, just kept on nodding for him to go back and run again and again ... at the end of the sixth run he made the three repeat the whole exercise. Terry wanted to put his arm around the big man's shoulder, but he didn't like to, he knew Harry was hurting. Harry had mentioned that this may be his last job, maybe he was getting old, maybe! He saw Harry walk over to Jimmy Nunn. The next time they did the rehearsal, Harry drove the bread truck. Terry knew from now on, Jimmy would be in the car with them.

The security wagon hardly had any more space to blow, and on the last rehearsal, the petrol tank blew up, the black smoke was sickening. Joe could feel the smoke fill his lungs, he walked away from it.

Jimmy was over the moon, he was not only in the team, but now on a bigger percentage of the take, he rubbed his hands. Trudie, his lady, would be knocked out. She'd been getting very touchy lately, she wanted him to get in with the big mob. Well, now he was.

Harry was getting back into his suit, the smoke was making him cough, he was tired. Joe began collecting the markers along the runway, he watched Harry drive off before he went over to Terry. Both men knew how much it had meant to 'step down', give way to a younger man. Both felt for Harry, now he would be taking the most vulnerable position, it would be up to him to hold the two front guards of the security wagon. It would be Harry facing them with the shot gun, Harry waiting until his team was clear. Still, at least he hadn't called the whole thing off. Harry never liked changes, he was so methodical, every detail worked out down to the last second. Any change usually made him tread water until he was sure, one hundred percent sure. Joe looked over the airstrip, it had gone well, too well for Harry to wait, all three had known it, but Terry and Joe were relieved.

Jimmy Nunn was ready to go, he had cleaned the bread truck, checked over the engine and was ready to drive it to Eddie Rawlins' yard where it would be hidden until the day of the raid. Jimmy walked over to Terry and Joe, they fell silent. Jimmy stopped and picked up a couple of cigarette ends and pocketed them. Joe smiled, he was okay this kid, a good 'un.

Jimmy sniffed and coughed, the black smoke from the charred out security van made him feel sick. 'I hate this smell, burning rubber, makes me sick ... always scared of fire, since I was a kid ... funny!'

Terry clipped him one, good naturedly, and grinned. The three men set about leaving, none looked back. The tick of excitement was already building, and everything had gone perfectly. They were high, and over the next few days they would get higher and higher until the day of the raid. The black smoke hung over the airstrip long after the men had gone. The only thing left, was a blackened, charred out, unrecognisable van. No number plates, nothing to show the men had been there, just the smell, the smell of burning petrol.

Chapter Twenty

The girls were all feeling sorry for Dolly. She had packed up the picnic hamper, her mouth a thin tight line. They had run themselves into the ground. On the last run, they had made good time – without Dolly running with them it seemed possible they could do it. All three felt it, all doubts they had each had, and never spoken, were gone. They contented themselves with quick flicking eye-to-eye glances, then they would bend their heads and grin.

Linda was bursting with excitement. She thought Shirley and Bella were treating Dolly with kid gloves. She gave Dolly a hooded look, then nudged Bella. Dolly was staring at the windscreen of the old Morris Minor – the windscreen was about the only thing still intact. Dolly then went over to the pile of their belongings, picked up the sledge-hammer which was heavy. She seemed to weight it in her hand, while all three girls were looking at her.

'Might as well get in a bit of practice meself ...'

Dolly positioned herself in front of the Morris, legs apart, her right hand gripping the sledge-hammer. She stepped back, looked at the girls, licked her lips. The rain was pouring down, her hair clinging to her scalp, dripping down her face. Dolly ran forwards, the veins standing out on her neck and she let rip ... not a scream, it was a weird sound, coming right up from her belly. She seemed to fly. Her right hand raised the sledge-hammer, she aimed it at the windscreen, and hurled it with all her strength. It smashed the windscreen into smithereens, and was going through the air so fast it landed in the back seat.

Like three children, the girls gaped. Dolly had frightened them. She seemed a little crazy when she looked at them. She had an impish grin at first, but it spread across her face, then she threw back her head and roared with laughter.

The girls needed no other sign, they were with her. With her for the first time ever, each one, heart and soul, reached out to Dolly, loving her for that one lunatic moment. She was bloody human after all.

Chapter Twenty-One

Fuller's whole weekend had been spent with Boxer Davis' landlady. Fran had seen hundreds and hundreds of mug shots. She had sometimes pointed at faces, known by Fuller to be serving long sentences. Fran had discovered ex-lovers, her husband even, but the man who had attacked her? She just couldn't remember him.

Andrews had checked out a stolen vehicle brought in the Friday night. It had been the car used in the Boxer hit and run. There was not a print on it, just terrible deep red stains across the bumper and radiator; they had come to yet another dead end.

Fuller typed out his notes. He was methodically neat – as each key hammered down, he wished it was Resnick's head. The whole station was buzzing with activity as there had been a big jewellery raid in Mayfair the night before. Fuller should, or would have been assigned to it, if he hadn't been on the Rawlins case. He was getting sick and tired of the gags every morning from his mates. Fuller had had enough, he finished typing and yanked his report from the typewriter. The paper tore in two. He was blazing; furious he started again.

Detective Andrews came in. He, too, was angry. The Chief had hauled him over the coals for giving priority on the stolen Boxer Davis car used in the hit and run.

It was nine fifteen, and no sign of Resnick. Andrews was unsure what to do. It had been Resnick who told him to get Forensic onto the stolen car. Resnick who instructed him to override any other vehicle. Now he was up before the Chief, and it wasn't fair.

Andrews paced up and down the room. He knew enough not to interrupt Fuller. The typewriter was now being hit with such force it was moving across the desk.

Detective Sergeant Hawkes appeared. He grinned as he popped his head round the door. Hawkes had been removed from the surveillance on the Rawlins woman. He, along with his partner, Richmond, were now assigned to the Mayfair raid.

'Resnick know about this?'

Fuller looked at Hawkes.

'No I've not seen him, it's the Chief's decision.'

Hawkes left, knowing the effect of his news. Fuller very carefully took his papers out of the typewriter, clipped them into his folder.

Alice now knocked on the door and popped her head round, 'You're moving today – don't forget.'

Fuller was ahead of her, his desk cleared, all his files already moved down to the annex. Andrews slipped out to the canteen before he could be commandeered into 'moving' any office equipment.

'Resnick in yet?'

Fuller shook his head and finished tidying his desk. Alice came into the room, hands on hips.

'Has he cleared his office?'

Alice knew he hadn't, she was furious. Resnick along with all the other officers on this floor had been instructed to clear their files and desks. The decorators were due to start knocking down walls. She knew Resnick had not paid the slightest attention to any of the memos. She also knew that she would now have to begin clearing his office.

'When is he coming in?'

Fuller collected his brief case, and as he got to the door, said, 'I don't know ... I don't know.'

Fuller slammed out of the office. Alice stood wondering what to do. In a way she was relieved that she had been transferred up to Records. Although she was a group secretary, Resnick behaved as if she was his property, and his alone. Alice went along the corridor and stood outside the cracked sellotape covered door. She rattled the handle. It was locked.

The swing doors at the end of the corridor banged open, and Resnick strode up the corridor. He bellowed for Fuller and Andrews as usual, and was about to bellow for Alice but saw her by his office. 'Morning, flower.'

Resnick then stopped for a heaving coughing fit, then he tossed his keys to Alice.

The office was as shambolic as ever, he had made no effort to begin clearing up. He flung his dog-eared, chewed brief case onto his desk and picked up the phone.

'It's been cut off, you're moving into the new annex today.'

Resnick banged the dead phone down and stomped out. Alice surveyed the mess, she knew she would never be able to clear the room on her own. She decided to go and beg for assistance from the typing pool.

Alice never really knew why she bothered, but she had worked alongside the fat man for so long she just couldn't get out of the habit of running after him. It wasn't as if he ever gave her any thought. How many times had he told her to send his regards to her father?

'Give him a hot toddy darlin', best thing for arthritis.'

Alice's father had died over four years ago, but Resnick

had forgotten. Alice lived with her senile mother, and the pair sipped hot toddies. Alice knew in her heart why she ran after Resnick. She'd do anything for him ... she'd loved him for fifteen years.

Chapter Twenty-Two

Linda bit her nails, the throbbing music in the arcade was giving her a headache. She didn't like it, didn't like what'd gone on at the last meet. They had all been high after the rehearsal, then it had turned sour. The four had got into a blazing row. Bella had asked Dolly where she was going to stash the money after the raid. Dolly's reply had taken them off guard, she had told them that for their own safety, none of them would know, only she, Dolly, would.

None of them had said anything, just watched as Dolly carefully handed out their tickets. She instructed that each girl, after the raid, was to take a flight out of the country: different airports, different destinations. Linda was to go to Spain; Shirley, France; Bella, Italy. They would then all meet up in Rio two weeks later. Dolly, however, would not leave England until she had stashed the money in a safe place. She was worried about leaving Wolf, she had to arrange kennels. The girls had checked over their tickets, Dolly had even given them spending money. The tension was building, Dolly seemed unaware of it. 'I'll bring out a considerable amount for us to stay out of England for at least two months ... the longer we stay out, the safer it'll be.'

Eventually Bella was the one who brought up what was uppermost in all their minds. She felt that they should know where the main bulk of money would be. Dolly pursed her lips and shook her head.

'We work the way Harry did, none of his team ever knew.'

Linda sided with Bella, told Dolly that they weren't Harry's team, they wanted to know. Anything could happen, and she, Dolly, was the only one left in England. Dolly blew, she turned on all three, she was hurt more than angry, hurt because she knew they didn't trust her. Dolly demanded that if they didn't like the arrangements then they could call the whole thing off, she put her hand out, demanding they repay her all the money she had so far laid out.

'Go ahead without me and see how far you get, it's up to you!'

The girls gave way. Besides, without the ledgers and the security contract they knew they couldn't do it. It was agreed that Dolly would be the only one to know where the money would be stashed. Bella didn't like it. Linda didn't like it. Shirley trusted Dolly, so in the end it was agreed.

Dolly left, the three waited until they heard the garage door clang shut behind her before they spoke.

'I didn't lose my man in her precious Harry's raid, but I swear to God if she tries anything on, I'll kill her.'

Shirley had looked shocked, Bella wasn't kidding.

Linda chewed her last nail down to the quick, it began to bleed. She still didn't trust Dolly, Bella was right, they were all flying here, there and everywhere, and Dolly... She wondered if they could do it without her, get rid of her. She decided that she'd call round Bella's after she came off duty.

Shirley looked at herself in the long mirror. Her skin glowed, the face pack had done wonders. She began cutting her nails. The rehearsal at the beach had been murder on her hands. Shirley nearly shot out of her silk nightie. The doorbell was ringing and ringing. Her heart began thumping, if it was Tony Fisher, she was on her own, he could break the door down. He could rape her, kill her. Shirley looked at the clock, it was one-fifteen.

Linda kept her finger on the doorbell. She could see the bedroom light was on and wondered what the old slag was up to. She giggled, it would be a laugh if she'd actually caught Miss Goody Two Shoes with her leg over!

'Who is it?'

Shirley's voice was terrified. Linda could see the relief on her face when she opened the door. It was like Fort Knox, bolts and chains and double, triple locks. Linda had never been to Shirley's before. She was actually taken aback, it was so tasteful. It was like a magazine ... soft pale colours everywhere. Linda walked into the lounge, Shirley began rebolting the front door.

Linda was stunned. The lounge was immaculate, big thick fur rugs, stripped pine dresser. Shirley bustled in and pulled the pale pink curtains across the window. Linda couldn't help herself, she was jealous, jealous as hell. She also sussed out just how much money had gone into this place, how much money Terry must have earned, how much Joe must have picked up. Linda looked around, it was certainly a lot different from her stinking little basement. Joe had been a bloody charity, his family, flying them over, keeping them. Linda also knew that Joe had thrown his money around down the clubs, gambling, his little blondes. She was getting edgy, angry. She watched Shirley fiddle with the central heating, muttering about the dial not working. She could have throttled her.

'How about a drink then?'

Shirley pursed her lips, she knew Linda had already been drinking, she could smell it. She also had that look on her face, like a nasty little ferret. Shirley poured her a brandy in a cut glass brandy bowl, one of her best; she handed it over.

Linda noted the glass, but didn't say anything. She sat on the floor on the thick white rug and leant against the Heal's sofa. She swigged at the drink then decided it was best to come out with it, not beat about the bush.

'You think Dolly's straight?'

Shirley sat near the fireplace and stared at her.

'Bella an' me, we think maybe this rumour she started

spreadin', the one about Boxer Davis, you know, sayin' Harry was really alive. I mean, look what happened to Boxer.'

Shirley felt her legs tighten up, she looked hard at Linda, didn't follow what she was on about.

'I mean, what if he really is, an' we go away and don't even know where the money is. If Harry is alive, what's to stop him walkin' in and takin' the lot?'

Shirley tensed up all over, a small pink spot showed up on her cheek, but she clenched her hands for control. Linda was now up on her feet bending over, prodding Shirley with her chewed finger. Shirley's anger took Linda by surprise, and it quite surprised Shirley. She pushed Linda away from her and stood, hands on her hips. She didn't shout and her voice was calm, almost tough and she let Linda have it, have it all, the disgust at her even thinking Dolly was playing a double game.

'Who do you think she is, Joan Crawford? You think that woman's grief wasn't real? Harry's dead, and it broke her heart. He's dead, Linda, just like Joe, like Terry ... I trust her, trust her with my life.'

Linda felt ashamed. Dolly had never let them down, she had always done what she said she was going to. She had even stepped down by accepting Bella into the team, even let Bella take her place in the raid. Linda flushed, she looked away from Shirley. The tears started, she couldn't stop them. She didn't want Shirley to see her cry. She didn't know why she always started to cry.

'I'm sorry, all right? I'm sorry.'

Shirley wouldn't let her get away with it that easily.

'No, it isn't all right. You frightened me, you frightened me, understand? You had no right to come here.'

Linda knew she shouldn't have come, she reached for the bottle of brandy.

'I think you have had enough.'

Linda stuck her hands into her jeans pocket, she stood head down like a naughty school girl. Shirley sighed and unscrewed the bottle, she poured another brandy for her. Linda carried the glass over to the sideboard. A row of photographs, she drank and nodded to each one.

'This your mum? This your brother? This must be your dad then?'

With her back to Shirley the tears rolled down her cheeks. 'My mum dumped me in an orphanage when I was three, never knew me dad, never knew me mum for that matter, she never came back for me.'

Linda polished off the remainder of the brandy, turned and was back to her old grinning self. 'Eh, tell you what I'm going to do with my share? I want to be a racing driver. I'm serious, I'm going to buy a . . .'

Linda didn't finish her sentence, Shirley suddenly turned and ran from the room. Linda followed Shirley up the stairs into the bedroom. She was sitting on the floor by the dressing table with an open album of photographs. 'It's him, it's got to be him.'

Shirley was pointing to a photograph, a snap shot of Terry standing with his arm around a man in white mechanics overalls. 'Jimmy Nunn, he must be the number four man, the one that got away. I'm sure of it. Terry . . . I remember Terry sayin' something . . . he drove the lead truck, I know it, I know it Linda!'

The two passed the snap shot back and forth. Linda was ticking all over, if it was him. She turned to Shirley gripping her arm. 'I want to find him, let me find him, don't tell Dolly until we're sure.'

Shirley nodded, Linda was on her way downstairs before she could stop her. She stood at the top of the stairs looking down.

'Don't say anything until we're sure, promise?'

Linda would prove to Dolly that she wasn't the only one in the team with brains. She, Linda would show her, she was going to find that bastard that left their men.

Chief Inspector Saunders listened intently to Detective Sergeant Fuller, his face expressionless. Occasionally he would look up from his empty writing pad, then look down again. Once or twice he sighed, got up and walked to his window, stared out, returned to his desk. Although he was paying close attention to everything Fuller was saying he couldn't shake off the feeling of complete disrespect for him. He knew what he was saying had to be said, but somehow he wished Fuller had chosen another way, if there was another way.

Saunders had known George Resnick for years, and to hear this young smart arse telling him of gross unprofessional conduct by a man he had once admired, even liked, was distasteful, but he had to recognise it as being true. Resnick had been becoming a thorn in his side for years. He would not, could not, conform.

Saunders moved to the door and held it open, an indication he had heard enough and the meeting was now at a close. Fuller he knew, was a good, very good officer. The secretaries in the annex watched Chief Inspector Saunders standing at Resnick's untidy desk, he opened drawers, picked up folders, his face was tight and angry.

'When Inspector Resnick comes in, ask him to see me.'

The secretary nodded and made a note, she also saw out of the corner of her eye, Fuller seated at his own desk measuring the space his chair seemed to be crammed against the partition. She sniggered to herself.

'Any idea where he is?'

Fuller jumped to attention and rounded the partition, he shook his head with a slight gesture of his hands. Saunders looked over the piled, untidy desk, he picked up Resnick's report diary, opened it ... page after page was blank, no indication of his whereabouts, not only for that morning but for what appeared to be the whole week. He snapped the diary shut and walked out. Now he couldn't resist a smirk, he tried to lean in his chair and caught his elbow, he then realised his office had shrunk.

Chapter Twenty-Three

Linda was feeling very pleased with herself, she had found out Jimmy Nunn's address. It had been quite simple really, she had contacted all the racing circuits she had ever heard of. Jimmy Nunn had not been seen for a considerable time, in fact the mechanic at Brands Hatch even asked that if she did find him, he would be grateful if she'd jog his memory about the fifty quid he owed him.

Linda sat in the Greek cafe, she had positioned herself near the door, by the window. She would be able to see Dolly, before she saw her, she could hardly wait.

The Merc pulled up, Linda waved to the owner for coffee, he looked and pointed to the espresso machine and Linda nodded. She watched Dolly lock up the Merc, and with Wolf tucked under her arm, stare at the crummy little cafe. Linda could see the look of distaste on her face, she was going to get that cow now, really show her that she wasn't the only one with know how.

Dolly sat opposite Linda, she couldn't stand the smell of the place, hated knowing that whenever you left one of these greasy spoon cafes, you reeked of the food. The Greek carried the coffee over and wiped his hands on his trousers, then, with a look to three swarthy looking men, he turned the juke box on. Demis Roussos tinkled out.

Dolly didn't touch her espresso. She sat stony-faced as Linda told her all about Jimmy Nunn, finishing with opening her handbag and placing a torn scrap of paper in front of Dolly. 'That's his address ... bet your life he's the number four bastard who left our men and here's a photo.'

Dolly still didn't give an inch, she picked up the photo and paper, looked at it, looked up at Linda, then turned and waved her hand to the Greek owner.

Linda was slightly off guard, Dolly still hadn't said a

word. As the Greek came over Dolly asked for a chocolate biscuit, not for herself, but for Wolf. Linda swore inside, that bloody Shirley must have told her after all. Dolly broke a piece of Penguin biscuit and fed the rat, still she didn't say anything. Linda waited, she could play the same game.

'So you're still seein' this Italian then?'

Linda was taken by surprise, so much so she couldn't cover fast enough, she felt the colour flood into her face. 'No ... I'm not seein' anyone.'

Dolly looked at her hard, icy, her hand still stroked the dog, 'You bloody lied to me, lied to my face, you stupid bitch.'

As Dolly talked, Linda felt her stomach turn over, she heard that quiet icy voice telling her that the 'Italian' was bent, bent in more ways than one, lover boy was no more than a little queen, hopping from Linda's bed straight into Arnie Fisher's. Dolly repeated herself, kept on about Arnie Fisher. Arnie Fisher, maybe she wasn't actually repeating the name, but that was all that was zinging through Linda's head, Arnie Fisher, Arnie Fisher.

'He's Arnie Fisher's bum boy you stupid ... stupid bitch.'

Then silence. Dolly fed another piece of chocolate into the rat's mouth, he licked her hand, wanting more.

Linda couldn't speak, her mouth had dried up, her tongue stuck to the roof of her mouth, eventually a strangled hoarse sound came out. 'That's not true.'

Dolly stared, and, again, Linda felt that pulling in her stomach, that quiet voice, the Greek music, that voice telling her that if she'd said anything, told this poof anything about their business the whole thing was off. Dolly leant over the table and gripped Linda's hand, so tight it hurt, Dolly's nails were cutting into her palm, but she couldn't even take her hand away, her mouth began to tremble, the tears began, she could feel them pricking at her, hurting her. 'I told him nothing, I swear, before God I swear I've told him nothing. He's just a screw, he means nothing, honest to God.'

114

Dolly released her hand, lightly as if she had never held it. She leant back in her chair and put Wolf onto the ground. Dolly told Linda to get rid of Carlos, he had to be got rid of, he was dangerous, dangerous because of who he knew, what he might put together.

Like a movie script, all those times you've heard gangsters say 'Get rid of him', then the cool nod of the henchman, and the next thing, whoever it is, gone. But this was a Greek cafe in Islington, it was 1983, it was real, how do you just get rid of someone? Dolly watched Linda, the mouth trying so hard to keep still. The eyes filling up with tears, but she couldn't feel sorry, she wanted to get hold of her by the scruff of the neck and belt her, really hurt her. She'd lied, lied to her face, she could have jeopardised the whole business. Right at this moment, Dolly was disgusted with this stupid, stupid girl who couldn't wait, just couldn't wait to set her oats off, she had to ... Dolly sighed.

'He's got a garage full of hot cars, he's the Fishers' wheels man, shop him, give a ring to the law, it'll keep him out of our way long enough.'

Dolly stood, she picked up Wolf, and leant over the table. 'Do it tonight, soon as you can.'

Then Dolly was gone, the address and photo of Jimmy Nunn gone. Linda sat, numb, shaking, aware of the Greek watching her, aware of the music still tinkling out, aware of the interested looks of the three swarthy, scruffy men. She couldn't move, legs felt like iron. Her right hand twisted a gold medallion, it was eighteen carat gold, with her birth sign on it, with an eighteen carat gold chain, a gift. A gift given to her when they'd been lying in bed together, he had taken it out of his pocket, made her close her eyes and he'd slipped it over her head, he'd kissed her gently and let her open her eyes.

She had looked at herself in the mirror, naked apart from the medallion, a gold medallion on a gold chain, one of the nicest presents she'd ever been given in her life, she loved him, loved him with every bone in her body, she kissed him, she cried, she was happy, in fact she had been so happy she had wanted to tell him everything about herself, tell him what she was doing, what she was about to do, but something, something had stopped her, instead, she had held him and they had made love together, standing watching each other in the dressing table mirror.

The anger rose inside Linda, that bitch, that twisted cow was lying, she must be lying, he couldn't make love to her like that and then go with Arnie Fisher, he couldn't... dear God, he couldn't, could he ...?

Chapter Twenty-Four

Dolly parked outside number forty-three, checked the address again, looked up at the row of squalid run down houses. A kid was hopping down the pavement on a skate board. Dolly lowered the window and yelled at him to come over. The boy went across. Dolly asked if he knew who lived in number thirty-nine. The kid didn't know, he looked over to the house, then back to the Merc. Dolly got out, said if he took care no one touched the motor he'd get a fiver. The boy couldn't believe his ears, Dolly on the other hand knew enough by the street, that the car was out of place, big enough prize for any punk to rip off, take a key down the side just because it was out of place, it represented something far away from this poverty reeking street and what you can't have, you destroy.

The house was even worse on the inside than she first thought. The hallway was full of black plastic rubbish bags, broken milk bottles, newspapers, used takeaway cartons. Dolly kept on going up the ill-lit hallway to flat number four. She got to the second landing, the smell was not too bad this high up. She stopped, number four was next to the stairs. As she knocked, a baby began to howl, Dolly knocked again, the baby cried, she waited, eventually a voice asked who was there, but Dolly just knocked again.

Trudie inched open the door, the baby in her arms. 'What do you want?'

Dolly was fast, almost pushing open the door. Trudie couldn't quite handle it, the quiet smiling woman holding the poodle.

'Mind if I just have a chat, love?'

Dolly was in, standing in the small cheaply furnished room, she could smell the girl's perfume, cheap, cloying, she smiled. 'I'm looking for Jimmy Nunn.'

Trudie watched as Dolly looked round the room, watched her as she put her dog down and sat on the sofa. She talked softly, telling her how she was looking for Jimmy Nunn, wanted to have a word with him, then she turned a sweet smile. 'I'm Mrs Harry Rawlins.'

All the time Dolly was taking in every inch of the room, the baby clothes on the heater, the untidy shoddy furniture, but most of all Trudie. The girl was beautiful, beautiful in a cheap tarty way, good figure, sexy, blonde hair, heavy pouting mouth, and big innocent wide eyes. Dolly knew she could handle her, she was easy. She relaxed, took out her cigarettes, offered her one. The girl refused, Dolly noted it, noted it because on the table, on the side of the easy cheap arm chair were ashtrays, ashtrays overflowing with cigarette butts. So sex bomb might not smoke, but someone here did.

Trudie couldn't believe the woman's cheek, the way she looked over the room, but she couldn't help herself, she answered all the questions.

'Jimmy Nunn? Yeah, he's my husband, no I've not seen him in months.'

Dolly showed Trudie the photograph. 'This Jimmy is it?'

Wolf was off the sofa and up onto the easy chair, scrabbling, digging with his paws. Dolly quickly lifted him off, scolded him and put him back on the sofa.

The girl seemed unimpressed when she mentioned Harry Rawlins, in fact, she seemed stupid, standing, rocking the baby backwards and forwards, as it began to howl. Dolly moved up closer, closer to the smell of that cheap heavy perfume. The baby was lovely, pretty, only about six months old, pretty. Dolly patted the baby's cheek. Trudie stepped back a fraction. Wolf went over to the easy chair, he jumped up, began scratching with his tiny paws. Dolly ignored Wolf, she opened her bag and took out five crisp new ten pounds notes. 'This is for the kid, an' if Jimmy comes back, tell him I'd like a word – Mrs Harry Rawlins.'

Dolly wrote down her number on a page from her diary, tore it out and placed it on the cluttered mantle shelf. Trudie looked at Wolf. He was still scrabbling at the chair. Dolly scooped him up in her arms. She saw something hidden in the arm of the chair, and bent down to pick it up. Dolly, bending over the chair, had her back to Trudie. She picked up a gold Dunhill lighter, the initials she knew before she turned it over in her hand, H.R. Dolly let the lighter slip from her fingers. It was as if someone had punched her in the stomach. She felt winded, a pain shot through her body and the blood drained from her face. Dolly had to grip the chair to steady herself.

Trudie looked out of the window. 'If that's your motor down there, Mrs Rawlins, you'd better go an' see to it, looks like you lost a wing mirror already.'

Trudie turned to see Dolly already at the front door. She didn't look back, she couldn't. Dolly was shaking, she fumbled with the latch of the door, wrenched it open and left.

Trudie watched from the window, saw Dolly exit into the street, saw her clip one of the kids standing by her car. Trudie grinned, tough old bird, that Mrs Rawlins.

The door from the kitchen opened, Trudie turned smiling, she still held the fifty pounds. 'Eh, she just give me fifty quid, for your kid.'

Chapter Twenty-Five

The arcade was almost empty. Linda sat in her booth. She kept on repeating over and over the words Dolly had said. It wouldn't sink in, she couldn't make herself believe it. Her heart lurched, her knees tightened. He was there. Carlos was standing at the entrance to the arcade.

Linda began frantically counting out already counted change, she knew he was walking towards the booth, she couldn't look up, she kept on clicking the ten pence pieces along the rows of change.

Carlos was wearing a cream suit, silk by the look of it, very smart, very expensive. He was also wearing heavy eau-de-cologne, she could smell it. He leant towards the booth's opening, smiling, his dark handsome face freshly shaved, he leant in and touched the gold medallion around her neck.

'Looks good, suits you.'

Linda eventually met his gaze, she was trying so hard to keep her nerves steady, her voice was sharp. 'Goin' someplace? All dressed up like a dog's dinner?'

Carlos held her hand, told her he was seeing people for dinner, just up the road. Linda wanted to ask who, but she couldn't, withdrew her hand and began counting out two pence pieces.

'Maybe I can see you later, after?'

Linda mumbled that she was busy, Carlos leant further and further in trying to tilt her head towards him.

'Something the matter?'

Again, Linda moved away, told him that she was tired, on late, couldn't see him, she began to twist the medallion nervously. Carlos stepped back, looked at her, she looked away, he gave a slight shrug and stood for a second, waiting, hoping she would say something, but she still kept her head down.

'Suit yourself.'

Carlos turned abruptly and walked to the exit. Linda didn't know why, or what made her say it, but she blurted out. 'Twelve, I'll be finished at twelve.'

Carlos smiled back at her, said he would be waiting for her, and left.

Linda bit her nails, then opened the kiosk door, she yelled for Charlie to take over, she didn't wait for a reply, she hurried after Carlos.

The white suit made him easy to follow, she kept well back, watching him looking at his reflection in a shop window, he patted his hair, straightened his tie and continued on down Wardour Street. Linda watched him cross the road and enter a small French bistro. She waited until he actually entered before she crossed the road.

The bistro was dark with red lamps, but Linda could see over the red curtain across the main window. She stared in. Standing on tiptoe, she saw Carlos talking to what looked like a head waiter. He was then led over to a small table at the back. A blonde woman smiled, waved to him. Seated with his back to Linda was Arnie Fisher. As Carlos joined the table he stood, touched Carlos on the shoulder, and kissed his cheek. For a fraction of a second Linda saw his face clearly. Arnie Fisher, then it was true, dear God, it was true.

Linda ran back down Wardour Street, ran across the road, making a car toot its horn, swerving to miss her. She ran towards a telephone kiosk. She remembered she didn't have any change, then remembered you didn't need it, didn't need any money for a 999 call.

Charlie knew something was up. Linda was bad-mouthing everyone who came in, mixing up change. She was twisting the gold medallion round and round, chewing at her nails. Twice he saw her crying, he would be glad when the night was over. Eventually, putting it all down to 'womens' trouble', he went about his business. He would have to tell the Boss, she was getting too out of hand, not doing her job properly. Charlie rather fancied himself in the kiosk, get some other sucker to wander round. Yeah, he'd see if he could ease her out, get a nice little teenager, blonde, one that would do as she was told. Charlie grinned to himself, he was already lying in bed with the replacement.

Later that night Linda lay next to Carlos, they had made love, and she didn't think he knew there was anything wrong. He was lying, seemingly asleep, and for a while she listened to his breathing, but then slid out of the bed and wandered round the room.

Carlos knew she was up, he could hear her wandering about. He opened his eyes a fraction, she was sitting staring at herself in the dressing table mirror, the medallion hanging between her breasts. She looked beautiful, her thick black hair, her dark eyes. He wondered what the matter was, she had been edgy all night, then that business at the arcade. He stopped thinking. She was getting back into bed. He pretended to stir, turning towards her, he slipped his arm round her. Her skin felt cold, like satin, he stroked her gently, they made love again. Afterwards, she cried, he held her tightly, lovingly. He had never told her he loved her, but he did, he thought he did. He would have told her that night but he felt her body relax, heavy in his arms. She was sleeping, he gently moved a strand of hair from her face and turned his back. Linda wasn't sleeping, she felt as if her heart was turning into stone, her body, her head. Dolly was wrong, wrong. In the morning she'd tell him, tell him everything.

The alarm had gone off, Carlos was up and dressed before Linda could shake herself awake. He knelt up on the bed, but she edged away and began dressing, insisting she drive him to work. Maybe in the car she could ask him, but she didn't, and they drove in silence. Carlos had his arm along the back of her seat, his suit was crumpled, his tie flung on the dashboard. The stubble on his chin gave his face a dark swarthy look. He turned on the radio. They were getting closer and closer, the mews was only half a mile away. It was too late, she couldn't say anything.

Carlos' garage was in a horseshoe mews. Linda parked

at the entrance, he had opened his door before she had time to turn the engine off. It was seven-thirty, he was late, he liked to start work at six-thirty, before the mews was full of cars. He leant in and grinned. 'See you.'

He kissed her on the cheek, leaning in, then cupped her chin in his hand.

'You okay?'

Linda nodded, and then he was gone, whistling, his hands stuck in his pockets. Linda started the car and began to reverse.

Positioned in the mews were two police cars. Two officers in plain clothes sat waiting, they had been waiting since six o'clock. Inside Carlos' garage, his young assistant sat between two uniformed officers, waiting. They heard the whistle, the footsteps. The young boy froze, the officers tensed up. Linda, as she was backing the car, saw Carlos' tie, she opened the door leaving the engine running and walked after Carlos to return the tie.

The garage doors were closed, Carlos fished in his pocket for the keys and as he did so, he heard the shout.

'The law ... IT'S THE LAW.'

Johnny hurled himself towards the doors to give Carlos the warning, it all happened in seconds. The two officers waiting in their cars moved at the same time. Carlos took in the situation fast; he turned and ran, running towards the blind exit at the other end of the mews.

Linda dropped the tie and ran back to her car, the engine was still running, she slammed the door and screeched off down the road. She didn't really know which way she was going, but she drove straight to the top of the road and made a left, then took the first left again. As she was turning she heard the crash, the squeal of brakes, the glass breaking, she stopped. Up ahead of her was the second exit of the mews, the exit Carlos was making for. He had run from the mews, running crazily, blindly, run directly into the road, straight in front of a red Post Office van - it was crashed into a lamp post, half up on the pavement. Linda's breath heaved out of her in short sharp gasps, but she couldn't see, couldn't see if he had got away, maybe she was even trying to help him, perhaps she was. She was confused, muddled, hysterical, pulling at her hair, but there was no sign of him. The police came running out of the mews, followed by a police car, the siren screaming. Linda craned her head to try and see what was happening. The men were clustered around the Post Office van. The driver was standing, holding his head, the blood dripping from a cut over his right eye.

Linda put the car into gear and moved slowly forwards. As Linda passed the Post Office van, an officer stepped out and waved her to move on, she passed the men and looked into her mirror. She saw him, his body rammed between the Post Office van and the lamp post, a pool of blood had already seeped onto the pavement, deep red blood, as red as the Post Office van.

The officer standing over him was shaking his head. Another, on his knees, looked up. The officer placed a jacket over Carlos' head. Linda saw it, saw it through the mirror, the white suit getting redder and redder.

Bella thought she was being busted, the hammering on the door nearly gave her heart failure. She heard Linda sobbing, shouting, screaming to be let in. Bella couldn't calm her down, she was hysterical, babbling on about how she had killed him, she had killed someone. Then she began to vomit, heaving all over the small hallway. Bella washed her face, still getting no sense, just a babble of words, and terrible, terrible, shuddering shaking sobs. She half carried Linda through into her main room, helped her onto the bed and stood helpless, watching Linda weeping, twisting the gold medallion round her neck. She yanked it off, threw it across the room, she was swearing, shouting abuse against Dolly.

It took Bella a long time to get the full story out of Linda; all she could say at the end of it was, 'It was an accident Linda, it wasn't your fault.'

Linda was quiet now, Bella gently put the medallion back into her hand, closed Linda's fingers over it. She saw the red weal round her neck where she had torn the chain, her heart went out to her. Linda leant on Bella's shoulder, holding her tightly like a child would do, she cried softly, this time not from hysteria or fear, this time she wept for Carlos. Bella rocked her gently back and forth until she was quiet, then she tucked her up in her bed and sat holding her hand. Linda still held onto the medallion. Bella thought she was all right, but a chill went up her spine when Linda said, 'I hate her, I hate her guts, an' I'll get her for this.'

Chapter Twenty-Six

Dolly was parked in the car park of the Little Chef, half-way to Brighton.

He was late, she had been there over half an hour. Dolly fingered the brief case, looked around, there was still no sign. She began to get edgy. To keep herself occupied she began working out the last details still to be organised. Dolly flipped through her note book, that truck still not found yet. She sighed, Linda had to be watched. She was supposed to have got them a heavy truck over a week ago. Still, if this didn't work out the whole thing was off. Again the panic rose up in her, where was he! Why was he late? Then she saw the car.

Brian Marshall had already had half a flask of brandy, but he was still shaking. He parked his Rover and looked around. He saw the Merc and wondered if that was to be the contact, his hand reached to his pocket for the flask. He was disgusted at himself, with himself, he had been for more than ten years. He made himself not have another drink, this time he would fight back, he couldn't go through it again. Brian Marshall aged forty-three, public school, head boy, rugby star, failure. He had begun to fail when he was thrown out of the team for drunkenness, he knew he'd let them down, just as he had let everyone and everything down, all his life.

Marshall's drinking went hand in glove with his gambling. Ten years ago he had allowed Harry Rawlins to pick up a seven thousand pound marker. He had used Harry's club, drifting from the straight gambling houses, priding himself that he could control his gambling, even quite liking the idea of mixing with villains, knowing them.

He had liked Rawlins, he had seemed a decent man, and he had helped Marshall. Fools like Marshall accept help from dangerous places.

Rawlins had known that Marshall was married to the sister of the owner of one of the biggest security firms. Samsons Security Firm. That had been Rawlins' reason, and his sole reason, for the helping hand. Rawlins knew that one day that so-called helping hand would have to be repaid. Marshall did work for his brother-in-law. He was the family charity, the family drunk. But he was well-educated, and was useful in the office, when sober. Rawlins had let Marshall off the hook for five years. It was as if the debt had never occurred. Then Rawlins had reappeared and demanded the return of the seven thousand pounds. Marshall, of course, hadn't got it. In return for the debt being cancelled out, and with a seven thousand cash gift on top, all Rawlins wanted was the route Samsons' security wagons took.

Marshall, under pressure, had agreed, and accepted the pay-off and the promise of the returned marker when the raid was over. The men had died, Rawlins being one of them. When Marshall had read of Rawlins' death he had heaved a sigh of relief. His relief was short lived. Five months later he had received a phone call. The call that made him drunk for three days. He knew what this meeting was about.

Dolly sat next to Marshall. She could smell the booze. She made a quick run down of him. His handsome puffy face, his pin-striped suit, the dandruff on his collar. She felt safe. She knew this wasn't going to be too difficult. Dolly also noted the child's bucket seat in the back of his car. Yes, she thought, Mr Marshall will cough up.

Dolly was a little too cocky. She flipped open the suitcase and showed the rows of bank notes, then she snapped it shut.

Marshall wasn't that easy. He began to get stroppy. He wasn't prepared to play, not this time. Rawlins had promised him a deal. He, Marshall, had done his share, but he had not got his marker returned. He wasn't going to be made a fool of again. Marshall looked at the woman sitting next to him, he disliked her. He didn't know who she worked for, he didn't care. He could feel the brandy giving him confidence.

'No deal, I worked for Rawlins, I did my part.'

He was shocked at the strength in the voice, it was icy.

'You got it wrong Mr Marshall, we know what happened to Rawlins and his men. No money was taken, but you got paid and now that marker belongs to the Fishers, you heard of them?'

He felt the brandy ebbing away. He didn't know the Fishers, but he had seen them ... that was enough. All they wanted was the route, just like Rawlins, that was all. Marshall could feel his mouth tremble but he wouldn't, they could go to the bloody law, he didn't care any more. The woman got out, she leant in and nodded to the petrol pumps. 'You have a think about it. I'll be over there.'

He saw her look to the baby seat on the back and she slammed the door. Marshall bent his head and leant on the steering wheel. The brandy flask felt hard against his chest, this time he drank, seeing his wife, his kids; he gulped at the drink. He hated himself, he wanted to die, he wanted to be free of all this. He felt the tears welling up inside, and that voice, that second voice talking to him, telling him it was all right, his brother-in-law was insured, he was the family drunk, the charity case, he was as disgusting to his brother-in-law as he was to his wife. He needed that money, he could pay off debts with it, maybe even start up his own business.

Dolly was beside herself, she had been too tough, too hard, she should have cajoled the man, been nice to him. As she put the petrol pump into the tank, she could see his reflection, see the Rover, see Marshall sitting there, she began to will him to come over, praying.

The Rover started up, moved towards the petrol pumps, Dolly was on tenterhooks, he looked as if he was heading for the exit. Then it was all over, they exchanged money for the route map and details. Marshall, without a word, picked up the suitcase from her car, he placed the envelope on the driving seat.

The agreement was, if the raid was accomplished, the law not tipped off, Marshall would get the return of the marker. Dolly would make sure of it. She felt sorry for him, even sorrier for the woman that was married to such a weak, boozed, shadow of a man ... so unlike Harry.

She didn't even notice the petrol on her shoes, she was buzzing all over, as if she'd had a shot in the arm. In fact she was so damned pleased with herself she nearly forgot to pay. The girl in the kiosk had to yell at her, she could have called Dolly anything she liked that morning. Dolly felt like kissing her, she couldn't wait to get to the meet that evening, to tell them, tell the girls. Dolly smiled at the thought of them, right now she loved them, as if they were her children. Her girls – even Linda on this morning was all right.

Dolly had to check the route, go over it in every detail. She and the girls had to get know it backwards. First, Dolly would time it. She drove off, she hadn't felt so good in years.

Chapter Twenty-Seven

Resnick and Andrews had been waiting outside Fran's since nine o'clock, it was now ten-fifteen. The car was full of cigarette smoke, the heater blowing. Andrews was getting red in the face, he could hardly breathe.

Fifteen minutes later they saw her, waddling along,

heaving her bulk. She kept leaning against the wall and having a breather, then she would start off again. Fran carried a carrier bag, you could head the clink of bottles as she waddled. They watched her turn into the scruffy overgrown path, the gate hanging by a rusty hinge. She leant against the front door and took out her key.

The smell was overpowering; cats, food, stale booze and body odour. Fran's bedsit was dusty, untidy and dark, the heavy velvet moth-eaten curtains looked as if they had never been opened in years. Resnick pulled up a chair and indicated for her to sit, she slumped into a low, easy chair, her fat hand still clutching the carrier bag. Her face had sticking plasters over the cuts, and one side of her head had been shaved at the hospital. The dark bruises over her right eye were now a strange yellow and purple.

Andrews watched Resnick go to work on her, his voice was gentle, friendly, he helped her take her coat off, folding it neatly for her, and all the time talking. 'Now love, isn't it about time you told us who did this to you?'

Fran smiled, and patted his hand. He was a nice man, very kind, but she still couldn't remember, she still couldn't help them. All she wanted was to be left alone. Resnick persisted, he asked her over and over the same question, and she began to cry, blubbering, awful child-like sobs. Resnick took out his handkerchief and wiped her face. She blew her nose, and suddenly he stood up, knocking the chair over, jerking his hand to Andrews.

'Take her in ... come on love, I've had enough.'

Fran wailed, held her hand out to Andrews to help her, begged him to take this man away, she didn't know anything, she wanted Boxer, she wanted to talk to Boxer.

Resnick was cruel, he spat out that Boxer was dead, killed by the same man who did this, and he pushed at her face. Fran was moaning, rocking back and forth.

'Who paid you to keep your mouth shut, eh? Who's given you money for all this?'

Resnick held the precious carrier bag in the air, he let it drop. The bottles crashed onto the floor. Fran lurched forwards with another howl. 'I told you, I told you everythin' I know ... ahhhh not me bag.'

Resnick was getting redder and redder in the face. He turned and shouted for Andrews to bring his brief case in from the car.

Andrews had no idea what had gone on when he left the room. Fran was now hunched in her seat, head in hands. Resnick sitting opposite.

'She ever say anything about a woman calling? On the night Boxer got it?'

Andrews shook his head.

'You say she called twice? What time was that?'

Fran told Resnick it was during Coronation Street, that was all she could remember. She wouldn't give her name. The second time she called, Boxer had already left.

'Who with? Who was it?'

Again, Fran shook her head, she was getting more and more confused by the barrage of questions. All she knew was that the man Boxer had left with, was not the man that beat her.

'Who was that, then? You know him, don't you? Don't you?'

Fran sobbed, she looked to Resnick then clung to his arm, she was like a pitiful washed-up whale.

'Dear God! They came to the hospital, they said they'd kill me.'

Resnick stood and leant over her.

'Who said?'

Again, she went into her sobbing routine. Resnick flicked his hand for the brief case. He took out a photograph of Harry Rawlins. Andrew watched him, he seemed a little crazy. Resnick was sweating, his face a beetroot colour.

The radio crackled, Andrews couldn't make out the call. Resnick now turned on him, told him to get outside with his bloody radio. The call was from Fuller, they had picked up the Fisher's wheels man in a raid earlier that morning. Resnick was wanted down the Yard.

Andrews stepped back into the room to repeat the message to Resnick. He stopped short. Resnick was leaning right over Fran. He held in his hand the blown-up photograph of Harry Rawlins. He was pushing the photo into the poor womans face.

'This him? This the man that did this to you ... THIS HIM?'

Andrews thought Resnick had gone mad, why was he showing her a photograph of a dead man?

'No ... no it's not him ... it ... it was Tony, Tony Fisher.'

Resnick straightened up, turned his puce face to Andrews. 'Let's go ...'

They drove back to the Yard in silence, Andrews took sidelong glances at Resnick. Why on earth had he shown Fran a picture of Harry Rawlins.

Chapter Twenty-Eight

Fuller was pleased with his morning's work, he had the report all ready for the little fat man. It looked like they could pin something on the Fisher brothers at long last. One of the cars, a brown Jaguar picked up at Carlos Moreno's was 'wanted' for a job up North. It had Tony Fisher's prints all over it, they now had enough to go on to search the Fishers' place. Fuller had already passed all the information onto the Chief; he sat smugly waiting, he knew any moment the bomb was going to explode. He knew Resnick had still not read all the reports from the past few days. When he did, the fuse would be lit.

Resnick and Andrews arrived back, the Chief requested to see Andrews first and then looking over the half moon glasses. 'George, say in half an hour ...'

This is it, Fuller thought, he couldn't help the smirk, Resnick caught it. 'What you lookin' so bloody happy about?'

Fuller covered and indicated the reports of one Carlos Moreno. Resnick sat in his annex, he opened the file and began to read, picking his nose he bellowed. 'Boxer's landlady admitted it was Tony Fisher that beat her up.'

Fuller was round the annex beaming.

'That's great, we put 'em away for ...'

Resnick looked up at him and shook his head, he tapped the report. 'This is a bloody cock-up isn't it? Fisher gets a good lawyer, we won't have a leg to stand on. Fran's an alcoholic, great witness eh?'

Then Resnick read the tip off was a woman.

'A woman rang Boxer Davis' place the night he was killed, where's the surveillance reports.'

Resnick clicked his fingers, Fuller passed them over, then ... now the bomb would go off. He hovered at the partition. Fuller watched Resnick's face as he read the surveillance reports. He flipped over the page, looked over at Saunders' office, lit a cigarette.

As Detective Andrews left Saunders' office, Resnick entered, the glass framed door shuddering as he banged it shut.

Andrews crossed to Fuller, he dug his hands into his pockets, chewed his lip, then tried to flippantly laugh it off. 'Suppose you know ... I'm back on the beat as from next month.'

Fuller knew perfectly well, but he put on a hurt expression. He was sorry for Andrews, but he was inept, he'd never make a good detective.

The explosion went off, the whole annex heard it, the boom of Resnick's voice. He was shouting, shouting at the top of his voice. All eyes looked over to the Chief's annex, Resnick's head could be seen over the glass partition, red faced, red necked. He was thumping Saunders' desk, he turned, he actually caught Fuller's eye staring towards him, he flung open the Chief's door. 'You all gettin' a bloody good earful? Are you? WELL, ARE YOU?'

Then he slammed back into the room, the whole annex suddenly becoming extra busy, people rushing, gathering papers, typists typing. Andrews looked at Fuller, and knew he was loving it, he also knew then that Fuller was a bastard. He turned and walked out.

Chief Inspector Saunders looked down onto his memo pad and tapped it with the point of his sharpened pencil.

'I withdrew the surveillance off the Rawlins woman over two days ago, it was my idea.'

Resnick sucked in his breath, he was trying so hard to keep control of his temper. He'd already blown his top once, he knew he could go so far with Saunders, then the knife went in. He knew he had to tread carefully. The wind was taken right out of him when Saunders placed the pencil down and leant forwards on his desk.

'The Rawlins case is closed, I'm sorry George, but that's final.'

Resnick could hear his voice, begging, pleading to be given more time. He knew there had to be some connection between the women. Why had a woman rung Boxer's that night? Why did a woman give the tip off for Carlos Moreno? It was as if he was hitting his head against a brick wall, Saunders wouldn't give an inch. Resnick tried once more, pleaded for just a few days.

Saunders snapped the pencil in two, and spoke very quietly. He went all over the cases requiring immediate attention, removed his glasses and leant back. 'You were given the Rawlins case, George, I wanted you to have it for God's sake, I know what that bastard did to you, but now I think you're carrying on personal grievances too far, you've had little results, if anything at all. Should anything come up the case will of course be re-opened and I will make sure ...'

Resnick interrupted him, he repeated. 'Personal grievances?'

'You heard what I said.'

Resnick leaned over the desk, he slammed his fist down. 'The man's a bloody villain, all I'm trying to do –'

This time Saunders interrupted, his voice icy. 'The man is dead, George. I suggest you bury him.'

Saunders changed his tactics, he had other cases he wanted George to work on, he had spoken to the Super.

Resnick interrupted again, he was quieter now, his breath rasped. 'He say anything about my application?'

Resnick watched as Saunders squirmed his way out of it, muttered how they had other officers to interview, he was not the only applicant. He knew what a good officer George was, how he was sure this time he would get the promotion. He knew that by rights George should be sitting where he was, but it wasn't just up to him.

Resnick leaned on the desk again, he pointed, stabbing towards Saunders with his finger. 'Too right, sonny. I should have been sitting where you are, I should have been there years ago. You know why I wasn't, the whole bloody place knows why ... Rawlins. Well you can stuff my application. I resign, it'll be on your desk tomorrow morning, SIR.'

Saunders sighed and he stood up. This wasn't what he wanted, but at the same time, George had over-stepped the mark, he'd had enough. 'I think you had better take that up with the Super.'

'I'm taking it up with you, and mark my words, you haven't heard the last of Rawlins. It's all yours, and don't think you'll get your hands on my pension. My resignation will be on your desk first thing in the morning ... that's what you've wanted all along, isn't it? Well I hope your head bloody well rolls.'

Resnick slammed out of the office. Saunders was furious, his mouth tight. He followed George out and stood at the office door. The whole annex kept their eyes down. Resnick walked over to his desk, picked up his brief case and walked out. Saunders nodded for Fuller to come into his office.

Resnick was half way up the corridor towards the main exit when he stopped. He could hardly catch his breath, he had a coughing fit. His heart was hammering as if it was going to leap out of his chest. Alice came round the bend in the corridor, she saw Resnick leaning against the wall, he looked ill, coughing, walked over to him.

'Do me a favour, Alice, love, I want you to write a letter.'

Alice interrupted him, said she wasn't working for his department any more. He would have to use one of the group secretaries.

'Not this time, it's my last, it's my resignation.'

Alice wanted to touch him, pat his arm, anything. He stood, head bent and told her exactly what he wanted written. It was to be on Saunders' desk first thing in the morning. Resnick tried to grin.

'Eh! an' when you do the whip round for the retirement pressie, no Teasmaid, all right?'

He turned abruptly and walked down the corridor with his old coat flapping and his moth-eaten brief case. Alice watched until he turned the bend in the corridor before she moved away. When she sat at her typewriter she burst into tears.

Chapter Twenty-Nine

Bella took the paint-mask off and gasped for breath. Sniffing, her eyes running, she surveyed her handy-work. Bella was respraying a white Ford Escort van. This was to be their getaway vehicle and Dolly had bought it over a month before. The number plates were changed, and Bella was giving it a new coat of paint.

Shirley was painting two signs for the sides of the van. Bella went over to see how they were coming along. Shirley was making a good neat methodical job, her tongue sticking out of the side of her mouth. She looked up.

'You think it's okay?'

Bella nodded, then went back to her own work. She looked at Linda on the far side of the lock-up. Linda was sitting cleaning the shot guns. Her face was ashen, her mouth a thin tight line. She kept flicking looks towards the exit, she was waiting for Dolly.

'Everything okay, Linda?'

Bella was worried she was going to blow her top. She had been with Linda all day. She had tried to persuade her to go home, but Linda wouldn't hear of it. Linda was like a taut wire ready to snap.

Dolly at last breezed in. She was still very 'up', and called out to the girls as she plonked her shopping bag down. 'It's on ... we've got the route.'

Shirley and Bella crossed to Dolly, picking up her 'high'. Dolly waved her hand towards Linda to join the group. She laid out the plans, and lit up her usual cigarette. She had certainly done her home-work as usual. All day Dolly had been driving backwards and forwards inspecting the roads they would be using. She knew exactly how long it would take the security wagon to leave their headquarters, how many seconds it took for them to move into position. Dolly instructed that each girl go over the route, just as she had done. They must know every inch of the road.

'You do it in the rush hour?'

Dolly looked to Linda as if she was stupid and ignored the question. The raid was to take place two weeks earlier than first anticipated. Dolly's instructions continued. The girls were to prepare their 'holiday' stories. Linda was either to leave the arcade or get herself sacked. Bella to quit her jobs at the clubs. No one must suspect the women had any contact with each other, their plans were to be above suspicion.

Dolly was perkier than they had ever seen her, checking and double checking they all had their passports and flight times. She ticked off each item in her precious note book. The girls went back to work, leaving Dolly going over her accounts. She then inspected their work. She was pleased, the van paint job was really very good and with the two mock signs and two sets of number plates, not easy to trace. She watched as Bella demonstrated how fast the signs could be switched, the number plates changed.

'What about this truck you're supposed to have found?'

Linda couldn't look Dolly in the face, she stared down at the floor.

'Dry cleaning truck, it'll be perfect, and a doddle to nick.'

Dolly tapped her with the pencil, she didn't give a damn what kind of doddle the thing was, she wanted it in position and ready two weeks before the raid.

'I'll get it, all right? all right?'

Linda turned abruptly and crossed the lock-up.

'Make sure the doors are strong at the back, the bumpers have got to be big.'

Linda ignored her and picked up the shot gun. She would have liked to turn it on Dolly, blast her right there and then.

'What's the matter with Linda?'

Bella shrugged and busied herself cleaning her hands with a rag.

Again, Dolly looked to Linda, Wolf padded round her feet. Dolly saw Linda kick the dog. That was it, she strode over. 'Don't you ever kick him!'

Linda looked at her insolently.

'Come on, out with it, what's the matter.'

Linda kept her head down and muttered that nothing was the matter. She told her that everything had been done. She had got rid of the Italian.

Dolly nodded, so that was it. She put her hand out to touch Linda's arm. She was shocked by the way Linda jerked away and looked at her with such hatred it made her freeze.

'He won't bother us, he's dead, want to know how it happened? Or is it good enough to know he's dead, just like you wanted. I did just what you told me, I grassed on him, SATISFIED?'

Dolly took a deep breath, again she tried to touch Linda.

'I'm sorry, I never meant that to happen. I'm sorry. Look at me Linda, Linda!'

Linda did – a hard cold bitter stare. Then she turned and walked off. Dolly did not know how to handle the situation. She went to Bella.

'She all right? How did it happen?'

Bella told her, and Dolly stood wringing her hands,

136

shaking her head. Sometimes she floored Bella, one minute she could be 'Pussy Galore', the next she acted like a maiden aunt, tutting and shaking her head.

'She's hurting, Dolly, she liked him, liked him a lot. She blames herself, but it was an accident. She'll be all right, just leave her alone for a while.'

Bella left Dolly standing alone, she joined Linda and slipped her arm around her shoulders. They watched Dolly pick up the shot gun. She cocked it, and caught her finger on the hammer. Linda couldn't help smiling, she hoped it hurt. It did. Dolly shook her finger and tried again. Three times she cocked it, then slammed her finger. It was red, raw and bleeding by the time Dolly got the hang of it.

'Okay. Let's have a rehearsal!'

The girls moaned. Every time they met at the lock-up Dolly made them rehearse a part of the raid. This time she wanted to practise unlocking the body harness, picking up the sledge-hammer and shot gun. Shirley had devised the harness. They couldn't afford to take any risks. Dolly would be ramming the security wagon and the jolt could unseat her. It was imperative she had full control of the truck to enable her to move it backwards and forwards at full force.

They moved out of the annex into the large filthy main garage. A furniture truck, minus wheels and one cab door, would act as the lead truck. Dolly got into the driving seat, again remarked to Linda that they must get the truck to be used in the raid. She had to practise on the real thing.

Shirley, Linda, and Bella lined up at the back doors of the furniture van. They heard Dolly shouting out by numbers the routine.

'Break ... ram backwards ... move forwards, ram back again!'

Dolly swore, she couldn't undo the harness. Shirley jumped into the cabin and re-tied it. She fixed the shot gun by a cord round Dolly's neck. This gave her hands freedom, and yet the gun was ready when she needed it. All she would have to do was release the harness, and pick up the sledge-hammer. She would need both hands to hurl it through the air.

Linda and Bella leaned against the truck. Again, Dolly began shouting out her routine. Suddenly the back doors of the van flew open and Dolly stood there holding the hammer. One door clipped Shirley on the shoulder and she fell over. The shot gun swung up and hit Dolly on the chin. Any other time Linda would have creased up laughing, this time she snarled. 'Bloody joke that was.'

Bella gave Linda the eye to cool it. Dolly was getting very uptight.

'It's her voice, sounds like bleedin' Bambi. They know we're women and forget it.'

They rehearsed over and over until Dolly could handle the harness, hammer and swing the gun into position. No matter how many times they did it, Dolly's voice still sounded high-pitched.

Shirley was the one eventually to call it quits for the night. They could all have a think about what to do with Dolly's voice. The four went back down to the annex and began changing into their street clothes.

'You've not changed your mind then, Dolly?'

Dolly looked up from putting her shoes on.

'Still not going to tell us where you're stashing the money?'

Dolly picked up her tweed coat, her mouth tightened.

'I thought we'd gone over that!'

Shirley gave Bella a steely look, but Bella persisted.

'I mean we all fly off all round the world, leaving you with a boot full of money.'

Dolly picked up her handbag, she twitched slightly.

'That is the way it was arranged, that's the way it's going to be.'

Dolly suddenly flung her bag down and turned on them.

'Come on, get it all off your chests now! You want it any different, them I'm out, I want every cent back, every penny I've laid out. Seven grand today just for starters. You think I'm doing it for any other reason than to safeguard the lot of you? You think that she, you think

Linda with a few drinks inside her could keep her mouth shut, and Shirley? We'll not only have the law after us but every villain in London. You didn't cope too well with the Fishers did you? DID YOU!'

'That's not the point Dolly.'

Dolly crossed to Bella, she was red in the face with fury.

'You tell me the point, because I can't bloody see it, all I can see is that after all we've bloody well been through, you don't trust me ... YOU STILL DON'T TRUST ME, what do I have to do? eh?'

Shirley sided with Dolly, she trusted Dolly, she wanted to go along with the arrangements. She also knew that Dolly was right. She wouldn't be able to take any pressure, not from animals like Tony Fisher.

Dolly picked up her bag and began pulling on her gloves. Her hand throbbed with pain from the shot gun. 'You know where I live, what you think I'm going to do? Run off with the money is that it?'

Bella shrugged. 'We got to get it first darlin'.'

Dolly whipped round on her. 'You said it, and it's up to you now if we do it or not.'

Bella shrugged, she picked up Wolf and handed him to Dolly, and after a moment said, 'Okay, the arrangements stay, but I don't like it!'

Linda agreed. Dolly, without a word, moved to the exit. She turned back to the three girls. 'Thanks, thanks for nothing ... goodnight.'

Dolly had to get out fast, she didn't want them to see that she near to tears. She felt cheated, betrayed, she hugged her little dog to her. 'Let's go home baby, home.'

Bella gave Linda a hug and a kiss, told her that if she needed her she'd be at the club. Bella put on her crash helmet and grinned.

'Maybe see you later?'

Linda shook her head, she was very tired, it had been a long day. Bella slipped out, and Linda collected the dirty coffee mugs.

'See you Shirl ... don't forget the lights.'

Shirley was standing stock still in the centre of the

annex. She listened, then turned to Linda. 'You hear that? You hear something?'

Linda listened from the office annex. A train rumbled overhead. Linda dumped the mugs into the sink and shouted.

'It'll be that bloody dog from next door.'

Linda didn't bother to wash the mugs, she picked up her bag and made her way to the exit. 'Ta-rah, see you!'

Linda didn't wait for Shirley's reply, the door closed after her and Shirley was alone. Shirley buttoned her coat up. It was odd, she hadn't heard the dog from next door all night. The outer main doors clanged shut after Linda. Shirley turned the main overhead lights off and went towards the annex. She heard it again, like a scuffle. She listened, the drip, drip of water. Suddenly she felt scared, she shivered. Shirley turned the annex lights off and switched on her small torch. She shone it round the lock-up.

Bill Grant pressed his face against the cold wall. He stared through the slits in the bricks. The blonde seemed to stare straight at him. Bill held his hands up and whispered without turning. 'One more to go.'

Bill heard the small inter-locking doors open and shut. The key turning in the lock. He then heard Shirley's footsteps moving out of the main garage. Clang went the outer door. Bill straightened up, he turned from the wall. 'Eh, who'd have thought it, the chicks are pullin' it.'

Bill chuckled and brushed the brick dust from his coat sleeve. The lock-up was identical to the girls', just dirtier. Lines of wrecked cars covered in dust and rubbish. A flashlight shone in his face, he held his hand to his eyes.

'Do me a favour.'

The light clicked off. Bill heard him laughing. A deep throaty laugh. He looked towards one of the wrecked cars. Harry Rawlins' teeth seemed to shine in the gloom. He held the Alsatian by the scruff of the neck. The dog's jaws were tied with a rag. Harry released the straining animal. The dog, without its muzzle, hurtled forwards, choking itself on its chain. Bill, scared, backed off. 'Fuckin' hell . . .'

The dog couldn't reach him, the chain was too short. Harry laughed even more. For a split second Harry was like the animal. His mouth snapping open and shut as he laughed.

'She's going by the book, you hear? She'll be the only one who knows where the money's stashed.'

Bill was grinning now, but when Harry spoke, his voice was quiet. 'Be like taking candy from a baby.'

Chapter Thirty

Linda was wearing old jeans and a sweater. She waited at the corner of Lanark Road, Maida Vale. The dry cleaning van turned the corner from Sutherland Avenue, just as it had done every Tuesday and Wednesday for the past four weeks.

Linda watched the driver slow down and park outside the back entrance of a block of flats. Linda hurried along the road. The driver got out, walked round the back of the van and opened the doors. He removed four heavy boxes of clean laundry and walked up the path to the flats. Linda ran along the road, she knew she had about two minutes to get into the van and drive it away before the driver returned. She had checked him out, he always left the keys in the ignition, she kept her fingers crossed. The porter let the driver into the flats. Linda got into the driving seat. Sure enough the keys were hanging in the ignition. The van started after the second try and Linda drove it from Lanark Road to Church Street, Paddington. A doddle, just as she had known it would be.

Shirley waited in the underground car-park. This was used by market stall holders as their dropping point. Lorries, vans and trucks were lined up with fruit and veg' deliveries. Towards the back of the parking bays was a large empty space. Stacks of orange boxes and cardboard boxes were thrown into piles. Shirley had cleared a space large enough for a big vehicle. She also had a spare set of number plates, cans of spray paint and a tarpaulin made from old sheets.

At long last Shirley saw Linda, and the truck lumbered into the yard. She waved Linda over to indicate the safest place for her to back up.

Linda was cocky, proud of herself, she showed the truck off to Shirley.

'See it's perfect, look at the size of the bumpers.'

Linda slid open the driving door, there was only one seat. Again this was perfect to store the sledge-hammer and the shot gun. The doors at the back of the truck opened; reinforcing the bumper, were small iron steps. Dolly could reverse back into the security wagon with ease. Linda showed Shirley the inside of the truck which was spacious. Dolly could move from the driving seat back up the truck with plenty of room to spare.

'What's the engine like?'

Linda was already heaving the sheets up and over the truck, hiding the dry cleaning sign.

'Leave the engine to me, all right?'

Shirley handed over the market keys. Linda had a lot of work to do when she opened the engine bonnet.

'Looks a mess to me, you sure it'll be all right?'

Linda looked at Shirley, 'I know all about engines, all right? You just get on and tell Dolly. I won't leave this place 'til it's runnin' like a Maserati.'

Shirley turned and stomped off, she was really fed up with Linda. Not a word of thank you, though it had been her that had arranged the hiding place, the keys cut, the tarpaulin, the paint.

Linda squinted into the engine, and scratched her head. 'Fuck me, which are the bloody spark plugs?'

Shirley was still tetchy when she arrived at her mother's. At first she thought she'd walked into the wrong flat. The place was tidy, not a dirty dish in sight.

'I've bought your keys back, mum? ... MUM?'

Audrey dived in from the bedroom. She was made up to the nines, her hair lacquered stiff. Shirley almost keeled over from the smell of Revlon's 'Intimate'.

'What do you think of this? Fiver, back of a lorry job.'

Audrey paraded in front of Shirley in the sequinned crimplene.

'Great, where's Greg?'

Shirley was still having a spot of bother with the Mini Estate. The knob kept falling off the gear stick.

'Don't you ask me about him, look, look what he was doin'.'

Audrey rabbited on as she opened a closet. All the tidying which had been thrown into one cupboard, all fell out. Dirty washing, shoes, groceries, ironing board.

'He was sniffin' glue with this on.'

Audrey held up a gas mask, she put it over her head and continued moaning about Greg. She didn't know what to do with him, he was out of his head.

Shirley stared at her mother. The voice barking at her through the gas mask was low, deep, with a strange echo. Shirley inspected the gas mask as Audrey now prattled on about her date for the night. Some bloke in the market had a brother-in-law, who knew this other bloke with a lot of money.

'What?'

'I said I'm going out tonight to the Golden Nugget.'

It took another ten minutes of chatter before Audrey went into the bedroom to re-fix her hair. Shirley slipped the gas mask into her carrier bag. She stood at her Mother's bedroom door. The kitchen may have been tidy but the bedroom looked like a bomb had hit it.

'Tarrah Mum, won't be seein' you for a bit, going off, holiday.'

Audrey looked at her through the dressing table mirror.

'Have a nice time then!'

A look passed between them, Audrey didn't even harp on about not being taken on the holiday. She followed Shirley to the back door. She didn't know why, but suddenly she felt frightened, in almost a whisper.

'Good luck!'

Shirley gave a strange half quizzical smile, then she
was gone.

The tension was building in the lock-up. Dolly had spent
two hours with Linda and the dry cleaning truck. They
had driven the van around the back streets. Twice it had
stalled. The paint wasn't dry on the sides. Dolly, however,
did admit that it was certainly strong enough.

Linda stood covered in oil and paint, she was getting
very worked up. In the end she said that to make sure the
bloody truck was in perfect working order she would sleep
in it the night before the raid.

Bella zipped up the hockey bag. The shot gun and
sledge-hammer, along with the harness, were now ready
to be stored in the truck. The getaway vehicle was
standing-by, ready to be driven into position.

They had all double checked passports, tickets, suitcases. Shirley had gone over their overalls so many times
she knew every inch of them. Each girl had instructions
about their own vehicles. Bella had given notice in the
clubs over a week ago. Linda had been fired from the
arcade two days previously. Shirley had laid the plans for
her holiday.

There was nothing more to do but wait, wait until the
day itself. They were just one day ahead of themselves,
Dolly had insisted that the day before the raid the girls
stay away from the lock-up, rest and just go over details in
case, just in case, something had been overlooked.

Dolly tried on the gas mask. She stood, legs apart in the
centre of the lock up, she screamed with all her force.
'DON'T MOVE!'

The three looked at each other. Her voice sounded low,
distorted, you couldn't tell if it was man or woman. They
agreed Dolly should wear the mask.

Linda went back to work on the truck. Shirley hovered
for a while, but eventually thought she should check over
the Mini, see if she could find her brother.

Bella had a feeling Dolly wanted a word, she waited until Shirley had left before she moved over to her side.

'Voice sounds good with the mask.'

Bella was slightly taken aback, Dolly seemed terrified. Her eyes flickered, she gripped Bella's arm. 'You think we can do it?'

For an answer, Bella gave a mock punch and grinned. Dolly seemed very vulnerable. She was twisting her wedding ring round and round. 'You'll have to keep your eye on Linda, don't let her go crazy. I don't want her shooting that gun off.'

Bella shrugged and sat up on the wing of the Ford Escort. 'Wouldn't matter, it's only full of rice.'

Dolly was pacing up and down, her hands still twisting the ring. 'Shirley will be scared, but she's all right, she'll come through. You back her up, know what I mean?'

Bella nodded, swinging her legs. She was a little worried, Dolly seemed to have cracked. Dolly was, after all, the main back-up to the three of them. If she lost her bottle then they'd all be for it.

'It's easier for us, Dolly, I mean we're together. Tough on you on your own, you okay?'

Dolly's head jerked up, her eyes narrowed.

'Don't you worry about me, I won't let you down.'

Bella jumped off the van, the oil boiler was back on top.

'Well good luck then!'

Dolly was putting her tweed on, she nodded, without looking at Bella.

'Yeah, that goes for all of you, for all of us.'

That was the last time Bella saw Dolly before the raid.

Chapter Thirty-One

The day before the raid Dolly went to the convent. She checked that the new lockers she had given as a gift were being installed.

Later that morning she stood by Harry's grave. She spent a lot of time tending to the flowers.

Lunchtime Shirley couldn't resist going to the lock-up. She just wanted a final check.

Bella missed Shirley by half an hour. She double checked her own gear and then left.

Linda drove the truck onto the motorway. She dumped the remaining laundry boxes and returned to the carpark. She then drove her Ford Capri into the West End.

It was getting dark by the time Linda returned to the truck. This time she carried the hockey bag with the gun and sledge-hammer. The harness was already bolted to the floor. The gas mask Dolly could bring herself. Linda sat wrapped in a blanket in the back of the truck. The chewing gum was tasteless, she chewed her finger nails. She could taste the engine oil. It was going to be a long night.

At two thirty a.m. Bella drove the getaway Ford Escort van into position. She placed a 'Meter out of order' on the two meters either side. Bella checked the florist sign, and the second set of number plates. Bella was wearing black motor-bike leather. She had her helmet and visor down. She now made her way to the three level car-park in Covent Garden.

Bella went up the back stairs. On level one she checked that Shirley had parked her Mini Estate. She moved up to level two. Linda's Ford Capri was parked as arranged near the exit door. Bella checked the boot. Both suitcases were side by side. One more to go.

Bella stepped out onto level three. Dolly's Mercedes was parked next to the Ladies' Room. Bella checked that the boot was unlocked. The time was by now four o'clock. Four hours to go.

Shirley was sweating, she threw off the top cover. She got out of bed and paced up and down the bedroom. Shirley hunted through a dressing table drawer. She took out a packet of cigarettes. She lit up, coughed, and stubbed it out. Shirley looked at herself in the mirror. How many nights had she watched Terry. He used to sit chain smoking the night before he was on some 'little bit of business darlin'.' All those nights, well now, now she knew just how he felt. Sick! Terry? . . . Terry? It had been a long time since she had thought of him. She felt that he had been a long time dead.

Linda squinted at her wrist watch. It was still only five o'clock. She stretched her stiff cold body. She made yet another inspection of the harness, the shot gun and the sledge-hammer. Took yet another look at her watch. The place was like a tomb, and she was desperate to have a pee.

Dolly got back into bed, she had been up to the loo six times. She lit yet another cigarette and stared at the alarm clock. Five-thirty, no good trying to sleep now. Wolf snuggled up next to her.

Dolly's eyes kept straying to the blink, blink, of the digital alarm clock. The photo of Harry next to it seemed to light up. Dolly turned on the pillow and looked at the photo. She could remember the exact day it had been taken. Their eighteenth wedding anniversary. Eddie stood next to Harry with his arm slung round his shoulder. Both men were looking at the camera, Dolly was gazing up to her husband, her hand on his arm. The alarm suddenly went off, and she nearly had heart failure.

Chapter Thirty-Two

Linda wasn't the first to arrive at the lock-up. Shirley was in the small annex, chucking up. Linda could hear her heaving and wretching.

'You okay?'

Shirley looked up, she was ashen, her eyes seemed three times their normal size. She managed a weak nod, then heaved over the sink.

Shirley was wearing her overall. It looked good. She had bandaged her chest flat, it gave a muscular look to the top half of her body.

Linda stripped off and prepared to get into her overall. She began to wind the bandage round her chest. She also wrapped them round the top part of her arms.

Bella strode in. She didn't even try to act casual. She went straight for her stack of clothes. Shirley was still vomiting. Bella looked to Linda and raised an eyebrow.

'You okay, Shirley?'

A feeble moan was all the reply. Linda was putting her gloves on. 'Okay everyone, remember gloves ... GLOVES from now on, nobody touch the van without gloves.'

At seven o'clock Dolly walked down the ramp towards the truck. She wore a heavy black overall, padded out, she seemed to roll as she walked. Her hair was greased and flattened to her head. She wore a ski-mask as a hat, ready to be pulled over her face.

There were two men already unloading crates of fruit. They paid no attention to her but continued to work. Dolly took off the tarpaulin and chucked it into the back of the truck. She then felt for the key beneath the right wheel. She had to get down on her knees, still she couldn't find it. The two men looked over, Dolly was beside herself, she felt all round the wheel, under the bumper. Dolly's hands were black by the time she located the ignition key. She was so angry that it seemed to calm her. The harness was in place, the sledge-hammer and the shot gun. Dolly tied the harness tight. She fitted the loop round her neck for the shot gun.

The truck wouldn't start. Three times she turned the ignition on. It caught on the fourth try, then went flat again. The two men turned and grinned. Dolly was praying under her breath they wouldn't come over.

At last the engine ticked over, she crashed the gears, the truck lurched forwards. Dolly slammed on the brakes.

'I'll kill her. I'll kill her, I knew it, I knew it!'

Dolly then realised she still had the hand brake on. As the truck roared out of the yard the men watching nudged each other. 'Not his morning is it?'

Bella tested the saw engine over and over again. Her hands were sweating inside the leather gloves. Satisfied, she carried it to the back of the van. Linda gave her the once over, she was obsessive about them wearing their gloves.

'I got 'em on, I got 'em on, all right?'

Bella bent down and placed the saw position. She had also built up her shoulders. She looked like a giant.

'You got eye make-up on, you've bloody got eye make-up on!'

Shirley shouted back that she hadn't. Bella clocked that she was near to tears with terror. She went over and took a look. As Bella passed Linda she whispered. 'Lay off her, all right, you just keep it shut.'

Linda went and sat at the back of the van, she clenched and unclenched her hand. She heard Shirley vomit yet again.

'She'll be wantin' us to stop at the ladies' lav next!'

Shirley rounded the van in a fury.

'Leave me alone, just leave me alone!'

Bella, again, gave Linda a ticking off, it wasn't much good, Linda was as uptight as Shirley.

'What time is it?'

Linda suddenly snapped, she jumped down from the

van. 'Use your own soddin' watch, that's the tenth time you've asked me, look at your own watch!'

Shirley's mouth trembled. This time Bella pushed Linda hard.

'Lay off her, I'm warning you!'

Bella put her arm around Shirley's shoulders. 'I guess this is it. Dolly's on her way, so let's go!'

Eight months ago to the day, Terry Miller had turned angrily on Jimmy Nunn. Three times Jimmy had asked him the time.

'What's the matter with your own bleedin' watch?'

Jimmy kept tapping his own watch, he listened, it had stopped. 'I must have over wound the bugger!'

Before a row could get underway, Harry Rawlins slipped off his own watch. 'Here take mine!'

Harry Rawlins held out a gold watch to Jimmy.

Neither Terry or Joe could believe it. Harry always wore that particular watch. He caught them staring, rolling up his sweater. Harry had been wearing a watch on both wrists. 'Keep it!'

Jimmy's mouth fell open, he put it on his wrist beaming. Two minutes later Harry was gone, in another five minutes the men would follow. As the lock-up door shut behind him, Joe whispered to Terry. 'His old lady gave him that, must be true then.'

Terry looked puzzled.

'He's packin' her in after tonight.'

He bent his head closer to Terry. 'You know who it is, don't you? Must be crazy!'

Joe jerked his head towards Jimmy and grinned. Terry understood and shook his head. 'She's a little raver, don't blame him!'

Jimmy overheard the last remark, he turned to Terry. 'Who is? Who you talking about?'

Jimmy looked at Joe, he asked, 'Who's packin' who in?'

Joe broke away immediately and walked to their van. 'Time to move sugar, let's go!'

Jimmy Nunn took the full impact of the explosion not

more than twenty minutes later. His body was literally blown to pieces. When the petrol tank exploded, what was left went up in flames. The gold wrist watch remained intact. The gold watch that identified the charred body as that of Harry Rawlins. Terry Miller burnt to death. Joe Pirelli burnt to death.

Chapter Thirty-Three

Dolly had the security truck in view. As the heavy iron gates closed behind it, she moved into position. Leading the security wagon, knowing the route it would take, Dolly began the journey. It would now only be a matter of minutes before they rounded the corner into Waterloo Bridge Road. Dolly hoped to God the girls were in position.

The girls had no aggro leaving the lock-up. Bella heaved the garage doors shut. She did not see the open garage doors of the lock-up next door to them. None of the girls noticed him.

Bill Grant was driving Jimmy Nunn's B.M.W. He watched the girls drive into the street. He was so intent on watching their movement he did not see a dust cart. As the girls drove off and he was just about to follow, the dust cart drew up directly in front of the open garage doors. By the time the dust cart moved, the girls had gone. Bill Grant ran back into the lock-up and put in a call to Harry Rawlins. They could have taken any of five routes, he would try and pick them up, in the meantime Harry was to make sure that Eddie Rawlins watched Dolly's house. If she was going by the books she would return there.

Harry was angry, but not too worried. So far, Dolly had literally gone stage by stage. If she was going by his records, she would be the carrier. She would then hold the money until she contacted one of the fences known to Harry.

Eddie was already waiting at the house, it was now only a matter of time. That is, if they got away with it.

Dolly could just see a glimmer of light at the end of the underpass. She pulled her mask down, over her face, over the gas mask. With her foot pressed as hard as it would go the truck moved faster, forty, forty-five, fifty. Dolly flicked a look in the mirror, sure enough the security wagon was right behind her, right on her tail. As the speedometer reached sixty, Dolly slammed her brakes on. The unsuspecting security wagon driver crashed into the back of the dry cleaning truck.

With grinding gears, Dolly moved forwards, her foot still pressed to the floor, she went into reverse. The security wagon jolted backward, the driver frantic. Dolly could hear the crunch of metal, the shattering of glass. She thanked God for the harness, she was jerked so hard she thought her chest would crack open.

As Dolly rammed the security wagon the second time, Shirley flung open the back doors of their van. She hurled smoke canisters. The smoke began to billow and hiss, clouding visibility. The woman driving the Fiat directly behind the girls had been given a warning by Linda to slow down. The car behind the Fiat now slammed into her back, the woman began screaming.

Linda was second out, she carried the shot gun chest high. With all her force she smashed the woman's windscreen and grabbed her ignition keys. The terrified, screaming woman covered her face. Linda stepped back. Legs apart, she stood with the shot gun poised. She looked big, muscular, the mask covering her face completely. As Linda threw the woman's key away, Shirley was already half-way over the top of the security wagon. With wire clippers she snapped off the aerial.

Bella had run from the girls' van with the chainsaw motor already turned on. The saw was cutting through the side of the truck like butter. With two pieces of lead piping tied together to look like the barrel of a shot gun, Shirley stood by.

Dolly, after braking, had picked up the sledge-hammer.

She moved through the back of the dry cleaning truck. The doors she kicked open with all her force. She looked like a black devil, the hammer swinging over her head. The reinforced glass on the security wagon cracked but didn't break. Dolly swung her shot gun up into position, chest high, pointing directly at the two stunned, panic stricken security guards.

'DON'T MOVE.'

The voice was hideous, distorted. The men lifted their hands above their heads.

Bella cut through and Shirley handed her the lead pipes.

'OPEN UP.'

The guard within the wagon could see nothing but the barrel pushed through the gaping hole in the side of the wagon.

'They're armed for God's sake, OPEN.'

The guard did as he was instructed by his driver. As the rear doors opened, Bella was first in. The chainsaw still held in her hand, she threw it at the frightened man's face. He backed off, tripped and fell, his head banging against the grill. Bella kicked him out of the way. Shirley was already clipping through the wire cage surrounding the money bags.

Shirley began stuffing the money sacks into the open rucksack on Bella's back.

As soon as Bella's rucksack was filled she ran from the wagon and changed places with Linda. Bella now held the shot gun. Terrified spectators watched from behind the safety of their cars. No one made a move to stop the raiders. Shirley filled Linda's rucksack full of money sacks. Linda filled Shirley's rucksack.

Linda's breath heaved, her wet ski-mask dragged in and out of her mouth. She was gasping, the bags were heavy, cumbersome. Bella saw Linda run from the wagon, she began to back. Shirley came out, her rucksack caught on the side of the wagon delaying her for a fraction. Bella backed further and further up the tunnel. At last Shirley was free and running. Bella now took off;

as she was faster, she overtook Shirley. She tossed the shot gun aside and was heading for the tunnel exit. As Shirley passed Dolly, two men ran from the back of the tunnel. One man caught up with Shirley and dived in a rugby tackle.

Shirley crashed to the floor, the man on top of her. Dolly actually seemed to fire at the man. She was, in fact, aiming at the tiled wall above his head. The tiles blew from the wall. The man thought he had been hit, he jumped up screaming.

Shirley was back on her feet and running. She was in trouble – her ankle – she took three steps and then began a desperate hobble towards the exit.

Dolly turned to watch her, she was getting panic stricken. The guards saw their chance. Dolly was the only one left. To protect herself, and still holding the shot gun, Dolly began to back up into the truck.

Both Linda and Bella had made it back into the get-away van, but there was still no sign of Shirley.

Linda began to back the van down the road towards the high road. They saw Shirley limping out of the underpass. Linda rammed her foot on the pedal. The white van, with G.L.C. scrawled across the side, screeched across the traffic. Oncoming cars braked, crashed into each other. The van with the back doors open banged over the pylon in the road.

Bella with her arms outstretched, grabbed hold of Shirley and hauled her into the van. Linda, with gears grinding, now moved forwards. Back over the pylon, back across the traffic.

Dolly had made it into the driving seat. The engine still running, she yet again reversed into the security wagon. This time the windscreen shattered. Dolly, with a clear road up ahead, drove out of the underpass.

Dolly, her foot pressed down on the accelerator, drove across the oncoming traffic. This was made easier by the havoc Linda had caused. Dolly took the first turning on the left. She mounted the pavement to avoid an oncoming car. Turning right, she knew she was in trouble as she was

154

heading straight for Neal Street. Dolly grabbed her small holdall bag, slid open the sliding door and jumped.

The dry cleaning truck hurtled straight into a shop front. The glass shattered, two women ran for their lives. Dolly was already on the run, down the small alley, past the market store. By now her mask was stripped off. Covent Garden tube station was thronging with rush hour commuters.

Dolly, her breath bursting, walked across Long Acre and into the tube station. She pushed her way through the commuters heading towards the stair case down to the tubes. As Dolly ran down she could hear the rumble of the trains below. She began frantically stripping off her overalls. She had to sit on the steps to ease the overall over her plimsolls. She wore a sweater and trousers beneath. She stuffed the overall into her holdall.

The sound of the tubes was louder as she made her way down stair after stair, towards the platform. She had to stand pressed against the wall. Gasping, heaving, to regain her breath, she closed her eyes. 'I did it ... dear God, I did it ... HARRRRYYYYY HAARRRRRY. I DID IT.'

At Floral Street, Bella, her mask stripped off, opened the back door of the Ford Escort Van. She looked around, then quickly ripped the G.L.C. sign from the side of the van. The florist sign was beneath. She then casually walked around the back of the van and slipped off the top number plate. The street was full of people, but no one paid any attention to the nondescript florist van.

Linda watched as Bella removed the front number plate. They were on the move as Bella jumped into the back. Shirley was lying on the floor, surrounded by plants, surrounded by rucksacks. She was crying, sobbing her heart out. Bella hugged her, arms round each other they kept on repeating over and over. 'We did it, we did it, we did it!'

Dolly stood on the platform, stepped into the tube. Her holdall was left in the tube wastebin. She now carried her

155

handbag and a plastic shopping Waitrose bag.

The white florist van entered the three level car-park, not more than twenty yards from where Dolly had crashed through the shop window. Linda drove up to the top level. One by one the girls placed their rucksacks into the boot of the Mercedes. Shirley limped her way down to the first level. Linda and Bella had already made it down to the second. They picked up their suitcases from the Capri and entered the ladies' toilet.

Dolly got off the tube at Piccadilly, went across the platform and got onto the next tube heading back to Covent Garden. She had bought a weekly season ticket and came up in the lift from the tube this time. Casually, as if she was window shopping, Dolly walked towards the split level car-park. She took her time. She noticed the police cars, heard the sirens as they headed towards the Strand underpass. Rush hour traffic had come to a standstill. Lines of cars waited along Long Acre. Luckily for the girls, they would be driving in the opposite direction!

Linda was dressed and ready. She had done her lips three times. She had smudged her lips so much she had more on her cheek than anywhere else.

Bella was already on her way to take a taxi. She had walked from the car-park, leaving a black plastic bag in the rubbish container. The bag contained her overalls and plimsolls. Bella was now wearing a smart coat and matching chic hat, she carried a small suitcase. She hailed a taxi.

'Luton Airport, darlin'.'

The taxi driver couldn't believe his luck. It had been a hell of a morning. Something had gone on in the Strand underpass, traffic held up everywhere.

Linda with her black plastic bag filled, knocked on the toilet door. 'You okay in there, Shirley? You all right?'

Shirley, in obvious agony limped out. She wasn't ready, she still hadn't done her make-up. She was crying with the pain. 'Get rid of this for me, I'll be all right.'

Shirley handed Linda her black plastic bag and began

to apply her make-up, Linda waited for no more than a second, with both plastic bags and her own suitcase, she slipped out.

Linda dumped the bags in the bin on the second floor, pushing them well down, then covering them up with rubbish. She made sure no one saw her, then she was on her way. As Linda drove out of the car-park, Dolly entered the top floor, she could hardly stop herself running towards the Merc. She opened the boot, there were three haversacks, neatly laid together. Dolly opened her car door, a woman entered and walked towards a parked car half-way up the level, Dolly ducked her head down and opened the glove compartment.

Dolly checked the wig in the driving mirror, then put on a pair of dark glasses. Through the mirror she watched the woman driver exit, then she drove herself down to level two.

Shirley limped to her car, put her suitcase in the back, then limped round to the driving seat. Her ankle was so painful she took her shoe off, and started sobbing uncontrollably.

Dolly drove onto level one, as she passed Shirley she stopped, wound down her window.

'It's my ankle ... I can't ... I can't ...'

Dolly didn't wait for Shirley to finish, she opened the door and pulled the seat forwards. Over her shoulder she shouted for Shirley to get in, Shirley limped over and Dolly pushed her from behind, she fell into the back seat.

'There's a rug, cover yourself, over your head, hurry.'

Shirley in her haste had dropped her shoe, Dolly ran for it and chucked it in the back seat.

'The keys, the keys Dolly, they're in the ignition, my case what about my case?'

Dolly slammed her door shut. 'Sod 'em, we have to go.'

With Shirley still crying in the back seat, completely hidden by the blanket, Dolly began the drive home.

All around Covent Garden the police cars screamed, sirens blasting, and the traffic was still at a standstill.

The drive took for ever, Dolly went down the Tottenham Court Road, crossed Euston Road and then the traffic thinned out. It was nine-thirty-five when Dolly at last drove into Totteridge Lane, took a left into her street. It was deserted apart from a few parked cars.

Dolly's heart was thumping, she was almost home. She turned into the drive and drove straight up and into the open garage.

Eddie Rawlins tensed up, and he adjusted the driving mirror. He watched as Dolly entered her drive, leant forward and then turned in his seat. Well, she'd made it, she was home. He watched the heavy garage doors clang shut, checked his watch, thought he'd give it a few minutes, then he'd make a call to Harry.

Dolly locked the doors, then edged round the car, she pulled her seat forwards and leant in.

'We're home darlin'.'

The siren made her freeze, dear God, the police, the siren wailed closer and closer, Shirley started screaming ...

'They got, they got us ... it's the police ... police!'

Dolly ran back to the garage doors and peered through the small window. The police car was pulling up outside the house. Dolly's mind was like a race-track, she went back and shoved Shirley in the car. 'Stay put. Don't move, just stay where you are.'

Dolly was ripping off her sweater as she went through the adjoining garage door into her kitchen. She threw the sweater off, and grabbed a housecoat from behind the door. She turned on the coffee percolator, and with Wolf yapping round her feet opened a cupboard and took out a packet of cereal. She emptied some into a bowl, flung the fridge door open and grabbed a bottle of milk.

The doorbell started ringing, Wolf barked and scratched at the door, Dolly opened a packet of Ryvita and tried to get her breath, the bell rang again and again. Dolly tried hard to keep her breathing steady, she had a mouth full of Ryvita. 'All right, all right, I'm comin' I'm comin'.'

Detective Sergeant Fuller, with two uniformed officers, stood on the doorstep. He flashed a search warrant and entered, almost pushing Dolly to one side. One officer headed up the stairs, and the other began a quick search of the downstairs rooms. Fuller instructed Dolly to get dressed, he wanted her to accompany him to the Yard. Wolf bounded up and down the stairs, the officer could be heard running from bedroom to bedroom.

'What are you bleedin' looking for?'

Fuller paid Dolly no attention, just suggested she get dressed, unless she wanted to come down the station in her dressing gown.

Dolly's heart, thumping like crazy, went up the stairs and into her bedroom. Praying that the officers didn't search the garage, she kept up a steady flow of abuse. She got a coat and a pair of shoes on so fast, she was downstairs in two minutes.

Fuller stood in the kitchen, he took a quick look over the room, nodded to the adjoining door. The officer opened the door and looked into the garage, he closed it again and shook his head. Shirley heard the door open and bit into her hand. Her teeth cut through the skin, she was rigid, then the door closed again. The next thing she could hear Dolly's voice, it was coming from outside. She could hear her, carrying on about why couldn't she take her dog down to the station.

Shirley edged out of the car, limped over to the garage window and peered through. She ducked fast, Dolly was being pushed into the police car. Then silence, they were gone, Shirley leant against the car, her breath came out in heaves. If the officer had so much as touched the bonnet of the car he would have known, it was hot. Why? Why had they taken Dolly?

Eddie inched up into a sitting position, he could see the police car rounding the bend in the road. Eddie waited for a moment, thinking what he should do. Decided he would go into the house and call Harry from there. Check the money was in the car, yes that's what he'd do. What had gone wrong? Something must have gone wrong? What were they doing at the house? and so soon, something must have gone wrong!

Shirley could hear Wolf, yap, yap, yap, then again yap, yap, yap. She limped to the adjoining garage door. Listened: yap, yap, yap, silence. Shirley inched open the door and limped into the kitchen. The coffee was boiling over, Shirley pulled the plug out, then froze. She could hear someone, there was someone in the house. Yap, yap, yap, went Wolf. The handle of the kitchen door turned slowly, very slowly.

Eddie was sure he'd heard something, but wasn't sure what. He inched open the door, the dog was padding round his feet, sniffing, wagging its tail. He pushed him away with his foot and swung open the kitchen door.

Eddie and Shirley took each other by surprise. He stared, moved towards her. Shirley swung out at him. She made Eddie automatically move to protect himself. He swung his right hand up and caught Shirley on the jaw. She went for him, scratching at his face, screaming, kicking, screaming. Wolf thought it was a game, he was up on his hind legs yapping, his tail wagging. Shirley grabbed the coffee pot and hurled it at Eddie. He put his hands up to protect himself, he heard Wolf howl.

Eddie was screaming, the boiling coffee scorching his face, his neck, burning into his ear, he turned and ran crazily, running up the hall, knocking over a vase of flowers. Shirley heard the crashing of the vase, then the front door slam. Footsteps running down the gravel path. She crumpled into a heap on one of the kitchen chairs, her jaw ached, her ankle, her face, she began sobbing. It was the silence that made her stop, just her own voice, the sound of her sobbing. She turned in the chair, the coffee stains up the wall, dripping down, she followed the stain down to the doorway.

Wolf was lying in a pool of dark brown coffee, his little body was limp, the fur stained. A small trickle of blood was coming from his mouth, his head was bent into the side of the wall. Shirley knew before she even touched him, he was dead.

Chapter Thirty-Four

Dolly looked at her watch, eleven-thirty, she tapped her foot. The woman officer stood at the door, her hatchet face blank.

'Any chance of a cup of coffee?'

Dolly got no reaction, she sucked in her breath.

'Eh, you keep lookin' like that love, you'll be able to bend spoons!'

The officer didn't flinch, Dolly lit another cigarette. She looked over the table, which was strewn with photographs. She began to whistle, tapping her foot.

'It's my dog you see, his legs'll be crossed by now, did you hear? I've told them everything I know, I don't know any of these. Eh! I'm talking to you, you any idea how long they're going to keep me here? I mean what's this all about?'

Still Dolly got no reaction, so she began to whistle again. Detective Sergeant Fuller entered, he was harassed, edgy. The press office were going bananas upstairs, demanding press releases. He hadn't been able to get any sense out of Saunders, and the whole place was in pandemonium.

'You know how long you're gonna keep me here?'

Fuller looked at Dolly, he'd almost forgotten her. He opened the door as Saunders and two officers were passing. Dolly heard them conferring in hushed tones. They were bringing in one of the security guards.

Fuller instructed the female officer to clean up the room and bring some fresh coffee up. He turned to Dolly and told her she could go.

Saunders was still outside the office talking with his men as Dolly stood up. They led into the room one of the security guards. He passed within a foot of Dolly, who stepped back allowing him to enter the room. He had a plaster over one side of his face.

'Think someone would be good enough to show me the way out?'

Dolly was taken out of the room.

Fuller laid out the row of photographs along the desk.

'Think you could recognise any of these men as being involved in the raid this morning?'

The guard was shaking. All he knew was that one man was black, a coloured fella, he could tell by the eyes. Fuller sat down with a sigh. He began a detailed interrogation, but he knew it was hopeless, the man was still in a state of shock.

Dolly arrived back at the house in a taxi. She paid him off, almost danced up the drive, she felt so good, so damned good. As Dolly entered she yelled for Shirley.

'I'm in here in the lounge.'

Dolly was talking nineteen to the dozen, going over everything she had been through. The questions they'd asked her. The police were already onto the fact that the raid was a Harry Rawlins styled number. They knew it was the same security firm he had tried when all their men died. That was the reason they had called her in, to see if she could name any men who had worked for her husband. Dolly stood in front of the mirror over the mantle, patting her hair. She looked terrible, but she laughed.

'They know a coloured bloke ... BLOKE was on the raid. They thought our Bella was a man.'

Dolly hooted with laughter, then went into the routine about the police woman being able to bend spoons. Shirley sat with her head bent, her bruised eye and cheek turned away from Dolly. She knew she must tell her, but she couldn't say it. Dolly poured herself a heavy brandy and turned, grinning, to Shirley. The phone rang. Dolly let the phone ring once, twice, then it stopped. She crossed over, it began ringing again, and she snatched it up.

Linda was calling in from Heathrow Airport. Everything was fine, she was on her way!

162

Dolly was brief, just a few words. 'Have a nice holiday love, everything's fine here.'

Dolly replaced the receiver and swigged her brandy. She laughed, she was full of herself, so full of herself she didn't notice Shirley's face. Shirley sobbed, hunched on the seat.

'Eh! Eh! come on, your ankle hurtin' you, is it?'

Shirley slowly lifted her head. The bruise round her eye was red, her cheek bleeding.

'Dear God, what's happened?'

Shirley began to stutter out, how someone had been at the house.

'You saw him? You know him? Did he touch the money?'

Shirley shook her head.

'No, I don't know, I don't think I know him.'

Dolly's whole manner changed, she toughened up.

'You'd better have a good think darlin', how the hell did he get in?'

The telephone rang for the second time, and again Dolly crossed. This time there was just one ring before it stopped. Dolly knew it had to be Bella. Bella was ringing in from Luton. All was fine, she was about to board her plane, she asked if everything was all right Dolly's end. Dolly spoke fast, sharply. 'Everything's just fine, Shirley didn't catch her plane, she'll be coming on later. Have a nice time.'

Dolly replaced the receiver before Bella could ask any more questions. Shirley turned to Dolly. 'I've never seen him before Dolly, I don't know who he was, he just came at me, he . . .'

Still Shirley couldn't get it out. She bent her head and covered her face.

Dolly became very motherly, she sat on the edge of Shirley's chair and put her arms around her. 'All right love, just calm down, it'll be all right. Soon as you are calm we'll go over it. Want a little drink. Here, have a sip of this.'

Dolly held the brandy glass to Shirley's lips. She looked

163

to the door, then back to Shirley. 'Where's Wolf, you've not locked him in the kitchen have you? he hates that.'

Somehow, Shirley got the words out. She told Dolly that Wolf was in his basket, in the kitchen. 'I'm sorry Dolly, I'm so sorry.'

Dolly's reaction was heartbreaking. Shaking her head, a child-like smile on her face.

'No! no! he's all right, he's all right, isn't he?'

Dolly plucked at her trousers, moving back from Shirley. All the time that pleading desperate look on her face. 'My baby's all right, he's all right, isn't he?'

Shirley watched Dolly bending over the dog basket. Her voice was hardly audible. 'Oh my little darlin'.'

Dolly seemed to stiffen, her whole body went rigid. Her mouth was hard and tight. She opened a drawer and took out a lace table cloth. Went back to the basket and lifted the still warm body. Gently she laid him in the cloth, she stood with him wrapped, like a baby at a christening. Dolly seemed unaware that her body was rocking, rocking slightly backwards and forwards. 'You bury him in the garden, in his basket, with his bowls and leads. Anything you see belonging to him, bury them with him.'

Dolly laid the bundle in the basket and picked up her car keys.

'You're not leaving me, Dolly? Don't leave me on my own.'

Dolly ignored her, and crossed to the back door. 'I've got things to do, we'll go together now, no reason for me to stay. We'll go together!'

Dolly was gone before Shirley could say anything. Shirley limped over to the basket and began putting the dog bowl and lead alongside Wolf.

Dolly opened the Mercedes door. She didn't want to think, but couldn't stop herself. The day she had had her third miscarriage, she hadn't known how she would tell Harry. He had been so proud, wanting a baby so much. She was more upset for Harry than herself. She'd wanted the baby, of course she had, but with Harry so happy, so loving. He'd taken such care of her throughout the four months. He hadn't let her get up, he'd waited on her, bringing trays to her bed. Now, now she'd lost his child.

The doctor had already told him, she knew by his face when he came home. In his arms he carried a tiny white bundle of fur. Gently he had placed the tiny animal on her lap.

'His name is Wolf.'

Dolly felt the pain, bursting her body open. A sound not a cry, but a deep low sound inched out of her. Dolly turned in the dark garage and smashed her fist against the brick wall. She hit out at the wall until her fist was bleeding, until the pain in her hand made her come to her senses.

Chapter Thirty-Five

Resnick wiped the egg remains from his greasy plate, he sucked the bread, then neatly placed his knife and fork back into place. He slurped his tea and looked round the neat, orderly, clinical kitchen. Only his dirty frying pan and plate were out of place. From upstairs Resnick could hear Katherine's radio. Terry Wogan burbled on, and he sighed. He was at a loss as to what to do with himself.

A set of clubs was under the stairs. He began chucking out wellingtons, shooting sticks and Hoover to find them. They were covered in mildew, but he dusted one down and fished in the smelly bag for a golf ball. Katherine could hear the bang, bang of the golf ball hitting the skirting board downstairs. She pursed her lips.

'George? George what are you doing?'

Resnick picked up the tatty golf ball and went upstairs.

'Playing a round of golf!'

Katherine lay in her bed, the newspapers and morning tea-tray at her side. She didn't look up as he entered.

'Have you finished with the middle section?'

Resnick nodded and placed the ball down on the floral carpet, it thudded against the skirting board next to one of Katherine's shoes.

'You want it?'

Katherine shook the paper, course she wanted it.

A news flash on the radio made Resnick dive across the bed. A news flash giving information on a security raid that had taken place that morning . . .

Harry Rawlins bent his head closer to the small transistor radio. According to the news flash the raiders had got away with between six and seven hundred thousand pounds. In a fit of fury Harry swiped at the radio, which fell from the table onto the floor.

Trudie made no move to pick it up, but continued bathing and cleaning Eddie's face. The scalds were now swelling and the scratch by his ear was a dark burning red. Eddie winced with the pain, but never took his eyes off Harry.

Harry lit a cigarette and took a lungful of smoke. It streamed out from his nose. He leant forwards and rubbed his head.

'She just came at me Harry, like a wild cat; I never seen anything like it, don't know who the hell she was.'

Harry ignored him and checked his watch.

'Your ear's really bad, Eddie.'

Trudie looked to Harry. He jerked his head for her to get out of the room. The baby started crying from her cot in the bedroom. Harry looked as if he was about to blow, so Trudie picked up the bowl of disinfectant and left. She turned at the door, was about to say something, but thought better of it. She quietly shut the door.

'The law was all over the place.'

Harry stood up and crossed to the window, he stubbed his cigarette out with his fingers, then flicked it towards an ashtray. It missed.

'Bill's back at the house is he?'

Harry leant his head against the cold window, and clenched his fists. He felt frustrated, helpless, caught up with these stupid bastards. His voice was quiet, hardly audible. 'Cash must still be at the house. I want it watched day and night.'

'Is she back then?'

Suddenly Harry blew. He turned on Eddie, his face ugly. He moved fast and swiped. Eddie fell off his chair with a howl, clutching his blistered ear. Harry felt better. He wanted to beat the hell out of Eddie, but he controlled himself.

Harry gave Eddie orders to return to the house. Together with Bill he was to watch every move Dolly made. So far she had gone by the ledgers every inch of the way. That meant the money had to be in her possession. If she fenced it according to the book it would be easy to step in. If she didn't then they would have to pay her a visit.

'She thinks you're dead for Christ's sake.'

Harry smiled. 'Well she's in for a surprise then, isn't she? Now get out, go on.'

Eddie crossed to the door; he was frightened,

'I don't want to hurt her. Not Dolly, I couldn't.'

Eddie saw the look on Harry's face and edged further away from him. All his life he had been scared of this man, tormented by him, used by him. Eddie had taken it, even gone along with the 'death game', but he would draw the line at physically hurting Dolly.

'You'll do what I tell you to, you hear me?'

Harry shoved Eddie, he caught his foot in the carpet and toppled over. Harry looked down at him and walked into the kitchen. He slammed the door behind him.

Trudie opened the bedroom door. Eddie was sitting on the sofa crying, he held a handkerchief to his bloody nose.

'Did he just do that?'

Eddie looked at the girl, standing in a cheap dressing gown. He looked at the curve of her breasts, he could smell her. He loathed her, it was all her doing. He just couldn't understand Harry. What had this cheap little tart got that was so special. The baby howled, and Eddie looked to the bedroom, then back to Trudie. Maybe that was it. The kid. Eddie stood up, he was damned sure the brat wasn't even Harry's. Bloody fool, stupid stupid fool. He'd left Dolly, left her for this.

'You all right, want anything?'

Eddie moved to the door and opened it. He turned to Trudie. 'You think you're so damned special, don't you? He's using you just like he's used every other bastard in his life. You're nothing, you hear me, you're nothing, an' as soon as he's got what he wants ...'

Eddie heard the clink of a cup from the kitchen. He was out and the front door closed before Harry entered the room.

'What did you hit him for?'

Harry ignored her and walked into the bedroom, Trudie followed and leant on the door. 'What did you hit Eddie for? He was crying, you shouldn't push him too far you know.'

Harry ignored her and drank his tea. He began to undo his shirt.

'Where's the money then?'

Harry looked at her, then continued to undo his shirt.

'You're not going over to the house are you? What if you're seen? She thinks you are dead, Harry.'

Still he ignored her. He pulled off his shirt and sat on the bed. His body was tight, muscular, Trudie could feel the pull inside her. He always had that effect on her – he had it the first moment she had set eyes on him.

Trudie had first met Harry Rawlins the night he came round to meet her husband, Jimmy. Harry had sat waiting for him for over an hour. Just before Jimmy arrived home, Harry had leant forwards and touched her neck. He had touched her so lightly, just his hand on her neck, but it had sent an electric shock right through her.

All the nights that followed, all the seedy meetings, the cheap hotels, Trudie got that same electric shock. She remembered his face the night she told him she was having his baby. Harry had held her to him, resting his head against her belly. She couldn't see his face, but she knew he had wept.

'You're not going to hurt her, are you?'

Harry reached up for her, pulling her to him. He slid his hand inside her dressing gown.

'Harry answer me, what are you going to do?'

Harry looked at her and smiled, pulling her closer, slipping her dressing gown off. Trudie found it hard to believe that this was the same man. The same man that no more than two minutes ago had frightened her, frightened Eddie. When Harry smiled it altered his whole face. His eyes softened. His heavy dark eyes. Harry was kissing her breasts, easing her knickers off. Trudie held him, held him tight. Her whole body started to quiver. She had never known such flooding inside her. All the men, none of them, not one had been able to open her up like Harry. Trudie lay back on the bed, he began kissing her, kissing every inch of her body.

All the weeks of being closeted up with him had made no difference. All he had ever had to do was touch her. She wanted him inside her all the time. She couldn't keep her hands off him. If anything, the time spent shut up together had made their relationship even stronger.

Trudie just wished that once, just once, he would tell her that he loved her. When Harry made love to her, he never spoke, never said a word. The fact that Harry always could, always would, make love to her should have been enough. Trudie had the same effect on him.

Sometimes Harry couldn't understand it himself. All the years with Dolly, all the little girls on the side. None of them, not one had been able to turn him on like this little slut. Harry knew her for what she was, but she made him wish he was ten years younger. He wished that the baby had been a boy, a son.

Chapter Thirty-Six

Dolly could feel the sweat trickling down her arm pits. She was working fast. Any minute now the children would be coming back from lunch. She had to get it finished. Dolly's gift to the convent of new lockers was now being put to use. The lockers were in bright colours – the bottom row five feet high. These would be used for the children's coats and play equipment. The top row however, the small top row, Dolly was using to stash the money.

Each top locker had a key, a key for each of the girls: Bella, Linda and Shirley. Dolly had stashed the money in each. She was now pasting large nursery posters across the doors. She still had one locker to go. The trestle table was covered in pots of glue. Dolly began pasting 'Little Miss Muffit'. Sister Theresa entered. She was surprised to see Dolly.

'Hello Mrs Rawlins, not gone on holiday yet?'

Dolly almost knocked the glue off the table, a holdall near the edge of the table was open. Stacks of bank notes could be seen sticking out. Sister Theresa didn't notice. She stood back beaming at the display. 'Why, that looks lovely, really pretty, please let me help.'

Whilst Sister Theresa stuck up the last poster, Dolly zipped up the holdall. She breathed a sigh of relief. Suddenly the play room was full of laughing, chattering children. Dolly, as she tidied, mentioned that there were a few personal belongings left in the poster covered lockers. Just a few things she may collect at some time.

Dolly remained with the children for the rest of the afternoon.

At four o'clock Dolly said her farewells, promised she would return to work as usual, after her holiday. At four thirty Dolly called into a travel agent. She booked a first class ticket to Rio. At five o'clock called into a second travel agent. She booked a second class ticket for Rio in the name of Shirley Miller.

It was dark when Dolly eventually drove up the pathway to her house. She was exhausted. Her shirt stiff from sweat. She wanted a bath more than anything, sleep. Dolly was so tired she couldn't even think about Wolf. So exhausted it was even hard for her to think what had taken place that day. It all seemed so long ago.

If Dolly hadn't been so tired perhaps she would have noticed. Seen Eddie Rawlins waiting outside, waiting and watching. Eddie was using Jimmy Nunn's car. Eddie nudged the sleeping figure of Bill Grant. 'She's back.'

Chapter Thirty-Seven

Resnick had waited all day for a phone call. The ashtray was full, but he lit up, and had a coughing fit. Kathleen Resnick was in the kitchen. He could hear her banging around, cleaning the already cleaned kitchen.

The phone rang, and he snatched at it, but it was Kathleen's bridge partner. He was furious, and shouted for his wife.

'Don't talk too long, I'm expecting a call.'

Kathleen arranged a game and replace the phone, pursing her lips. 'You might have at least been civil to her, it was Margaret.' Resnick had another coughing fit, his neck and face turning bright red. Kathleen sighed.

'Why don't you face up to it, they're not going to call you. Why don't you call them? You're just being stubborn.'

Resnick could have throttled her there and then. 'They'll bloody well call me, you'll see, they'll want me.'

Kathleen began dusting round the desk, she was smug.

'I'm sure they will, but it's been all day now, and you are retired. You retired yourself, so why should they call you, you're finished.'

Resnick stood up. In a fury he snatched the duster out of his wife's hand ... she pushed him away.

'It's true, you've stayed here all day, it's been on the television, it's been on the radio. What do you want, an emergency call just for you?'

Resnick turned on her, shouted that he knew that the raid was going to happen, he'd warned them but they wouldn't listen, he'd told them about Harry Rawlins.

Kathleen Resnick snapped. All she had heard for the

past fifteen years was that man's name. Resnick had blamed him for everything that had gone wrong in his life, his lack of promotion, his retirement, everything was Harry Rawlins until she was sick of the sound of the man's name. 'He's dead George ... dead, why don't you forget it, forget him.'

Resnick grabbed his coat and hat and waddled to the door. It wasn't even worth speaking to her. Stupid woman, stupid irritating nagging frigid woman.

'Where are you going?'

The front door slammed behind him. Kathleen sighed, she couldn't take much more, she'd taken too much as it was. She should have divorced him years ago. She looked at the dirty, overflowing ashtray with disgust, and bent to throw the filth into the wastebin. As she bent down she looked at the photograph of George, George Resnick. Slim, proud, smiling into the camera holding his medal. She sighed, it had all gone wrong, terribly wrong. There was a time when he had been just like that ghost in the photograph. She had been proud of him, had loved him them, Kathleen dusted the empty ashtray and replaced it. Harry Rawlins did have a lot to answer for, her marriage for one. She remembered the terrible day she had seen the newspapers ... 'officer accused of taking bribes'. The face in the photograph was the same one smiling at her now. Well, that was a long time ago, too long for her to start thinking about it now, she would be late for the bridge game.

Resnick got into his battered Granada and made his way to Rawlins' house. He didn't know why he was going there, the car seemed to drive itself. He felt better than sitting waiting for those bastards to call. He hoped all hell was let loose at the yard. He hoped that Saunders would get a bullet right up his arse. Maybe this is what Saunders wanted all along, maybe they had wanted him out so they could take over the case themselves. The more George thought about it, the more he thought he was right. They'd stopped him all along the way. Blocked him off, wanting him out, well he'd show 'em there was life in the old horse yet. He'd bloody sort it out himself.

Resnick drove into the road, it was dark, few lights. He slowed down and cruised very slowly past the Rawlins house. He could see a bedroom light on, but the rest of the house was in darkness.

Resnick parked his car about twenty yards up from Dolly's. He walked slowly back on the opposite side of the street. Eddie Rawlins could see him out of the driving mirror, he nudged Bill Grant.

'You see him, it's law, that's a ... it's Resnick.'

The two men sat still, Eddie adjusted the mirror.

'He's clockin' the house. Christ he's coming right up behind us.'

Resnick could see the movement of the man's hand, he couldn't see their faces, but he knew there were two of them. He continued on and past the car. He stopped as if he had trodden in dog shit. He walked to the curb and scraped his shoe. Resnick made a note of the number plate, then turned and walked back to his car. Resnick sat for a couple of minutes. He was sure one of the men was Eddie Rawlins, but he hadn't seen the face of the second man. He wondered what they were up to, started the engine and drove off.

The two men watched the tail lights until they disappeared.

'I'll go and give Harry a bell, see if I can get any joy from "Ray the Rash".'

Bill eased out of the car and stretched. He had left messages all over London with every fence Harry had named, but so far, nothing. He leant into the car.

'I'll pick up your motor and get a bite to eat, a few hours kip, then I'll relieve you ... in more ways than one.'

Eddie nodded, shivered and opened his door. He stood up and stamped his feet. 'Bleedin' freezin' out there, my piles are playin' me up an' all.'

Bill grinned and dug his hands into his pockets. He moved off.

Shirley stood hidden by the bedroom window, as she peered down. For a moment Eddie's face was clear, then he got back into the car. Dolly came out of the bathroom en suite, and crossed over to the bed. 'Everywhere locked up?'

Shirley nodded. Every door and window had been bolted. Dolly picked up the glass of hot milk. She took out a sleeping pill.

'You want one? Be able to get some sleep.'

Shirley indicated for Dolly to come to the window pointing to the car. 'Been there all night long, there were two of them, now just the one, is watching the place. You think it's the law?'

Dolly stood behind her and looked down. She couldn't see Eddie's face and she didn't recognise the car.

'What we going to do?'

Dolly was already getting into bed, she took the pill, and sipped her milk. 'Sleep . . . if I don't get some sleep I'm finished. Here take one, they work fast and you won't feel drowsy in the morning.'

Shirley sat on the edge of the bed, took the pill, Dolly pulled the covers over herself.

'You put the electric blanket on in the spare room? Don't go asleep with it on, it's dangerous.'

Shirley nodded, and held the milk for Dolly, but Dolly shook her head and Shirley finished it. Dolly had made no mention of Wolf, hadn't asked about where she had buried him, so Shirley said nothing. She looked down at Dolly, her face was haggard, she looked old, worn out. Shirley touched her hand lightly. Dolly without opening her eyes gripped Shirley's hand tight, so tight it hurt, then she released it. 'You get some sleep love, go on.'

Dolly could feel the pill working, her head felt heavy. Shirley bent to turn off her bedside light, but as she did so she looked at the anniversary photograph of Harry and Eddie with Dolly. Shirley picked up the photograph and stared at it.

'Who's this, this man with you?'

Dolly's eyes were heavy, she opened them and looked. 'Harry's cousin, that's Eddie, Eddie Rawlins.'

'Would he have a key to get into the house? Did Wolf

174

know him? He was yapping, Dolly, not barking like he
didn't know someone, it was yap yap yap. Dolly it was
him, it was this man that did it. It was him that hit me . . .
Dolly . . . Dolly.'

Dolly lay still with her eyes closed.

'You sure?'

Shirley nodded, she was sure, sure it was him.

'He can't do anything, the money is safe. I can't think
now, I've got to sleep, go to bed. We'll sort it out in the
morning.'

Dolly turned on her side, her face away from Shirley.
After a while Shirley got up and switched the bedside
lamp off, she crept out, the door closing softly behind her.

The curtain was still slightly open. A chink of light
semmed to arrow its way to the photograph. Dolly, as she
turned her head on the pillow, could see clearly. The three
smiling faces. Harry, Dolly and Eddie.

Dolly sighed. 'Eddie, poor stupid Eddie, never could do
anything without Harry.'

It was as if a blade of ice cut through, right through her.
The jigsaw pieces began to fit, crazy, crazy pieces. The
lighter at Jimmy Nunn's flat. Dolly sat up in bed,
gripping her head, Shirley had said Wolf seemed to know
the man. Dolly's lips moved soundlessly.

The rumour, Boxer Davis, what if she had . . . what if . . .
what if it had been the truth?'

It all made sense, terrible sense.

Sleep was gone, Dolly lay there, her eyes wide open. Her
heart wanted to stop beating.

She whispered over and over. 'No . . . no . . . no . . . no.'

Chapter Thirty-Eight

Kathleen Resnick looked at the bedside clock: it was three-thirty. She could hear George moving about down stairs, the ping ping of the phone. She slipped a dressing gown on. He would be drunk, sprawled in the chair, well, she'd had enough.

Kathleen opened the door into the lounge. George was sitting hunched over his desk, the phone hooked in his ear. He still wore his coat and hat. The room was full of cigarette smoke. Kathleen went to speak but George held up his hand, turning round in his chair.

'Yeah, what, James what? Nunn, and the address?'

Resnick scribbled down the information on a scrap of paper. He wasn't drunk, far from it. He was bursting with energy.

'Thanks me old darlin' I owe you one. Will do, ta.'

George replaced the receiver and opened his diary.

'What are you doing?'

Resnick thumbed through the diary.

'What's Alice's home number. You got it?'

Kathleen couldn't believe it, but crossed to the desk.

'It's three-thirty George, you can't ring that poor woman now.'

George looked up, his face was hard, cruel.

'Just bugger off will you, bugger off.'

Kathleen turned and slammed out of the room, the phone pinged. She was furious, he was actually ringing that poor woman at this hour.

Alice thought her mother had died. The phone was the ambulance siren. She could see her mother being carried out on a stretcher. The frail hand waving Alice goodbye. In actual fact, the frail bony hand was shaking her awake.

'Call for you, telephone.'

Alice ran down the stairs. Her mother stood on the landing sucking in her gums, grinning.

'Boyfriend, Alice? Alice got a boyfriend?'

Alice had a hard time getting her mother back to bed. She could hear her still singing.

'The boy I love is up in the gallery . . .'

Alice wasn't angry, more puzzled than worried. Maybe Resnick had been drinking, but he didn't sound it. She wondered what he was up to. She knew she would do as he asked. It was easy, working in records. Alice smiled, the old boy had sounded like his old self. God, thought Alice. 'Old'? what on earth did that make her? She sighed, wished in a way it had been the ambulance. She then prayed to God to forgive her.

Chapter Thirty-Nine

Bill sniffed. The flat smelt of baby's piss. Harry came out of the bedroom wrapping a towel round himself.

'Not a fence in London, nothing, not a dickie.'

Harry moved into the kitchen, over his shoulder.

'You think she's still got it in the house?'

Bill shrugged, hovering at the kitchen door.

'I could do with a cuppa.'

Harry gave him an odd stare, then he put the kettle on.

'She was missing for over three hours yesterday afternoon, right. Maybe she's stashed it someplace?'

Bill shifted his weight. He was getting pissed off with all the hanging round.

Harry carried the tea into the lounge and sat down. Bill sat on the edge of the sofa.

'Eddie's gonna need a break, his piles playin' him up.'

Bill slipped his tea. He watched Harry wipe the rim of his mug, then in disgust place the mug down, away from himself.

'Okay, you take over from Eddie, let him have a kip. If

nothing has moved by, what, say five o'clock? we'll go in, you and me.'

Bill chewed his lip, he slurped his tea down. 'What if something does?'

Harry stood, he shrugged. 'You know what to do!'

Bill muttered that if he'd had his way he would have moved in bloody hours ago, all the footsying around.

Harry had him by the scruff of his neck, and the tea jerked out of his hand. 'But you're not me ... and you'll do as I say!'

Bill could have got into a row with Harry, but the bedroom door opened and Trudie stood there.

'I'm on my way, all right?'

Bill left and Harry stared after him, trying his towel tighter round his waist.

'What happened, they got the money yet?'

Harry picked up his tea mug.

'Why don't you stand outside and tell the whole bleedin' house?' Trudie sighed, looked at the spilt tea on the carpet.

'Here, see if you can wash some of your bloody lipstick off.' Harry slammed into the bedroom, and the baby howled.

Bill Grant left Jimmy Nunn's flat. He got into Eddie's car. Resnick, parked five motors down, pulled out. He began to tail Bill Grant.

Resnick followed Bill, followed him right back to Dolly Rawlins' street. Resnick didn't tail him into the street. He parked near a pub along with other parked cars.

Resnick was unsure of his next move, he sat back 'thinking'. He clicked his fingers ... 'Bill Grant' the face was Bill Grant. Resnick mused that he thought he was still in Brixton.

Eddie Rawlins drove past, and Resnick hunched up in his seat. He needn't have worried. Eddie was more interested in getting a cup of tea. More important he needed a crap. Resnick had three names: Eddie Rawlins, Bill Grant, Jimmy Nunn. All three seemed to be connected, like bees round a honey pot. The pot being Rawlins' house.

Shirley had seen the changeover. Seen Eddie's face clearly. She knew it was the man that had killed Wolf. Dolly stood behind her at the window. They watched Bill Grant sitting in the B.M.W. picking his teeth.

'You know him Dolly?'

Dolly said she didn't. In a way it was true, she didn't know him. But she had seen him before. He was the mechanic that had called round to the girls' lock-up all those weeks earlier. It meant they must have been watched – watched from the very beginning.

Dolly was exhausted, she had hardly slept the night before the raid, and not a wink that night. Shirley had slept like a ton of bricks. Her ankle was better, she felt stronger and hungry.

Dolly couldn't eat and the smell of bacon and eggs made her want to throw up. All she wanted was time alone, time to think. Dolly knew they had to leave by four o'clock, leave the house right under Eddie's nose. Leave with the money – she didn't know how. She paced up and down the hall. Up and down, up and down.

'How about some toast Dolly? You should eat something you know.'

Dolly ran to the kitchen.

'Get your mother here, soon as you can, and that brother of yours, what's his name?'

Dolly's mind began to tick over. She gave Shirley the instructions for their get away as fast as they came into her head. Shirley was to get Greg to pick up her car, the one left in the car park. He was to bring it to the house, parking it a short distance away so as not to warn Eddie. Greg was to leave the keys in the ignition, call them by phone when it was done, not come to the house.

'What if the car's not there?'

Dolly ignored Shirley, still pacing up and down 'Shut-up, just get cracking, get that mother of yours, here, at the house, soon as you can.'

Shirley picked up the phone, while Dolly ran up the stairs to pack. Shirley was still trying to contact Audrey fifteen minutes later. Greg, she had tracked down, but had to promise him fifty quid.

'I can't get hold of Mum! She's not answering!'

Dolly leant over the bannisters – she looked a little bit crazy, a pair of scissors gripped in her hand. She shouted 'Keep bloody trying, you're to get her here.'

Shirley rang again, this time she let it ring and ring. She heard Dolly's bedroom door slam shut. She could smell burning, she sniffed, looked to the kitchen.

' 'ello? 'ello? 'ello?'

Shirley shouted into the phone.

'Mum? ... mum?'

Dolly set light to the last page. The leather cover of the ledgers wouldn't burn, she pushed the charred pages further into the bath, and then turned the tap on. The bathroom was thick with smoke.

Dolly stood at the dressing table, cold cream and spilt nail varnish littered on the top. She swept them onto the floor. Stood back and looked at herself. She was ready, her face ashen beneath the heavy make-up; she put more lipstick on.

Shirley shouted up that her Mum was on her way. Dolly sighed with relief. She picked up her suitcase, handbag, and looked round the room, looked at the smashed photo frame and closed the door.

Dolly carried her case into the lounge. Shirley sniffed, she could still smell burning, but now Dolly's heavy perfume filled the air.

Standing in the centre of the room was another suitcase, identical to the one Dolly had brought down. It was open, the bottom covered with rows of bank notes, over one hundred thousand pounds worth. This was spending money, enough to keep them out of England for at least two months, keep them out living well and travelling. Dolly had creamed off one hundred thousand from the main bulk of stolen money. Dolly sat down and crossed her legs, she patted her stockings, 'Go on, let's hear you, go from the beginning, go on?'

Lying over a chair were trousers, shirts and two jackets

- Harry's clothes. Shirley put her gloves on and like a parrot began to repeat the instructions. 'Two identical cases, one yours, one with the money. The "money" case had a red tag, Dolly's a blue one. In the money case Harry's clothes.'

Dolly interrupted, told her harshly that it didn't matter that they were Harry's clothes, important thing was that they were men's clothes, and that the suitcase had no prints, not one print from either of them. Shirley sighed, she knew that, she'd spent half an hour wiping it down with Vim, she also knew that they were men's clothes, she'd just said Harry's clothes because they were Harry's clothes. Sometimes Dolly treated her as if she was a bloody idiot, she was getting sick of it.

'Well go on, carry on, then what?'

Shirley began again.

'Okay, now the suitcase with the money and the "men's" clothes with not be touched by either of us - only with gloves on, right?'

Dolly nodded for Shirley to go on.

'Right, now, I take this case, the money case, with my own case to the baggage collection at Victoria. When I get there I have to find a pigeon - right?'

Dolly snapped,

'Man, it's got to be a man, we want a) a man's prints all over the bloody thing b) because it's full of men's clothes - what the hell is the matter with you? We've been over this twenty times.' Shirley now began to pace the room, her gloves on, she began chewing at the fingers.

'Now I pick up a man, the pigeon, a man with little or no luggage - I have to somehow persuade him to take one of my cases, the money case through the baggage check-in - I have to tell him I am overweight, yes? Can he help me?'

Dolly was trying to keep her patience but it was getting increasingly more difficult. Shirley seemed so damned stupid. Dolly, like a school teacher, went over the details one more time, very slowly.

'So you find our man, he takes the money case, I am carrying the identical one. When we get to Rio, I take the luggage off the turntable, the money case – I take the money case through customs, if and only if I am asked to open up that case, then we do the wrong case routine – it's full of men's clothes! So I then go for my own case, show them my gear – are you listening? Jesus Christ, are you listening to me?'

Shirley's mind had gone like putty, she slumped into an armchair.

'I'll never do it, I'll never get through it!'

Dolly could have thumped Shirley, but she controlled her temper and sat on the arm of the chair. All she needed now was for Shirley to lose her bottle, she had to calm her down.

'Course you can do it, it's the oldest switch in the world, go over it one more time!'

Shirley began again, but Dolly wasn't really listening, her eyes were on the clock – where was that bloody Audrey?

Dolly got up and crossed to the window. She flicked the curtains back slightly. He was still there, still watching, she replaced the curtain. Shirley was standing over the money case still going over the routine. She stopped. 'I still don't see why we're taking such a risk, I mean why do we have to take this amount out with us, it's crazy, we don't need all this, why? What if you're caught?'

Dolly saw red, clenched her hands, her face twisted. 'You just said it. It's me taking the risk, me carrying it through. You've got bloody sod all to do except carry the thing. I'm the one that could get caught, so shut your face and just get on with it.'

Shirley picked up the clothes and threw them into the case.

'Why can't we use straight money? I mean you've got enough, enough to last us haven't you?'

Dolly blazed, she had been forking out all along the line. So far it had cost her thousands. These bloody girls thought she was a God-damned city bank. Dolly didn't have any more money, well any she could get her hands on, and they needed cash, hard cash.

182

'I'm out of money sweetheart, we need it, and fold those trousers, don't just chuck them in, pack the case properly.'

Shirley got on her knees. Dolly was really getting on her nerves. This was crazy. After all it wasn't just Dolly's money, it was hers, Linda's and Bella's. It belonged to all of them, why should Dolly be the only one to decide what to do.

'Still don't think we needed all this, it's not just your money Dolly, it belongs to all four of us. Maybe they wouldn't want you to take so much out.'

'We need a lot, we've got months of freedom. We don't come back to England for as long as possible, the more we take out, the safer we'll be, I want everything to cool down before we collect.'

Shirley tightened her lips and continued packing, Dolly was pacing up and down and up and down. She kept flicking the curtain aside and staring through the window.

'He'll see you Dolly, why don't you sit down? you've not had anything to eat, why don't you have a cup of tea?'

Dolly crossed to the drinks cabinet and poured herself a brandy. Shirley looked from the packing and gave her a frown. Dolly dug her heel into the carpet, then looked round the room. She could get a good price for this, she'd sell, the lot, furniture, everything. She twisted her heel, digging it further into the carpet. Everything was in her name, she'd tell her lawyers to sell, sell the lot. She got up and opened the desk, she took out the deeds to the house and placed them in her handbag. Yes that's what she'd do, she wouldn't come back, she wouldn't come back to this house ever again, maybe she could buy a place in Rio. Yes, that's what she could do. She'd have enough money, she needn't come back for years. The lawyers could sell for her, send the money on, she could get at least, what? Dolly looked round the house. At least a hundred grand for this place. In the meantime she, Dolly, needed the money. Bugger the girls, *she* needed it.

Shirley repeated the question for the third time, Dolly was miles away.

'I said, I'm through, it's all packed. Shall I lock it?'

Dolly nodded and swigged back the brandy. It hit her stomach hard, warming her, and she looked at the clock. Where was that bloody woman?

Shirley sat on the chair opposite Dolly, swung her leg, then she too tapped the carpet with her heel.

'So it was Eddie, Eddie Rawlins outside was it?'

Dolly looked up, shook her head and poured another brandy.

'Take it easy Dolly, you don't want to get pissed.'

Dolly slowly, carefully, replaced the bottle. She went and sat down and took out her cigarettes.

'Chuck one over, Dolly.'

Dolly did so, remarking that Shirley was smoking like a chimney now. The telephone rang, Dolly nearly jumped out of her skin, Shirley answered, she nodded, repeating yes, yes, yes over and over then put the phone down.

'Greg has parked the car outside number fifteen, keys in the glove compartment, fifty quid, I promised him, fifty?'

Dolly nodded, now all they needed was Audrey, she twitched her foot.

'Seems funny, me having to ask you for fifty quid, silly considering how much I'm worth now. How much you reckon?'

''Bout two hundred and fifty grand each, take a few grand either way, then I've got to be repaid, say two thirty each.'

Shirley whistled and got up, she crossed to the window.

Eddie drew up in his Granada, got out and went over to the B.M.W. He leant in, looked at his watch, looked over at the house, and changed places.

'Eddie, your cousin's just arrived, they're changing places.'

Dolly lit another cigarette from the stub. She threw it into the the ashtray, her foot was now jerking, twitching all the time, and it was getting on Shirley's nerves.

The two sat in silence, the clock ticking away on the mantle shelf. Shirley watched Dolly out of the corner of her eyes, she seemed to be sweating, her face shining, beads of sweat stood out on her nose, she constantly pushed her hand through her hair. Twice Shirley saw her lips moving, as if she was talking to herself.

'What's he want, Dolly?'

Again, silence, and Shirley stood up and with her back to Dolly watched out of the window.

'Where in hell's name is your mother? If she doesn't come soon we'll never get away in time. They'll see us go, it'll be over.'

Shirley, still with her back to Dolly, quietly asked who 'they' were. Dolly always referred to 'they', her cousin Eddie and who else? Shirley wanted to know why 'they' were outside, how did 'they' know? Shirley turned to Dolly.

'What's to stop them from coming into the house? "They" seemed to be waiting, waiting for us to go, go with a hundred thousand pounds, leaving behind the bulk of the money. What was to stop them? after we've flown the nest? What was to stop them walking in and picking up the rest of the money? Only you know where it is - I don't - Bella and Linda don't.'

Without asking, Shirley opened Dolly's cigarettes, and lit up. She blew out the smoke, was very calm, tough almost.

'Where's the rest of it, Dolly?'

No answer.

'It's your cousin out there, not mine. He's going to walk in and pick it up, that what you arranged, is it?'

Dolly's face twitched, and then she was up and on her feet, and she swiped Shirley hard across the face. Shirley took it, hardly flinched, then returned swipe for swipe, and Dolly was the one to fall back into her seat. She touched her burning face.

'I want to know Dolly, not just for me, for Linda and Bella.'

Dolly was at breaking point, she seemed to cave in. She picked up her handbag, opened it and took out three sets of keys.

'It's in the top row of lockers, convent, children's playroom, nursery posters cover them, there's a locker each, you can pick it up at any time.'

Dolly dropped the keys onto the table and poured herself another brandy. She was shaking.

The doorbell rang, shrill, once, twice, Shirley ran to the window.

'It's mum.'

Eddie watched as Audrey, wearing her tatty coat and boots, a head scarf wrapped round her head stood at the front door. Audrey looked like a cleaner, he squinted towards the house, the door opened and Audrey stepped in, he couldn't make out who had opened the door.

By the time Shirley and Audrey entered the lounge Dolly was composed and smiling. Audrey, for two hundred pounds, and fifty on top for Greg, was to dress as Dolly and drive out in the Mercedes. The girls hoped Eddie would follow, it was their only chance.

Audrey looked round the plush room, her head felt like lead, she had been out on the town the previous night, and had in fact been at home all morning, but was in a coma, passed out, still in her evening clothes.

Dolly looked Audrey up and down. She had Dolly's wig on, but the coat was awful, Eddie would never mistake her for Dolly. She went to the hall closet and brought back her black mink. The mink had been a present from Harry, she flung it to Shirley. 'Put her in this.'

Audrey was beside herself – the mink felt like silk. She looked at her reflection in the mirror. She looked great, the face could do with a bit of work, but the coat, she touched it lovingly. Shirley pointed to her feet. The market woolly lined boots weren't right. Dolly moved to the door to go upstairs to her wardrobe, but Shirley was ahead of her.

'Okay, I'll do it.'

Audrey sat and smiled at Dolly. Odd woman she thought, edgy. Mind you so was Shirley. Must be worried about flying, never had bothered her, that trip to Jersey, she'd never even felt a flutter. She wondered why Shirley hadn't told her she was going away with Mrs Rawlins. All Shirley had said was that Dolly was being harassed by villains, friends of her dead husband. They were watching the house, Audrey wondered why, why all the James Bond tactics? but for two hundred quid she'd have done a tap dance stark naked on her doorstep.

'You can keep the mink, just do another little thing for me.'

Dolly handed the speechless Audrey the deeds to the house and the instructions for her lawyers to sell. All Audrey had to do was post the envelope. Audrey was not sure she was hearing correctly – post a letter for a mink coat – bloody hell she'd eat the letter if she wanted her to.

Shirley entered Dolly's room, the smell of burning was in the air, she sniffed. So this was where it had come from, but she saw no sign of fire, or anything burnt so she crossed to the wardrobe. The two identical wardrobes stood next to each other, Dolly's and Harry's. Shirley opened Harry's by mistake, she gasped, stood back and stared. There was not an article of clothing that wasn't slashed to pieces, make-up, cleansing cream covered the cloth, nail varnished dripped hard from the hangers, like dark red congealed blood. Even the shoes were covered in glue, cream, and slashed. Shirley shut the door quickly and went to Dolly's wardrobe, she took out a couple of pairs of shoes from the neat rack and ran from the bedroom.

Shirley never mentioned the clothes to Dolly, she couldn't, and there wasn't the time. Audrey pushed her feet into the patent leather high heels. They were too small and were crippling her. She stood up, she'd manage.

Eddie watched as Shirley walked out of the front door. She walked down to the front gates and shouted back to the open front door.

'I'll get the gates, you open the garage.'

Eddie saw Dolly clearly standing in the doorway, then she was gone. He started the engine, looked like she was on her way.

Audrey sat in the Merc, it was automatic, she had never driven an automatic before, she fumbled with the gear stick.

'You just put it into reverse, NOT yet.'

Dolly leant over Audrey, she hit her left leg hard, on the thigh.

'You don't use that leg, ever, just the brake and the accelerator. D is for drive, you got that?'

Audrey rubbed her thigh and nodded. 'Bloody hell,' she thought, 'I'll never get beyond the bleedin' gate!'

Eddie watched as Audrey hurtled down the path, she braked, then skidded out into the road, the car moved backwards first, then screeched off down the street.

Eddie followed, did a 'U'-turn and disappeared after the Merc. As he turned the corner, Dolly was already at the front door with her suitcase. Shirley followed, they ran out into the street to the waiting car left by Greg. Dolly knew they had very little time. At the rate Audrey was driving they'd be lucky if she made it down to the end of the road.

First they couldn't find the ignition key, Greg had hidden it in the glove compartment. Both girls were shrieking at each other, Shirley wanted to drive but Dolly was already in the driving seat.

The key was found, then the car wouldn't start. Shirley shouted that she should drive, but at last Dolly got it going – but it stalled yet again. Dolly banged the steering wheel in fury. Again she started it up, and they were away, they'd done it.

Audrey crashed into a wall a mile further down the road. Eddie hauled her out of the car. She was terrified, the wig slipping over her face, he pushed her against the crashed car, she began screaming at the top of her voice. Two passers-by ran over to see what they could do. Eddie backed off, returned to his car and drove to the nearest telephone box.

Chapter Forty

Alice knew she could get into trouble, but she did it all the same. She hurried down the corridor clutching the files and her neatly typed notes.

Resnick was waiting round the corner near the exit doors. Alice had got very little information on James Nunn. Ex-racing driver, unemployed for two years, and according to the labour exchange had disappeared over seven months ago. Two visits from the social security had been made, and his wife had informed them that she didn't want any money, and that Jimmy had gone.

William Grant had been released from Brixton nine months previously. Unlike Jimmy, he had a heavy record, and was a very unpleasant customer. Alice handed over all her notes, and then let Resnick have a look through the file on the 'girls'' raid, all the police procedure up to date. Resnick read fast, flicking over page after page. Alice began to get nervous, people could be heard entering the corridor.

Resnick handed back the report, and took her notes, patted her cheek and was about to leave when Alice stopped him.

'You're not doing anything ... stupid?'

Resnick grinned, he gave a bravado gesture with his hands.

'I'm coming back Alice, I'll be back, you'll see.'

Resnick felt foolish, he wanted to bite his tongue off. Alice's worried face, her big hands clutching the report. She had done him such a good turn, in fact he knew Alice would do anything for him, he leant over and placed a wet kiss on her cheek. 'Don't pay any attention to me, just interested in what's going on, that's all.'

Alice watched him as he pushed through the doors.

Interested? she knew he was up to something, and she knew it had something to do with Harry Rawlins, everything always had, she sighed. For the first time in all the years she had worked alongside Resnick, she felt sorry for him. George sat in his car re-reading Alice's notes. He wasn't sure what his first move should be, he decided to take another look at Jimmy Nunn's gaff.

Bill Grant was out of breath, he had run up the stairs three at a time, he hammered on Jimmy's door, Trudie opened it startled, Bill pushed past her and shouted for Harry. Harry came out of the bedroom. He was about to give Bill a back hander for shouting out his name when he realised something was wrong.

'She's on the move. Eddie's lost her, she did a runner.'

As Bill filled Harry in on all the details, he collected his coat, pulled on a pair of sneakers. Trudie hovered, kept on trying to stop Harry from leaving, frightened he would be seen. Harry wrapped Bill's scarf around his neck, pulling it up and over his face, he didn't even say goodbye. Trudie was pushed aside, and then they were gone.

Trudie ran to the window, she stared down and saw Bill run from the house followed by Harry, they got into Eddie's Granada. She saw them move off, she also saw a car switch on its lights further up the street, then the lights went off, fast, just on and off, she craned forwards trying to see. The car pulled out after Bill and Harry. Trudie knew, knew Harry was being followed, she shouted his name but it was pointless. The baby began to scream from the bedroom, it was all going wrong, she could feel it, something terrible was going to happen. She began sobbing, the baby still crying, standing up in her playpen, holding onto the bars, its wet nappy, its red face. Trudie slapped her, then picked her up, the baby went quiet, shaken by the slap. Trudie sobbed.

Dolly pulled up outside Victoria baggage collection. The street was full of passengers being dropped off, taxis, cars. Dolly had got herself back in complete control again. Shirley was beginning to crack up. She didn't want to go by train to Gatwick, why should she go by train and Dolly by car? She was scared, Dolly took it that she was just worried, that even now Dolly would try and make off with the rest of the money. Dolly loathed her, wanted to push her out of the car.

Shirley stood on the pavement with the heavy money case and her own suitcase. She was holding onto the driving window, still wanting Dolly to come with her, she didn't think she could find a pigeon to carry the case through. She tried every angle. Dolly drove off, Shirley clung onto the window and eventually had to let go, either that or be dragged down the street. She shouted after Dolly, 'Bitch, you bitch, I'll show you, I'll bloody show you.'

Shirley lifted the cases and entered the baggage weigh-in. She was angry, angry at Dolly, 'just wait till she saw her at the airport, she'd give it to her then, she'd tell her exactly what she thought, and when they got to Rio she'd tell the girls, tell them everything, they could all have a go at Dolly, nobody liked her anyway.'

Shirley managed to work herself into such a state of 'fight' that it actually calmed her, and she got down to the job of watching the passengers entering. She needed someone on that Rio flight, someone with very little luggage. She wheeled her trolley up and down watching, waiting. She saw no one, she was there over fifteen minutes, and began to get edgy.

A hitch-hiker with just his rucksack moved towards the flight board, looked up, then back to his mound of papers, his coloured travel brochures.

'Excuse me, are you on the Rio flight?'

He was nice boy, very helpful, and he did only have his rucksack. He lifted the money case from Shirley's trolley. He thought it must be his lucky day, he gave Shirley the 'eye', she smiled and pouted, thanked him, talked on and on about her beauty costumes being so heavy, she was going to enter 'Miss Rio'.

Shirley kept up the chat until the money case disappeared down the ramp. She put up her own case, her own safe case, onto the scales. He was still hovering, still talking to her, still thinking he had cracked it. She could see him getting all hot under the collar. She knew she would have him with her on the train, but she hoped to God he wouldn't be in the same row of seats on the plane, it would be too much. Luckily he was on a standby ticket, he would be at the back of the plane. She heaved a sigh of relief. He still nattered on about places he had been to, how he had gone round the booking and travel agents until he reckoned he had found the cheapest and most economical way to fly.

Shirley watched her bag checked in and go down the chute. Together with the pigeon she crossed to the trains. She could smell his heavy BO, it would be a very boring smelly train journey, but it was worth it, she had done it, and she could have kissed him.

Bill Grant adjusted his driving mirror. The car was still behind, still following. Harry leant over and looked through the mirror, then sat back in his seat and shook his head.

'Some flies, no matter how hard you hit them, keep on buzzin' round.'

Bill wasn't sure what he was talking about, he was worried about this bugger behind. He didn't like it, but he seemed to be on his own. Bill knew it wasn't a police car and he had seen no sign of anyone else following. Harry looked out of the back window.

'I thought I'd seen to him a long time ago, long time, over fifteen years, he was trailing after me like a blood hound, fifteen years later, he's still at it.'

Harry went silent. How come Resnick was still on him? how did he know he was alive? He took another look in the mirror. Maybe it was just a stroke of luck, he touched the scarf, he knew his face hadn't been seen when they left the house, it must be luck. 'Well Resnick, George Resnick, your luck just ran out.' Bill parked the car a good fifty yards up the road.

Eddie was already on his way to meet them, and he leant into the passenger seat. 'She got me goin' Harry, I could have sworn it was her, they must have done a runner when I followed her, couldn't get much out of her, she started up screaming, then the whole place was alive with nig nogs. Next thing the law would have shown up so I thought it best to move, get hold of Bill.'

Harry could have pushed his stupid face through the car window, but he nodded and opened the car door, he kept this scarf pulled up almost covering his face. Bill caught his arm.

'You want me to say hello to our friend?'

Harry nodded, then very quietly whispered something to Bill, Eddie craned forwards to hear but missed it.

'What ... what you say?'

Harry ignored him and began to walk over to the house. Bill watched them crossing the street, Eddie hovering around Harry like a lap dog. He adjusted the mirror and saw that Resnick was watching, craning his head almost out of the window. Bill moved very fast, slipped out of the car and edged his way up the street. Under cover of a number of parked cars, he made his way towards Resnick.

Harry stood on the doorstep, and took out his key. Bill had still not made it to Resnick's car. They waited, wanting the attention to be on him, he then pulled his scarf down, lit a match and turned to face Resnick.

Resnick stared, pressed his face against the window, the flame went out, the men entered the house, but that face, he knew it, knew it, it was him, it was Harry Rawlins, he had been right all along the line. Resnick's stomach heaved over, the sweat stood out on his face, he was right! He was right!

Resnick was taken completely by surprise, his door yanked open. Before he could defend himself he felt a blow straight into his face, he was trapped by the steering wheel, he felt his head being yanked forwards, then he could remember nothing, just a grinding noise as time and time again he felt his head crash against the steering wheel, it was black, red, blue, bright colours, terrible pain, and that grinding noise, the noise of his own nose, his cheek being crushed.

Bill pushed Resnick over. He was limp and fell forwards, then sideways, slipping out of the car. With his boot, Bill kicked him back into the car, kicked him hard in the groin, then gave four or five heavy blows to the ribs, Resnick was finished.

Bill slammed the car door, he heard the bang and presumed it was closed, he crossed over the street. The vicious attack on Resnick had taken no more than a minute. Bill joined Harry and Eddie in the house.

Resnick's right arm dangled, his right hand had caught in the door. The blood streamed down his fingers, but he felt nothing, no pain now, nothing, just the cool air as the door slowly inch by inch swung open, but he couldn't move, he couldn't cry out, nothing, everything went dark, dark mulberry red.

Eddie went into the garage and began covering every inch, searching. Bill was going through the lounge, he had already done over the dining room. They had found nothing and Bill was getting angry. He opened a flick knife to rip the cushions open, cushions that had already been slashed before, and neatly sewn up again.

Harry had left the bedroom until the end. He had searched the two spare bedrooms, one had been used, and had looked over the bathroom. He couldn't put it off any longer, and walked into his own bedroom.

Harry stood in the doorway, he sniffed, something had been burned, smelled like charred paper.

He looked over the dressing table, it was obvious that Dolly had left in a hurry, always so immaculate. He touched a spilled bottle of cream and stood it back into position. He knew this room, knew it like the back of his hand, he sat on the dressing table stool and looked round. His eyes narrowed when he saw the glass by the bed. He crossed over and picked up the broken photo frame, he looked down at his wife's smiling face, his mouth twitched, hardly noticeable but he replaced the frame exactly where it had always stood, right next to the bed.

Harry crossed to her wardrobe, opened it, and there were the rows of immaculate clothes, the rows of shoes.

194

The colours of some of the dresses caught him off guard, colours and the memory of times and places, the occasions. He caught the sleeve on a green dress, the lace sleeve, he gently held it to his nose, and there it was, the smell of Dolly, that perfume she wore, the perfume he had always bought her, he let the sleeve drop as Eddie shouted.

'Eh you found anything yet? Sweet bugger all down here.'

Then the thud, thud of Eddie coming up the stairs, Harry moved away from the wardrobe.

'You come up with anything?'

Eddie was in the room, he looked around, often the wealth and style of the way Harry lived had this effect, always took him slightly off guard, it was so plush, so unlike his own pad, but then he had three kids. 'Anything here?'

Harry shook his head, he looked over the bed, it was untouched, Eddie took it as a sign and pulled the bed canopy off, he then got on his hands and knees searching under the bed.

'Gawd Almighty, when I look a' this gaff I dunno why you ever took up with that piece, I mean you could have kept her on the side. You always did before, what's so special about this blonde. All look the same to me you know, an' that kid, all right so she's got a kid, but it could be his couldn't it, could be Jimmy Nunn's.'

Harry kicked Eddie across the room, kicked him hard. It caught him on the shoulder, and he rolled across the floor. Harry stood over him.

'You'd better do something about that mouth Eddie, do it fast before I rip it across your head. Now pack some gear up and let's get out.'

Eddie crawled round the bed, and rubbed his shoulder. Harry stood by the door of the bathroom en suite – he pulled it open.

The bath tub was full, full of burnt charred paper, Harry knew what it was, he didn't even have to pick it up, he could see the leather cover of his ledgers. His precious ledgers floating, the red leather dye seeping out over the hundreds and hundreds of charred pages. He clenched his hand and slammed the door shut. Eddie stood at the open wardrobe and his mouth gaped.

'Jesus Christ, Harry, look.'

Harry stared at the mess, his suits, shirts, shoes, everything destroyed. For a moment he couldn't register, couldn't take it in. He punched at the fragile door, his hand went straight through it, and came out the other side.

'I'll kill her.'

Eddie backed off. Harry was like a devil, his face twisted and the violence which he kept under control was surfacing, fast - Eddie backed to the door.

'I'll go an' see what Bill wants ... he's out back.'

Eddie ran down the stairs into the kitchen and then into the garden.

Bill was searching every inch of the garden.

Harry stood in the centre of the room, a long time, it seemed a long time, his mind felt like it was exploding. He had underestimated her, she was winning, she was one up on him, and she knew, knew he was alive.

The phone rang, a soft burr burr burr; Harry took his time to cross the room, he stood over the ringing phone then made the decision, he picked it up.

No one spoke, like an echo chamber, but no voice.

'Hello?'

Still no one replied, Harry held the phone to his ear, somehow he knew it was Dolly, Dolly at the other end, he knew it, he could feel it, he licked his lips, then sat on the bed, his voice gentle, loving. 'That you Doll? ... Doll this you?'

The phone went dead, in a fury he hurled it across the room.

Chapter Forty-One

Linda replaced the receiver, she felt cold, her hand was shaking. Bella stood at their en suite bathroom door, in yet another creation she had bought from the boutique downstairs. This one was green and white silk, yards of it, she was swathed in it from head to foot like a Greek goddess.

'Right now, tell me straight, do you think I should have this or the blue, or both?'

Linda ignored her, that voice, she knew that voice.

'There's a hat to match this, covered in sequins, what do you think?'

Bella crossed to her bed, which was covered in dress boxes, handbags, shoes, bathing suits. Bella, since she had arrived, had been going crazy, regardless of the fact she had already spent what little money she had, she was on a spending trip that had to be seen to be believed.

The hotel staff treated Bella as if she was Shirley Bassey, and so they should, she had so far spent thousands on credit, and was still going strong. Bella looked over to Linda, she was beginning to get on her nerves. If she called reception once a minute today she'd have a fit. All Linda could think about was why hadn't Dolly arrived! She had said she would be there, and she wasn't, nor was Shirley. Linda kept on thinking they had both run off with all their money, she had got herself into such a state that she couldn't eat, just waded her way through the bottles of miniatures stacked into the fridge bar in their lounge. She had been half sloshed since they arrived, now she was getting punchy and maudlin.

Bella began to strip off and get into another creation.

'Listen sweetheart, if we go round lookin' like a coupla' slags that might have to do a moonlight, then we'll be treated like slags, just go and get yourself down to reception, get the gear, then we'll have dinner on the roof garden, and enjoy ourselves.'

Linda got up and began pacing up and down, Bella threw her new creation onto the bed.

'They'll be here for Christ's sake, just stop this, you're driving me mad!'

'Oh yeah ... they'll be here will they? Will they? Well I just put a call in to London, and don't you start about we were told not to do it, I done it, and you wanna know who bloody answered the phone, you wanna know?'

Linda was ashen-faced. Bella felt a twinge of fear.

'It was Harry, Harry Rawlins. You was right after all, that bastard's still alive, and Dolly's with him, now you wanna go down reception buy some more gear, gear we got no money to pay for, no money to pay the hotel, and what's more we got no money to even get a bloody flight home!'

The pair argued and went over every sentence, every word of that phone call. Under heavy pressure from Bella, Linda began to give way. Maybe she had been mistaken, maybe it wasn't Harry. But that was all Harry Rawlins had ever been to Linda, a voice on the end of the telephone, a voice that just said a few clipped words, wanting Joe. A voice Linda could remember, she had to, Joe worked for him, he was Mr Big. When Harry Rawlins rang up it was business. The two sat on their beds, Linda began to cry, she was tired she couldn't take much more waiting.

Bella gave her a hug, always the calm one, always ready for the situation. She laughed, told Linda they were sitting on their fortunes, no sign of Dolly and they would be able to get back home, no problem, and they'd have the gear for it, just do a hop over the balcony.

Linda leant against Bella's shoulder, all those dreams, all the things she wanted to do with the money, she wanted to be a racing driver, she dreamt of giving James Hunt a seeing to, dancing in the Martini adverts.

Bella rocked backwards and forwards, began to sing,

she didn't know why. She sang an Ike and Tina Turner number 'River Deep Mountain High' singing softly at first, then stamping her foot, she bellowed it out, and Linda was up on her feet clapping her hands.

'Do I love you me oh my ... River deep mountain highhhhhhh.'

Together they danced, stamping, clapping and then, as it had begun, it stopped, the pair just stopped, it was no good, they were in trouble, no amount of singing the blues away could help.

Bella took her new creations and held them up in a mirror.

'She'll be here, she'll be here.'

Both knew there was a strong chance she wouldn't, but they'd give it a little more time before they did the moonlight, but the atmosphere had changed. Bella didn't feel like eating, she stared at herself in the mirror. If that bitch Dolly had bloody double-crossed them she would get her, pay her back, no matter how long it would take. Linda, sitting on the bed biting her nails thought, if that cow, if Dolly has done this to them, after all they had been through, she would kill her, and she hoped she'd get it like Carlos, running, running scared, straight into an on-coming truck.

Chapter Forty-Two

Bill bent down, he'd found something, he jerked his hand for Eddie to come over, he began digging. Harry came out of the kitchen, he saw the two men leaning over the spade, they were down at the bottom of the garden, so he walked over.

Shirley had been all over Gatwick, there was no sign of Dolly, she was getting into a state, she'd been in every Burger Bar, every wine bar, ladies room, nothing. She went back to the magazine shop, her flight was being called over the speakers, still no sign of Dolly. She made her way towards the gate. The pigeon waved, and indicated a seat next to him in the flight lounge. Shirley pretended she hadn't seen him, there were passengers already moving down the stairs to the coach, Shirley hung back as long as possible in the hope of finding Dolly. The stewardess called out for any first class passengers to please take their seats on the first coach ready to embark.

Shirley moved into the line of passengers, she knew the pigeon was behind her but didn't turn, she clutched hold of her ticket and passport, and began to shake, Dolly wasn't on the plane, she was sure of it, she was pushed towards the second class coach, there was nothing she could do, it was too late to go back.

Outside Dolly's house the police began moving in, they were positioned across the lawn, two officers were entering the house.

The police had parked cars either end of the street blocking any access. The passer-by who had given the call to the station stood holding onto his dog. He looked over to the group around Resnick's car, then back to Chief Inspector Saunders. The police seemed to be everywhere, moving silently, surrounding Dolly's house.

Detective Sergeant Fuller joined Saunders, he informed him that everyone was ready to move in, Saunders turned to the passer-by.

'I think it would be better if you went over to the police car sir, we'd like you down at the station for a statement.' Saunders, out of the side of his mouth, instructed Fuller to get rid of him, out of the way, he then crossed over to Resnick.

Fuller guided the passer-by away from the action.

'He kept on saying Rawlins gave me your number, wouldn't let me call an ambulance, is he all right?'

Resnick hunched over the wheel, the blood streamed down his face, his breath came in terrible guttural gasps.

Saunders leaned into the car.

'Ambulance on its way George, you hear me? it's on its way.'

Resnick just heaved for his breath unable to talk, and Saunders turned to an officer passing.

'Instruct that ambulance, no alarm bell, we're ready to move in any second now.'

'How is he?'

Fuller looked to the car, Saunders shook his head, he stepped off the curb.

'See if he's got false teeth, he seems to be choking!'

Fuller thought to himself, 'What a bastard'. He watched as Saunders made his way to the house, then he went over to Resnick.

Fuller bent down and looked at the hunched pitiful figure. Fuller eased his coat off and gently slipped it around Resnick's shoulders. Carefully he rested his head back against the seat.

'You took a fair old pastin' didn't you? Don't want you freezin' to death do we eh?'

Resnick's breath rattled, the blood still poured from his mouth and nose.

'You got false teeth George?'

Fuller opened Resnick's mouth, he slipped his finger in and felt his teeth, he could feel the plastic and eased it out, it was a plate with two side teeth on it, Resnick seemed easier.

'I'll put this in your pocket, you hear me?'

Resnick tried to turn his head towards Fuller, he gasped, then lifted his broken hand, the fingers were blue, the blood seeping down his coat sleeve. He indicated his top pocket, he tried to speak but Fuller couldn't understand what he was trying to say, the man was fighting to get words out but nothing would come, again he tried to lift his hand to his pocket.

Fuller looked, searching Resnick's top pocket, and took out a crumpled sheet of paper.

'Rawlins. Rawlins ...'

Then, Resnick blacked out, his head lolling on his chest.

Fuller stood up and looked at the paper, he hadn't understood what Resnick had said. He opened the slip of paper and began reading, then he was given a signal from the doorway of Dolly's house and moved off to join the men.

Bill and Eddie were on their knees over the huge black plastic parcel. Bill slit it open with his knife, it was a basket. He picked up a smaller tightly wrapped bundle, sniffed it, it stank, but he slit it open. The rotting body of Wolf, he threw it from him.

Harry turned to Eddie, he was blazing.

'You know about this? You bloody know about this, you stupid ...'

Harry picked up the corpse by its collar and held it in front of Eddie's face.

'It's her bloody dog, she's gone ... it's her dog.'

Harry slapped the tiny stinking body into Eddie's face. Eddie backed off terrified, then they heard it, the wail of the siren. Bill was running towards the kitchen door, he shouted something unintelligible over his shoulder. Eddie froze, panic stricken, looked to Harry then back to Bill, then he took after Bill, running.

'It's the law, it's the law.'

Harry moved back down the garden, scratched his hands on the blackberry bushes, swiping at them. He took a running jump at the six foot wall, the glass cemented on top cut through the palms of his hand, he dropped back down again, the pain flashed through his hands.

The house was suddenly full of light. Bill was held between two uniformed officers, he was like a mad bull, kicking, punching, they were having a hard time holding him down, he was desperate to make it back down the garden. The officers were hanging onto him as he dragged them further and further into the garden. Eddie ran backwards, fell over a shrub, picked himself up and half stumbling, tried to make it to the wall. Harry was already up and climbing over, he kicked out as Eddie clawed for help ...

'Give me a hand for God's sake ... help me ...'

Bill Grant was brought down squirming, swearing, still fighting, they handcuffed him, rubbing his face into the grass. They hauled Eddie off the wall, he was weeping like a baby.

Saunders was creating hell, he had instructed no alarm bell on the ambulance, suddenly all the well-laid plans were a shambles, there were officers running all over the house and grounds.

Resnick was lifted onto a stretcher and carried into the ambulance.

They brought out Bill Grant first. Handcuffed to one officer, he was quiet now, head bent. They hauled him out of the garage. He was followed by the blubbering weeping Eddie, Fuller could hear Eddie crying ...

'I've got a right to be here, I got a right to be here.'

They flung Bill over the bonnet of the waiting police car, he kicked out catching the officer in the groin. Fuller went up the steps into the ambulance, he leant over the ashen faced Resnick.

'Which one did this George, the big one in the leather George?'

Resnick's head lolled, the blood was dark congealed round his mouth and nose, but his eyes, like an animal's stared into Fuller's, he jerked his head once, coughed out thick red blood ... Fuller was already on the move, he didn't hear.

'He's alive, Rawlins ... alive.'

The two ambulance men set about setting up a drip, the engine was already ticking over, they worked fast, one holding Resnick's pulse, they tried to make him as comfortable as possible.

One officer looked into Resnick's face ...

'Sweet Jesus ... poor bastard.'

The ambulance began slowly to make its progress down the street, they were held up as the police patrol car had to be moved, then let rip siren screaming.

Fuller hoped Resnick knew he was doing this for him, a heavy hard blow to Grant's kidneys, the officer kicked in the groin had to hold Fuller off, he too wanted to beat the hell out of Grant.

Fuller felt guilty, guilty for his attitude towards Resnick, he got just one more punch before Grant was shoved into the car. The ambulance siren still persisted, their head lamps on full blast. The police car moved backwards allowing the ambulance through, their lights caught Harry Rawlins for a fraction of a second, who bent down low into the hedge, almost burying himself in it. Then it was dark again, and the police car moved back to the house.

Rawlins kept to the hedge, he crawled and inched his way further and further along each garden, until it was safe for him to stand, ease out into the street that was now filling up with by-standers, and he was free, hunched up inside his coat, head down. No one took any notice of him.

The police car carrying Grant passed Harry, followed by the second car carrying Eddie. Harry didn't attempt to run, not until he turned the corner at the top of the road, then he ran, ran until his lungs felt they were bursting open.

Chapter Forty-Three

Shirley moved down the aisle onto the plane, the curtained first class compartment was on her left. She stopped as the hostess looked at her seat number. She saw her sitting by a window reading *Vogue* magazine, calm as ever. Shirley felt herself go weak with relief, she craned forwards hoping Dolly would turn but she kept her head bent over the magazine.

Shirley sat in her seat, she was a bit miffed, it was an aisle seat so she couldn't watch the take-off through the window. She thought how typical of Dolly to travel first class and shove her into an aisle seat, typical.

Shirley enjoyed the meal, very nice, and she settled back to watch the movie, her headphones plugged in beside her. She was so intent on the movie she didn't notice Dolly moving down the gangway towards her, she felt a shadow move over her view and looked up. Dolly jerked her head towards the toilets and carried on. Dolly checked that the toilets were all vacant then leant against the wall, Shirley joined her, the headphones dangling round her neck.

Dolly didn't look at her when she talked, just kept her head bent looking at her shoes. 'We got trouble, the customs system at Rio, not what I thought.'

Shirley's heart sank, it was different all right, there was no red and green area, everyone went through the same barrier and they searched who they liked, they just swooped on anyone.

'I'm willing to risk it, what you think?'

Shirley couldn't believe it, there she was standing there, asking her, course it wasn't all right. What happened if they opened up the money case, it was crazy.

'I'm the one taking the risk, an' like you said, the money belongs to all four of us, what you think?'

Dolly tugged at the head set, it was Dolly taking the risk, but she had to back her up, she couldn't think straight, she said nothing.

'So, I do it? ... You keep your eyes on me, do as we rehearsed, you see me in trouble and let loose, you got that?'

Shirley didn't have time to reply, Dolly turned and walked back up the gangway. Shirley went into the toilet, she held her head in her hands, she felt sick ... when she got back to her seat the film was just ending, they had arrested the villains, caught them all on the Costa Brava. Shirley ordered a large brandy.

Trudie had waited, waited for hours, but eventually she had gone to sleep in her dressing gown lying across the bed. Harry moved around the darkened bedroom trying not to waken her. His hands were agony, the bloody handkerchief was sodden, he sucked his cut fingers and opened a drawer in the dressing table. He took out his passport and then began searching for some money. Harry had already packed a small holdall, now all he needed was money, he tried to remember where Trudie had stashed the fifty quid Dolly had given her. The thought of Dolly made him twist inside. Twist with hate, he would pay her back for this, he would find her, have her for doing this to him. He caught his hand on a pair of nail scissors and gasped.

Trudie woke, she went to scream, all she could see was a dark figure searching through the dressing table, Harry moved to the bed and put his hand over her mouth to quieten her, the last thing he wanted was the baby to start howling. Trudie grabbed his arm, pushing it from her face, she could smell earth, blood, Harry took his hand away.

'Quiet, keep it shut, don't wake the kid.'

Harry's blood had smeered across Trudie's face.

'What you done, what you done?'

Harry again told her to shut it, and went back to the dressing table.

'Where's the fifty quid she gave you?'

Trudie told him in the top drawer without thinking, then it struck her,

'What happened, you get the money, you get the money? where's Eddie and Bill?'

Harry ignored her, he found the money and pushed past her and out into the lounge. He stuffed his passport into his holdall.

'Where are you going? Harry? Where are you going? You're not leaving me?'

Harry turned on her and shook his head, he crossed to the front door, but she was ahead of him, holding her body against it so he couldn't get out. 'You going to her? You going to Dolly?'

Harry almost spat out the words. 'She's gone! Gone.'

Trudie grabbed hold of him.

'The money ... what about the money?'

Harry wrenched open the door and pushed her to one side. Trudie grabbed him, holding onto him, and then he caved in, he held her tightly, pulling her head into his shoulder. Trudie was scared, she began to cry, holding him, not wanting him to go. 'I love you, I love you ... Oh God! Harry what happened? I love you.'

Harry quietly lifted her face to him, he stared down into it, he whispered. 'Yeah I know, but I can't stay, they're onto us, the law, they got Eddie and Bill.'

Trudie let out a howl, he covered her mouth with his hand.

'I'll be back for you, just got to make it on my own for a while.'

Trudie tried to keep a grip of him but she couldn't, he moved out onto the landing.

Trudie was crying, grabbing onto his coat, pulling him backwards - 'No, don't, don't, please don't go.'

Again, Harry stopped, and jerked his hand backwards to get her off him ...

'No, I won't let you, I won't let you ...'

Harry held her face so hard it hurt.

'That kid, she's mine isn't she ... isn't she?'

Trudie was taken aback by the question, she stood looking into his face, his eyes were hard, cruel, his hand gripping her chin hurt, he was hurting her, she pushed him away.

'She'd better be, she'd better be mine!'

He moved off, she tried again to hold him, this time he jerked his hand so hard against her, she fell, her head cracked against the wall, but he never turned back, he was already round the bend on the stairs, running down. Trudie crawled to the bannisters and watched him running, she felt sick, sickened.

'Bastard, YOU BASTARD ...'

Then he was gone, she cried for him to come back, shouted for him to come back, she hauled herself up and hung over the landing ...

'You run to her, GO ON, RUN TO HER ... you ask me she was the brains behind you all along and you never even knew it!'

The front door slammed shut behind him and she knew he was gone. All the fight went out of her, she slumped onto the stairs and wept, sobbing, holding onto the rail, sobbing, begging him to come back.

Mrs Obebega came out of her flat she looked up ...

'You all right, Mrs Nunn? Mrs Nunn?'

Mrs Obebega began to move up the stairs towards Trudie when they heard the police siren wailing.

The front door sounded as if it was being hacked down. They came running up the stairs like a pack of animals. Detective Sergeant Fuller at the lead, he was the first to see Trudie. She staggered to her feet and began to back away, he flashed his warrant card.

'He's gone ... he's gone GETTTTTTTOUUTTTTT!'

Trudie began screaming hysterically, tenants were coming out onto their respective landings, the police swarmed everywhere, and then the baby howled. The police entered Trudie's flat, Fuller held her by the arm, he pulled her towards the front door.

'Jimmy Nunn, we're looking for Jimmy Nunn.'

Trudie could hear herself laughing, crazy laughter, then as if a record began playing inside her head. 'I don't know anything, I don't know anything, I don't know anything.'

Chapter Forty-Four

After two and a half hours Dolly was through the passport control at Rio. At no time during the waiting, the standing in the long queue, had Dolly so much as flicked a look to Shirley.

Shirley could just see Dolly's blonde head above the

group of passengers moving towards the luggage turntable. The waiting had made a number of people irritable and tetchy, they grabbed for their cases.

At the exit was a row of simple trestle tables, an officer standing at either end. Two officers stood by the exit doors, they were armed, and watched like hawks the passengers already wheeling and heaving their cases towards the customs control. The air conditioning made the vast room cold, the 'muzac' was some kind of Tijuana brass, tinny and repetitive, everywhere the jabber of Argentinian, the hundreds of passengers pushing and shoving and collecting their luggage, the noise level was deafening.

Shirley could feel the sweat begin to trickle down her forehead, she pushed her way towards the turntable. Dolly was already waiting, watching the bags, the turntable seemed to spin the whole room.

Shirley looked over to the trestle table. A line of passengers were waiting to go through, and her heart lurched, they seemed to be inspecting everyone's cases, articles were strewn the whole length of the trestle tables, arguments, shouting. Shirley pushed forwards moving closer and closer to Dolly, eventually she squeezed into a place directly behind her.

'They're searching everyone, don't do it.'

Dolly's voice was hardly audible.

'You know what to do, now get away from me.'

Up came the money case, the red tag visible, Shirley watched as Dolly leant forwards and lugged it off the turntable.

'Here's your case now.'

Shirley jumped out of her skin, the pigeon stood behind her.

'Want me to give you a hand?'

He pressed close, she could smell his BO even stronger now.

'Maybe we could have dinner, sight see whatever you'd like?'

Shirley turned on him 'Piss off.'

Taken aback, the boy stepped back, treading on a fat woman's foot, she shoved him, he turned to apologise and hit another man with his rucksack, embarrassed he moved off.

Shirley searched the crowds for Dolly. She was in line at the third trestle table her case at her side, the money case. Still on the turntable in front of Shirley was the identical dummy case, and Shirley's own case. She had to pretend she couldn't find them, looking over the bags with a worried expression, she didn't have to act it, she was more than worried, she was beginning to shake with nerves.

Dolly inched further and further towards the customs official. The man behind Dolly pressed closer. Shirley couldn't see, couldn't see if Dolly was next in line, if the case was on the trestle table.

Again, Shirley's bags passed her on the turntable, her mouth was dry, she licked her lips. She couldn't see Dolly, the man was directly behind her, Shirley craned forwards, desperate to get Dolly in sight.

Dolly lifted the case onto the table, she tried hard not to show that it weighed a ton, she carefully placed her small holdall on top, her bag of duty free. She rested her hands on the holdall. In broken English the official without looking at Dolly held his hand out for her passport and customs declaration.

'You have anything to declare? Any food, plants?'

Dolly's voice was soft, she smiled sweetly and shook her head.

'No nothing, I do have a bottle of gin, some cigarettes but I have written that down, do you want to see in my bag?'

Still he didn't look at her, just slowly thumbed through her passport.

'Holiday? You come for holiday?'

The man behind Dolly pushed and sighed, he checked his watch. The pigeon on the next trestle table was ordered to open his rucksack, he began taking out his crumpled clothes and shaving bag.

'Open please.'

Dolly slowly unzipped her holdall, she began taking out each neatly packed article, he prodded the bag, lifted it off and placed his hands on top of the suitcase.

Shirley saw it – she let rip, she started screaming that her passport had been stolen, tipping out her handbag onto the floor, shouting and screaming for help, she had been robbed! Pandemonium broke loose.

The two guards at the exit door stepped forward to see what the rumpus was about, the man next to Dolly threw up his arms in despair, he was shouting, arguing that he had an appointment. Then it was over, Dolly was waved through, her unopened case was pushed down the trestle table and taken off at the other end by another official. He handed the money case to her.

All eyes were looking towards Shirley who was still screaming about being robbed, two uniformed officers ran to her side. Dolly became just one of the crowd pushing her way through the exit doors.

It was not until the doors closed behind Dolly did Shirley 'find' the missing passport, she waved it above her head, she was laughing and crying at the same time. The two officers helped her take her two suitcases off the turntable, the dummy case and her own red one, they then led her towards the same 'search' room as the pigeon, it appeared that their interaction had been watched. Shirley was under suspicion, she had only one case ticket, the pigeon had only a ruck sack, and a case ticket but no case!

Shirley was interrogated for more than an hour, eventually everything was sorted out and both she and the pigeon were allowed through. Shirley apologised for the trouble she had caused him, it took another hour as they went for a drink, not that Shirley wanted one. She wanted more than anything to get rid of him, but she didn't want him to become suspicious. In the end she gave him the name of a fictitious hotel and said he could take her out for dinner later that week.

At long last she was on her way to the Sheraton, her whole body ticking, bursting, even the heat seemed wonderful, and the boiling hot sticky taxi ride. She had never known such an exhilarating feeling before – the whole world belonged to her, it was over, all over, she was free, free to do what she wanted, be what she wanted, and what's more she was rich, very rich.

The exhilaration never left her, hours later drinking champagne with the ecstatic Bella and Linda. Trying on dress after dress from the Elle and Yves St Laurent boutique – in fact the hotel suite looked more like a Harrods' sale than a room, everywhere boxes, gowns, furs, the three were like children running around, whooping and dancing with each other, the bottles banging open.

Dolly lay in the bath, she could hear them shouting and laughing with each other, she lit a cigarette, her hands were wrinkled from the water, her whole body seemed as if it was floating, as if it didn't belong to her, she dragged on the cigarette, she heard Bella shouting for her to come out of the bath, then bang went another champagne cork and more shrieks. Dolly stared at the soapsuds, she touched them with her fingers, white fluffy soapsuds, soft, like Wolf, like Wolf's fur, she felt sick, dizzy, the cigarette dropped from her fingers and floated on top of the soapsuds.

Shirley looked at herself in the long mirror, she should have put the blue dress on, but she stepped back, she looked good, and couldn't help admiring herself, she looked more than good, she looked beautiful.

Bella lolled at the bedroom door, she was draped in black sequins, and seemed to shimmer. 'Eh, sugar put the lolly away, Linda's sorted it out, don't want to leave it lying everywhere.'

Again, Bella shouted for Dolly to come out of the bathroom, even went to the door and banged on it, but she heard the water draining away so went back into the lounge part of the suite. Money was everywhere in bundles, in single notes strewn over the floor. Linda had a pile of it in her lap, she was singing at the top of her voice, Bella joined in, they sang their own version of 'My Way'

212

then roared with laughter. Shirley made yet another entrance and Linda whistled. Bella went into a Shirley Bassey stance and began singing 'Gold Finger', the atmosphere was getting crazier and crazier.

Shirley gulped more champagne and lit a cigarette, she began parading up and down the room as if she was on a ramp in a beauty competition, swaying her hips, spilling the champagne. 'An' now we have Miss Shirley Miller! And what are your hobbies Missss Miller ... Well I like children and ROBBIN' BANKSSSSS!'

Linda threw her a bundle of notes and told her to get packing them away, she had already stashed hers into her case and was beginning to do Bella's.

'Dolly not out of the bathroom yet?'

Bella shouted for her yet again, she had booked a table in the best club in town, they were going to celebrate, she was about to go into the bathroom when she began singing. 'Celebration, ohhhhh Celebration la la la.'

Dolly knotted the towel dressing gown round her waist, she looked into the steamy mirror, wiped it and stared at her face, her wet hair hung down like rats tails, her face was haggard, she looked old, worn out, old. She pressed her head against the cold mirror, the tears she had wanted to come for so long stayed locked inside her, the relief she thought would come didn't. She was dried up, empty, she felt nothing, she had no energy, no life left in her.

The girls had stashed all their shares. Linda stacked Dolly's onto the side of the sofa, then helped herself to some caviar from the trolley. Bottles and glasses were strewn around the room, but the trolley seemed like an Aladdin's cave, still more champagne, more caviar – as much as they could eat.

Linda fingered Dolly's pile of notes, she had fifteen thousand more than the rest of them, they had agreed that was fair. Shirley had given them each their keys to the lockers, but Linda felt a little niggle of anger, Dolly certainly was coming out with the cream on top. She made a mental note to get each girl to calculate just how much they reckoned Dolly had handed out, she was sure it wasn't as much as Dolly said.

'Bella, shall I tell Shirley about the phone call?'

Bella froze and gave Linda a dirty look.

'No, just forget it, you must have been mistaken, forget it.'

Shirley moved from the mirror patting her hair, 'Go on, forget what?'

Bella shrugged and snapped her case closed.

'You can't keep it shut, can you?'

Now Shirley was even more interested in what had gone on, she nudged Linda, 'Go on what, what she talking about?'

Linda gave a quick look to Bella then sat on the sofa. 'I put a call into London, don't say anything. I know we weren't supposed to, but well I did, I was worried, we'd had no word ...'

Linda gave another guilty look over to Bella, she looked down.

'Harry answered the phone, I know it was him, it was Harry, it was him Bella, I know it.'

Bella poured herself a drink. 'Nobody's arguing with you sugar.'

Shirley felt herself draining, she looked towards the bathroom.

'You sure? Sure it was him?'

Linda was getting uptight, she wasn't actually one hundred percent sure, how could she be? he'd only said a few words.

'He was the only one who ever called her Doll. The man said, "Is that you Doll?" It was him, I'd recognise the voice anywhere. He used to call for Joe, I know it was him, he's alive.'

They sat in silence, each thinking their own thoughts. Shirley was the first to break it. She told them what she had found at the house, his clothes, the clothes in the wardrobe, how they had been slashed, his cousin Eddie waiting outside, suddenly it all added up.

214

Linda was on her feet, her face tight, she looked ugly, she kicked at her case. 'What you all think this is? A kiss off? that's what it is? who's getting the rest?'

Now Bella stood, she put her glass down. 'Just take it easy, we don't know if it's true, we don't know if he really is alive ...'

None of them heard, she was suddenly standing there, standing at the door, the dressing gown hung on her, too large, the hotel motif on the pocket. They didn't know if she had heard or not, she paid no attention to them, she stepped into the room and crossed to her case, she opened it slowly and began sorting out the clothes.

Behind her the girls looked to each other, Bella gave the nod to Linda.

'I put a call into London, Dolly, your place.'

Dolly appeared not to hear, she continued sorting out the clothes, and held a grey dress up. 'I could wear this, won't be as dressy as you lot, but I could wear this, or I've got a cocktail dress, I think I put it in.'

'Is Harry alive?'

Still Dolly didn't turn round, she rummaged through the case. Linda went up to her and snatched the dress from her hands.

'Harry answered the phone, he's alive isn't he?'

It was like someone had kicked her, kicked her deep inside her groin. The burning feeling began to spread through her, but when she spoke her voice was calm. 'If you say so.'

Still Dolly kept her back to them, but now her hands began to jerk slightly.

'You'd better tell us Dolly, what about the rest of the money?'

Dolly was burning up, she swallowed. 'You think I'm working with him? You think I knew?'

Bella had to hold Linda back, she tried to grab Dolly's arm.

'We just want to know what's going on.'

Then Dolly turned, she looked at each girl, she was

215

trembling. She moved slowly to the drinks trolley, put out a hand to reach for the bottle, it shook so much she couldn't touch it, then her whole body started to shake, out of control. Linda moved forwards, this time Bella held her firmly. 'Is he alive, Dolly?'

The explosion took them all by surprise, frightened them. One minute Dolly was standing shaking like a frail old lady, the next she was like a mad woman, over went the drinks trolley, glasses, food, anything she could lay her hands on she clutched at and hurled through the air. Her voice was like a growl to begin with, repeating over and over, snarling out ... 'yes ... yes, yes, yes, yes, yes, yes, yes.'

The room was spinning and she had nothing left to throw, her face, twisted, she began pulling at the dressing gown, trying to rip it with her nails, her head shaking backwards and forwards. She glowered at them like an animal – it was hard for them to take it all in, it was ghastly, watching her. They were watching her mind slitting open, she began to scratch at her bare arms, deep red gashes, and her voice rose higher and higher. 'You want to know what t...t...t it feels like, what it felt like to find out? it was like this, this, inside me, it's inside me, he's inside me ... out, out get him out of me, dear God get him out.'

Dolly's hand still scratched at herself, Linda stood shocked, her eyes popping out of her head. Shirley's face began to pucker like a frightened child. It was Bella that grabbed Dolly, hit her hard across the face, so hard Dolly's head jerked back, they heard her neck crack, then she stood like a bird, her hands jerking and fluttering by themselves, her face was heartbreaking, the eyes staring helpless, then her body shuddered with a long terrible sob, and she slowly sank onto the floor, she held her head and the tears she had needed began, she wept like there was no end to the sobbing. None of them knew what to do, they looked down at the crumpled heap on the floor.

Shirley stepped towards Dolly but Bella held her hand

out, she knew enough that Dolly had to let it go, had to release the pain she had bottled up, and the sobbing went on and on and on until she exhausted herself, and she was still, silent, curled on the floor holding her head in her hands.

Bella knelt down beside her and gently held her, she rocked her back and forth and whispered to her that it was all right, it was all right now, it was all over.

None of them could believe that this was Dolly, this was the woman they had fought against for all those months. Linda couldn't look, she felt guilty, she sat twiddling her hands, clenching and unclenching them, Shirley lit a cigarette and bent down.

'Here, here you are.'

Dolly was too spent even to lift her hand to take it. Shirley held it to her lips and Dolly drew on the hot smoke, pulling at the cigarette like a baby with a dummy, she filled her lungs and let the smoke drift out, still Bella held her tight, she leant her head against Bella's shoulder.

The tears trickled down Dolly's face, big rolling tears. She made no effort to wipe them away. She turned to Bella and tried to stand, Bella helped her to her feet and guided her to a chair. She sat. Still the tears came, dripping down onto the open dressing gown, she sat there, naked, naked, until Bella tucked the gown around her exhausted body ...

'I knew when I went to Jimmy Nunn's place, I knew then, but I didn't want to believe it. I couldn't believe it. He let me bury that boy, I buried him, I buried Jimmy Nunn, it was him in that front seat, wearing Harry's watch, the watch I gave him.'

Linda looked at the hunched figure, then back to Shirley. Dolly's tears stopped, and held out her hand for the cigarette. Shirley gave it to her, and Dolly smoked in silence, none of them knew what to say, how to comfort her, almost as if it was too late.

'This girl, she knew who I was.'

Dolly's face twisted, her head jerked. 'The way she looked at me, and all the time ... I said, I said "I'm Mrs

Harry Rawlins", and he was there, he was there, he must have heard every word I said. She looked at me as if I was dirt.'

Dolly held her head in her hands, again her body seemed to jerk.

'I don't know what I did to him. I never did anything that would hurt him, all I ever did was love him, I loved him, I loved him. He was my life, I loved him, from the first moment I saw him, twenty years.'

Again her body jerked. Shirley took the cigarette end from her hand and stubbed it out. Dolly was calmer when she spoke again – 'When I pieced it together, when all the pieces came together and I knew, I still, I still … I wanted him back, I would still have him back, I couldn't tell you, I couldn't tell you that, I was too ashamed.'

Dolly wiped her face with the sleeve of her dressing gown, then she turned to the watching faces.

'I wouldn't have let him touch your money, he would have had to kill me first. Well, there it is, take it, go on, the three of you take it and get out.'

Dolly stared at the money she'd thrown around the room.

'TAKE IT!'

They all felt ashamed then, all of them, they had in their way betrayed her almost as much as Harry, and they knew it. Dolly rubbed her feet, she tightened her dressing gown belt round her, rubbed her hand through her hair. She was like an old fighter, there was fight left in her, it began to flicker. 'I've left him nothing, no money, no ledgers, nothing, not even a roof over his head.'

Now Bella stood, she put her glass down.

'Just take it easy, we don't know if it's true, we don't know if he really is alive …'

God knows where Dolly dredged the energy from, but she seemed strong again, maybe it was the fire of revenge in her, but there she was standing facing them again.

'What you going to do Dolly?'

Dolly smiled at Shirley and shrugged, she rubbed her hand through her matted hair. 'Buy my twenty years back, I'm going to get a new face, a new body even. They can do wonders nowadays, and God knows I'm rich enough. I'll buy youth with my share, and a couple of years from now I'll look as good as any of you.'

Dolly stared at them and swayed slightly, and then began to move back to the bathroom, to shut herself away from their watching eyes. She wanted to get out, she could feel her energy going again.

Bella had a flash, she saw Dolly at the beach, remembered the way she had punished herself, so desperate to be part of them. Bella knew Dolly was putting on a show for them, right now the woman was acting her socks off, and she was so damned good at it, so good at hiding her feelings, Bella looked to Shirley and Linda, they were taken in, they thought Dolly wanted to be on her own ...

'Eh come on Dolly, you got to get into your gear, the table's waiting, best club in Rio.'

Bella saw Dolly stop for a second, then up came the act again, she shook her head, said she was all right, she was tired, wanted to rest.

'We ain't takin' no for an answer darlin', here, get that rag off and try this for size.'

Linda and Shirley watched Bella, she was grabbing all the tension in the room, grabbing it with both hands and throwing it out.

'I can do your face for you Dolly, bit of slap and you'll look great!'

Bella grinned at Shirley, good girl, now it was Linda's turn.

'Where's the hair dryer Bella? She'll need her barnet seen to.'

Shirley was already pulling Dolly to the dressing table, Linda plugged in the rollers. Dolly wasn't giving too much resistance, she was childlike, sitting in front of the mirror like Cinderella.

'What you want, the silver lame or the sequins?'

Bella held up two evening gowns. Dolly looked at her through the mirror. 'Be a bit of a mutton in that, won't I?'

Bella laughed and chucked the lame to one side, the sequins would be just fine. She caught Dolly's eye through the mirror, and she gave her a wink. Bella looked away as she saw Dolly's mouth begin to tremble, but her eyes were bright, the colour coming back in her cheeks.

Linda began combing Dolly's matted hair, she lightly touched her shoulder. This was the first time Linda had ever made any gesture of friendship towards Dolly. Dolly caught her hand and gripped it. Nobody spoke, nobody needed to, all their emotions were covered with chit chat about hair styles, dresses, make-up, but there was a truce, and at long last an understanding between them.

Dolly, for that night, felt their love, it wouldn't matter if it didn't last, she felt it there and then, it warmed her, strengthened her, she felt wanted.

For that night Dolly was one of the 'Girls', but unlike Bella, Shirley and Linda, Dolly was not a widow, not yet, and she would not forget, or forgive.

One day she would face him, see him again, Harry was still alive and she would find him.